WINTER'S LIST

ALSO BY JORDYN KROSS

Melting Hearts Series

Prequel Novella - Jack's Frost

Book 1 - Winter's List

Book 2 - Xmas Angel

Dirty Daisy Mystery Series

Book 1 - Dirty Daisy

Anthologies

Falling Hard - 2021 Passionate Ink

WINTER'S LIST

MELTING HEARTS - BOOK 1

JORDYN KROSS

Scarlet Parlor Press, LLC

Published by Scarlet Parlor Press, LLC

Library of Congress Control Number: 2022900329

Publisher's Cataloging-In-Publication Data

(Prepared by The Donohue Group, Inc.)

Names: Kross, Jordyn, author.

Title: Winter's list / Jordyn Kross.

Description: [Albuquerque, New Mexico] : Scarlet Parlor Press, LLC, [2022] | Series: Melting hearts ; book 1

Identifiers: ISBN 9781733380843 (print)

Subjects: LCSH: Young women--Fiction. | Triangles (Interpersonal relations)--Fiction. | Male friendship--Fiction. | Vacations--Fiction. | LCGFT: Erotic fiction. | Romance fiction.

Classification: LCC PS3611.R776 W56 2022 | DDC 813/.6--dc23

ebook ISBN-13: 978-1-7333808-0-5

print ISBN: 13: 978-1-7333808-4-3

For my mother, who always believes I can do anything and tells me to raise my hand.

CHAPTER 1

*S*ex was supposed to be fun, but Missy Winter was bored.

"Uhn," Carter grunted as he slid into her, his rhythm rivaling a metronome.

She loved him for his steadfastness, but years of missionary position twice a week was a slow death. In the beginning, it had been exciting just to be with him. Increasingly, she craved more variety.

Travel posters used to help combat her boredom. She'd imagine the trips they would take after they finished law school. In final preparation for their relocation, she'd taken the scenic images down. Her home for the last seven years, the studio apartment hadn't been so empty since she moved in. Nostalgia washed over her before she remembered she needed to pay attention to what Carter was doing.

"Mmm, yes, Carter. It feels so good." Missy stifled a yawn and ran her hands down his smooth back. "Oh yeah. Do it."

Carter didn't respond as expected. No growls about the size of his cock and how he was fucking her so good. She held in another yawn.

It would be the last time they'd have sex under such stressful conditions. No more law school. No more avoiding Carter's parents. No more—

"Uhn," he grunted louder. Her cue to start moaning with him. She

1

squeezed her internal muscles lightly in a rhythm he believed indicated her orgasm. Having never experienced a real one other than by masturbating, she'd read online how to fake it.

Stroke, pause, stroke, pause.

And there it was. He came.

She smiled up at him, although his eyes were closed, and ran her hands through his shaggy chestnut locks. His untrimmed hair was another sign of how busy and stressful the last semester had been. He'd never let it go that long, but it would be a perfect beach look.

As he withdrew, he used one hand to grip the condom around his softening penis and pushed off the old futon she planned to leave behind. The usual gaze into her eyes to make sure she was happy, his touch of her hair while he lingered inside her...absent. Was something wrong? His confident swagger on the way to the bathroom reassured her that all was well in spite of his silence.

Once, giving in to a spontaneous urge to have the sex life she fantasized about, she'd tried to mix it up. With her ass in the air, she'd looked over her shoulder at him when he came out of the bathroom, condom already in place. Her long blond hair cascaded down her back, and she encouraged him to take her from behind. She'd been so wet in anticipation.

Instead of the turned-on sex god she'd wanted, his face flamed red, and his jaw dropped open. He slowly closed his mouth, and fire lit his eyes, accompanied by a huge load of brimstone. She'd expected surprise but not preacher mode. He accused her of cheating on him. For two weeks he'd withheld every bit of intimacy, even kisses. A shiver ran up her spine, still mortified by the memory.

"Are you ready for tomorrow?" she called through the bathroom door, over the sounds of him cleaning up. In less than twenty-four hours, they'd be lying on the sand, drinking umbrella-topped cocktails. She could almost taste the pineapple. A month in the Virgin Islands—away from the relentless humid heat of summer in Missouri. Hopefully, what they said about vacation sex was true and they'd have plenty of time to find out. Besides, they needed a restful break before moving to New York for her dream job.

Carter exited the bathroom, fully dressed. "I'm not going with you." His voice was emotionless as he eyed the small space.

"Haha. Funny." Missy, still naked, propped up on her elbows.

"What we had was fine. Now I have to consider my future."

She cocked her head, unable to wrap her mind around what he was saying. "What are you talking about?"

"I need to be with people who can advance my career. That's not you." Arms crossed, he glanced down at her but avoided eye contact.

She sat upright, drawing the sheet tight across her body as she stared at him. He had to be kidding. But his expression was deadly serious as he fiddled with the handle of one of his suitcases.

He'd leave? Right after he'd fucked her? Bile rose in her throat. She swallowed hard.

"New York was your dream, too." Missy hated that her voice was barely above a whisper.

"Doesn't matter."

"It does. It's all we talk about."

He winced. "Reality is, I can't do this."

"Can't do *what*?"

"Waste a month on some godforsaken island in the middle of the Atlantic."

"It's the Virgin Islands, Carter." The tropical getaway they'd planned months ago, every detail discussed and decided. Together. Her mind whirled through the events of the past few days. *What changed? When?*

"I have to take advantage of the opportunities I have—"

"Opportunities? Your father's law office?" Her voice rose as she pushed the words through her constricted throat.

"It's a very successful firm." He sounded stiff, as if he'd rehearsed.

"You were going to keep looking for a job once we got to New York."

His shoulders sagged. His mouth opened and then closed tight.

She struggled to take a breath as her stomach clenched. Carter was methodical. He didn't surprise her. Ever. They made a plan and it happened. It had been that way from the start. Her life had been a series of tragic losses, but not him. Carter was constant.

"You told me you loved me." She peered at him sideways, as if another view would change the situation. Pain saturated her system, but she held back the rising panic. They were good together, successful. He was supposed to be the One. Tears rolled down her face. If it were a nightmare, she'd wake up any second. "I—I don't understand."

"Goddammit!"

Missy gaped. Carter never yelled.

"You're so fucking needy."

Finally, he made eye contact. A hateful glare. He towered over her, hands on his hips. "I'm sick of being the only one who can bail you out. Do you know how much it sucks to have to attend fucking funerals for old people I don't even know?"

What the hell did he mean "bail her out"? And he dared to bring her grandparents into the argument? The two people who had loved her unconditionally even when she hadn't deserved it. Hugging her knees, she tried to protect herself from his verbal assault. "Why are you doing this?"

It wasn't happening. There was nothing she'd done to justify his betrayal.

"What, did you think we were going to move to New York and get married and live happily ever after?"

She stared wide-eyed at a stranger she'd thought she'd known.

He rolled his eyes. "I have a life here. In St. Louis. My family has been here for a hundred years."

The roar of his voice jolted her into action. She held the sheet to her shaking body as she stood to her full height and lifted her chin.

"Then why were you with me?" she screamed.

The neighbors were going to call the cops if they kept yelling at each other, but she didn't care. It wasn't like she was going to see them in the hallways after tomorrow.

"Because I like to get laid, and you were a good study partner." Carter sneered at her as if she were a roach in the kitchen.

She stomped toward him. "I should have listened to my friends when they said you were an asshole." Friends who had drifted away once she'd started dating Carter. "Instead, I believed everything you told me."

"A little lesson for the courtroom. People lie." He picked up his overnight bag and set it on his large rolling suitcase.

As the reality hit her, Missy saw her future. One where she was completely alone. An icy coldness filled her veins, and she shuddered. "You don't have to do this, Carter. I love you. I want to be with you, always."

A small twitch of his cheek was his only response before he walked out.

Missy leaned heavily on the closed door. Her muscles could no longer hold her, and she collapsed to the floor in the fetal position. There wasn't enough air in her lungs to scream.

He'd actually left her.

Not even the apartment was hers after tomorrow. What was she going to do? Everything was supposed to be different, brighter, better since she'd graduated. Instead, it was all gone. Her future had walked out the door. How could she have been so wrong about him?

Missy cried until there were no more tears left. Unsure whether hours or minutes had passed, she dragged herself into the bathroom. The cheap dinner Carter had bought her earlier in the evening didn't taste any better coming up than it had going down. She was covered in snot, sweat, and stink. Turning on the shower, she stepped under the spray. Its frigid temperature shocked her system. Sucking in a ragged breath, she waited, shivering.

Slowly, the water started to heat, warming her frozen core. Time to make a new plan. No one was going to rescue her. But Carter's leaving wouldn't destroy her. She'd survived much worse and, despite how she felt, she would survive his abandonment, too.

There were only so many options. None of them were good. To stay in St. Louis for the month, she'd have to beg her landlord, but all of her belongings were in a truck. The apartment in New York wasn't hers until next month. The urge to bang her head on the shower wall would result in a trip to the emergency room, also not a good choice.

The only place she had to live was the bungalow on the island, but a solo vacation didn't appeal to her any more than the Brazilian wax she'd had two days ago. Unlike the wax, there was no other alternative.

Before the water went cold again, she shut it off and wrapped herself in the oversized beach towel she'd bought for Carter. No. Not Carter anymore. The Shit. That would be his new name: the Shit. Kind of ironic since he thought he was "the shit."

Fuck him.

Not one more day would be wasted on him. Five years was already more than he'd ever deserved. Terrified and shaking, she vowed to move on. No way would she allow him to destroy her plans or prevent her from keeping her promise to the people who'd truly loved her.

Before she assumed her conventional career in New York, she'd go to the godforsaken island in the middle of the Atlantic. Take chances, have adventures, and experience the vacation of a lifetime. All by herself.

CHAPTER 2

Missy put her arm around the tiny white-haired woman in the terminal. "Thank you."

"Oh, dear, you made the flight a pleasure." Alice held Missy's hand as they walked up the ramp from the plane. "John always sleeps, and I love showing off my grandchildren."

"I'm so glad you did. I hope you have a wonderful visit with them."

"I'm sure to." The elderly woman shoved the well-worn photo album back in her purse with her free hand. "And you must have a marvelous adventure. One you may tell your grandchildren about one day." Her eyes twinkled.

"I will." Missy nodded, determined to follow the woman's wise counsel.

"Off you go. If you miss your connection, you won't make it to the island, and that wouldn't be a very good story." Alice released her hand, but Missy wasn't ready to leave them.

"Thank you for everything, especially the cookie." Eating had seemed like a bad idea after her sleepless night. Who knew the plane had no food other than a foil package containing six pretzels?

"I remember when they used to serve a full meal, with proper linens. But times change."

Alice's husband followed her and Missy down the concourse with their small roller bag. Her connection was probably in the opposite direction, but at least she'd make sure they found their way out of the terminal. The crowd of people moved much faster than the elderly couple.

"We have to leave you here, dear." Alice pointed at the sign for the baggage claim just outside the TSA-cleared area.

Missy gave the tiny woman a gentle hug and then waved goodbye. It was difficult to part from the older couple, knowing she would never see them again. Despite the years since her grandparents had passed, she still desperately missed them. They'd raised her after her parents were killed on a train they should've never been on.

Tears formed in the corners of her eyes, and she swiped them away. They weren't for Alice, but for her own grandmother, who would have told Missy to have a marvelous adventure, too.

A monitor suspended from the ceiling displayed the information for her gate. Unsure how long it would take to get there, she grabbed the handle of her carry-on tighter and dove back into the river of people. No time for tears. Her stomach rumbled like the low growl of an angry dog. As soon as she reached the gate, she would search for something to appease the beast.

Restaurant signs blurred by on both sides as she speed-walked to the remote terminal. Carter hated it when they were late. He would have told her to let the old people make their own way. How had she missed the fact he had no compassion for others?

When she finally got to the gate, she found a single shop cut into the wall displaying pre-made sandwiches and tired-looking oranges and apples. Not a great choice, but it beat starvation.

She hitched her purse up and wheeled her carry-on into the store. There wasn't a lot of room to move around, but she had no one to watch her things.

She dumped a sandwich, juice, and small bag of cookies on the counter, thankful she hadn't dropped them before it was her turn. The cashier barely acknowledged her before ringing up the items. "Twenty-three ninety-six."

"For that?" Missy retrieved cash from her wallet. If she wanted to eat at the end of the month, she'd have to find cheaper food. Hands overloaded, she turned to leave and crashed into a wall of hard muscle.

"I got ya." The masculine voice vibrated through her entire body and pushed the rest of the air from her lungs.

She gazed at the finest man she had ever seen. He was tall and radiated warmth and light like the sun. Blond hair fell across his tanned forehead to frame crystal-blue eyes that focused on her like lasers. Laugh lines softened the overwhelming effect.

He'd caught her sandwich out of the air while she was plastered to his chest and smiled down at her, revealing model-perfect teeth. She drew her first breath in a gasp and tried to slow her racing heart. Damn, he smelled good—clean linen and spring grass. Men like him belonged in magazines, not closet-sized food stores.

"Oh god, I'm so sorry." She stared at him wide-eyed.

He laughed. His mouth was right next to her ear and his breath tickled and teased parts of her that were nowhere near her head. "Usually, I have to get a woman naked before she calls me 'god.' Let me help you." Even his Texas drawl was hot.

"Um…thanks." Had she heard him correctly? She ducked her chin to hide the heat rising up her cheeks.

"Of course. In addition to being a god, I'm also a gentleman." He took the juice from her and followed her out of the store.

She sat in a nearby chair and took back the vital food he'd saved.

"I…you…" Her vocabulary evaporated in the sexy-as-sin man's presence.

"My pleasure, ma'am." His low voice rasped up her spine, spreading heat as it went.

She opened her mouth to bleat an appropriate response and came up with nothing.

"Well, have a good trip." He backed up a couple of steps before he turned back toward the store.

The stranger was as delectable from behind as he was from the front. His faded jeans molded to his tight ass. The white cotton shirt she'd had her hands all over was tucked in around his trim waist. Well-loved leather cowboy boots made his slow walk a strut.

A sigh escaped her lips. The opportunity to flirt, or whatever it was a woman did to get a man interested, was gone. She didn't know anything about dating as an adult, another thing she'd missed out on while she'd squandered her life with Carter. To have any kind of sexy adventure on her vacation, she'd have to figure it out. Maybe she could find some advice online. It had worked for faking orgasms.

NED'S EYES tracked his friend Jack as he navigated the people and suitcases packed into the tiny waiting area. The cocky half-grin Jack wore said there would be a story, most likely about a woman. Heads turned to watch him move, so comfortable in his own skin. Ned didn't remember being that confident, even years ago when he'd been the younger man's age. There was just something about Jack that drew people.

"You would not believe the woman I ran into." Jack handed him a bottle of water. "Well, she ran into me."

"And you're already back?" Ned shifted to prop his ankle on his knee. Airport chairs weren't designed for tall men.

"She didn't bite." Jack took his seat, leaving the mandatory empty chair between them.

"Not into you?" Despite the fact he didn't feel thirsty, Ned opened the bottle and took a deep swallow.

"Long blond hair with a body that won't quit. She'd be a typical princess type except for her eyes. They're unbelievable. Light brown, flecks of gold..." He craned his neck as if trying to locate her again.

"I'm shocked you remembered she had eyes, much less what color they were."

"She's over there. You can't see much but the top of her head. Did I mention she's tall?" Jack opened his water and took a swig. "I'm sure she's going to be on our plane."

A burning sensation flashed through his gut. What was that? A spark of... *Damn.* Jealousy? That he might not have his friend's full attention during the flight? It was ridiculous. "Sounds like love."

Jack shuddered. "Even I'm not cowboy enough to attempt that ride again. It's an unequivocal case of hard-core lust."

~

"WHERE'S FIRST CLASS?" Jack teased the flight attendant as he folded himself in half to board the small plane. The cabin had twenty rows with two seats on one side of the aisle and three seats on the other. His first time flying commercial to the island and damn he missed Ned's company jet.

He took his assigned window seat leaving Ned to take the aisle. Those had been the last two seats available when they'd booked a week ago, and some poor soul would have to wedge in between them.

Ned's eyes were closed, his head tilted back against the seat. After three years of mourning, the man's sadness had become a part of him like his eyes or his lips. Even his hair was grayer. It was time to get him back to the person he'd been or, if not back, at least better.

Jack tapped him on the arm with the in-flight magazine. "Thanks for working on this project with me, man."

"I need the distraction." Ned opened his eyes and turned his gaze to him. "Anything that doesn't require logging billable hours for assholes."

"I'll try not to be an asshole."

"And I'll take any excuse to get to the island." Ned laced his fingers and stretched.

Drawn to him, Jack noticed every movement. He forced himself to continue the conversation. "Are you going to miss it?"

"Eighty-hour weeks? Clients who won't listen, do stupid shit, then expect you to fix their fuck-ups?" Ned exhaled as if he were trying to blow those clients away. "No. I'm not giving it up, just limiting it to people who deserve my time. I only wish I'd wised up about a decade sooner."

"Wouldn't have changed anything."

"It would have changed the memories. I'd have a whole lot more of them." Ned's voice was so low, Jack strained to hear him.

"Hell, I'd love to go back and never have met Katherine." He kept his tone light despite the burning in his gut. "But then I probably wouldn't have met you. Everything happens for a reason."

"Sure." Ned lifted one shoulder slightly.

The lack of conviction in his friend's voice squeezed his heart. Ned was too young to give up living, and it was Jack's self-assigned duty to make sure he didn't. "So, what are we doing tonight, partner?" He slapped his hands together and rubbed them back and forth.

"I hadn't planned anything. The housekeeper stocked the bar and the fridge. If she got lobsters, we can throw those on the grill."

"I like the way you think." Jack closed his eyes briefly and could almost feel the ocean breeze that would stroke his skin while they cooked outside on the deck. "But we can't spend the entire month chained to the house, working, no matter how nice it is. I require more company than your old bachelor ass. And it's about time for you to get back in the game."

"I'm too old to play games."

Jack punched Ned in the arm. "You are if you say shit like that."

MISSY BOARDED THE PLANE, her pass clutched in her hand. Choking down the desert-dry sandwich meant she was one of the last passengers through the door. The plane was so small that the airline agent had to check her carry-on bag, but she had her purse, book, and what was left of her courage. Which evaporated when she verified for the second time that she was seated between two gorgeous men, one of whom was the sunshine god who'd saved her in the store. The man seated on the aisle was just as handsome but brooding, with dark hair going silver. Her pulse sped. Where were the doting grandparents when she needed them?

As tiny as the plane was, with so few seats, it wasn't at all unexpected she would be near the man, but right next to him? She was going to have to make conversation—an impossible task *before* she was stuck in a steel tube, thousands of feet in the air. Maybe she could read her book and ignore him since her headphones had been whisked away with her carry-on.

"Um, excuse me." She pointed at the empty seat between the men while trying to avoid eye contact.

"Of course," the dark, handsome man said, his cultured voice deep and smooth like expensive liquor. He unfolded his tall, lean form, and she couldn't help following his every move. She tottered back a few steps as he moved into the aisle.

Try not to crash into him, too.

She sat and attempted to take up as little room as possible, arms folded to her chest and legs pressed together. Wedged shoulder to thigh between the men, there was no space to spare. When she glanced up, they were staring at her, smiling. Suddenly, the plane was way too warm. She clenched her thighs tighter, trying to quench the source of the fire.

"Hey again." The man from the store held his hand out to her as best he could, given the cramped conditions. "Andrew Jackson. Friends call me Jack." A warm hand, slightly callused, engulfed hers. The heat of his touch traveled up her arm to her achy breasts. "This is my buddy Ned."

The other man held up his hand briefly.

"Missy. Nice to meet you both. Sorry again about the store. I'm a bit out of my element." Her cheeks burned. Had she really said that? She gave a slight tug, and Jack released his grip.

"You can run into me anytime." Jack nudged her gently with his shoulder.

"It's my first time flying. Except for the plane I took to get here. I mean, it's still my first time...uh, trip." And the stupid just kept coming.

"Really? You've *never* been on a plane before?" Jack asked like she was the only one on the planet who hadn't.

"My grandparents couldn't leave their farm." And they didn't spend money if they didn't have to.

Thankfully, the flight attendant interrupted their conversation with the safety presentation as the pilot moved the plane to the runway. Soon, they were in the air, sipping cold drinks.

"Are you visiting someone?" Ned's dark blue eyes focused sharply on her when she met his gaze.

"No, on vacation. I have a free month before I start my new life. I rented a bungalow. It's going to be great." She plastered a smile on her face.

"What new life will be waiting for you?"

Missy's smile wobbled. She drank some water to try to release the catch in her throat. Sharing so much with strangers was dumb, but she wanted to talk to them. It might have been their demeanor, or it might have been that she was so wrung out from her breakup and sleepless night. "I'll be working at a law firm in New York while I study for the bar. I just finished law school."

"Beautiful *and* smart," Jack said.

Missy ignored that. She'd heard it before. Why was it such a big deal when a woman was both? Men could be smart and sexy and no one batted an eye. Brains and boobs and suddenly you're a curiosity.

"What school?" Ned asked.

"Wash U."

"Congratulations, that's a top-tier program. Your family must be very proud of you."

"I'm sure they would be." Missy was surprised that Ned recognized the St. Louis university. It was an elite program, but not as famous as Harvard.

"Would be?" Ned's eyebrows were up at his hairline. She admired Ned's interview technique. Textbook trial lawyer.

"I don't have any family left."

"No brothers or sisters, aunts, uncles, cousins?" Jack asked. "No one?"

Ned rubbed his forehead. "Jack, I'm going to get you a mouth filter for your next birthday."

"They don't make 'em Texas-sized. Seriously, no one at all?" There was genuine concern in his voice.

"My boyfriend—ex—was supposed to come with me, but it seems he wanted different things." Missy sucked in a breath and blinked as her eyes burned.

"He's an idiot," Jack said, giving a final judgment.

She resisted the urge to laugh at Jack's succinct assessment. "Enough about me, what do you two do?"

"Well," Jack drawled, "I do a little bit of everything. Mostly, I work on business opportunities that capture my attention. Ned's a lawyer, like you."

Her instincts about the silver fox had been correct.

"I invited myself to his place to hash out some details on my next project." Jack stared at Ned as he answered her. "Possibly get him to work with me full-time."

"So, you're an entrepreneur?"

"That's about the best label."

The conversation lulled, but they remained focused on her. She conversed with others easily. Why was it so hard to find intelligent words around a couple of attractive men? "What do you recommend I see while I'm on the island?"

"The Diamond Dunes has a beautiful restaurant right on the ocean. It's out of this world," Ned replied. "You'll have to let us take you to dinner one night."

"Sounds nice. Will your spouses join us?" Missy wasn't sure about agreeing to meet the men by herself, and the place was probably way out of her league. She could let the invitation die after they went their separate ways.

"My wife passed away." Ned tugged his bare ring finger. "Jack's divorced. But don't worry, we'll meet at the restaurant." He patted her hand gently, much as Alice had on the first flight. His hand was firm and warm, and she had an unexplainable impulse to cling to it. She gazed into his dark sapphire eyes and basked in the kindness he radiated.

The flight attendant interrupted by offering additional drinks and snacks. Missy declined. She yawned deeply and, after loosening her seatbelt, tried to stretch in the tight confines. The exhaustion from her sleepless night hit her as soon as she closed her eyes.

Missy woke when the pilot announced they were descending, only to find she had curled up with her head on Ned's chest. The armrest was tucked away, and he'd twisted in his seat to accommodate her. Her bottom pressed into Jack. Sprawled sideways, she filled any space he might have claimed. Dizziness and heat swamped her as she tried to figure out how to disentangle herself from the two men and perhaps melt into the baggage compartment underneath the plane.

"Welcome back." Ned smiled at her and petted her hair, probably smoothing her bedhead.

"I'm so sorry." She cringed as she lifted her head from Ned's chest. She discreetly checked for drool, relieved there was none.

"Not at all. It was the best flight I've ever had."

"Me too." Jack grinned and a hint of a dimple formed on one side. He reminded her of a big, playful puppy.

Wow. Her trip had barely started and already she'd slept with two men who weren't her ex.

Jack laughed. "What was that?"

Missy swiveled her head to take in Ned's shock and Jack's lifted eyebrows and heated stare. "I did not say that out loud."

"Pretty sure you did." Ned chuckled.

Laughing, because what else could she do, she ran her hands through her hair and tidied up her space. Teasing two men wasn't quite what she'd intended when she'd planned a vacation. However, it might be the juiciest story she'd have to tell at the end of the month. No, she could do better than that. She would take risks while on the island before she left it all behind for her real life.

The plane landed, and the two men stayed with her as everyone exited. "Follow me." Ned touched her elbow briefly. "I know this airport like the back of my hand."

Her own private escort beat the heck out of stopping to stare at signs. They were at the baggage area in moments.

"Mr. Strauss?" A woman in coveralls waved over the crowd as she moved toward them.

Ned's face lit with a smile. "Cas." He shook the worker's hand.

"Long time no see."

"It's been less than two months." His chuckle was low and warm.

"Why aren't you in your plane?" Her barrage of questions didn't seem to bother Ned at all. Jack had wandered over to the emerging bags. Missy joined him.

She leaned to pick up her big suitcase, but a tanned arm darted in front of her.

"Let me help." Jack tugged the bag up like it was empty and set it on the ground next to her. She merely pointed at the next one, and he immediately snatched that one, too.

Ned joined them and took one of the two bags that Jack had pulled for her and one of the others. They moved toward the large sliding glass doors.

"Cas usually handles the luggage when I fly private," Ned said with a quick glance over his shoulder.

He spoke of the airport employee like a friend. Not a servant. So different from Carter. Missy made a mental note to add it to a list of criteria for her next boyfriend.

They guided her to the taxi line in front of the airport and got her settled in the first available car.

"Here's my number." Ned held out a cream-colored rectangle. "Promise you'll call us for dinner."

Missy nodded and took the offering through the open window, a warm feeling in her stomach and a smile on her face. She dropped it in her purse. It was a sweet gesture. Ned patted the top of the taxi twice, and it whisked her away toward the bungalow.

Everything was going to be okay.

CHAPTER 3

*E*verything was not okay.

The taxi stopped at the address Missy provided—the same address on the paperwork from the landlord.

"Um, sir?" Missy leaned forward and gripped the headrest of the passenger seat. "Are you positive this is it?"

"Sure am."

"Is there another Flower Street on the island?"

He shook his head.

Early evening light exposed the carnage clearly despite the tangled foliage that surrounded the structure. Gaping holes occupied the spaces that should have contained windows. The interior walls, visible from the street, consisted of exposed two-by-fours, and the roof lacked at least half of its shingles. Chunks of concrete from the exterior walls lay crumbled at the foundation. The bungalow was a disaster. So was her dream vacation.

Tears pricked her eyes as the sharp knife of betrayal sliced through her again.

Pity in the driver's dark eyes reflected through the rearview mirror, making her uncomfortable. Through gritted teeth, she asked him to return to the café they'd passed.

Homeless. She belonged to no one, no place. Her heart raced, and she gulped in the musty taxi air. Other people were scared of things, cockroaches or crowds. But the absence of everything was a true nightmare. Her plan had been sound, well-thought-out. Give up the apartment in St. Louis, live in the island rental for a month, finish the move to New York. Fear and regret wouldn't solve her problem. She had to stay calm. It was pointless to fly to NYC and spend a month in a shelter, but she had to do something because living in the back of a cab wasn't an option.

Using the manual crank, she opened the window. The island air reminded her why she'd come. Unlike the wet wool blanket that was a Missouri summer, the fresh ocean breezes gently hugged her. She sucked in a slow, shuddering breath.

The driver parked in front of the tiny diner. She paid him, then forced herself to open the door and get out. He set her bags at the entrance of the restaurant.

"Are you sure you don't want me to wait, miss?" he asked her.

"I'll be fine."

The booth in the restaurant was well-worn, the fabric showing through parts of the turquoise vinyl. Outside, the cab remained at the curb. The cabbie's eyes met hers through the window, but she turned away, surprised he hadn't sped off to the next fare. The smell of hot food filled her nostrils. A meal wouldn't sit well, but she could order coffee and buy some time. If she could overcome the latest hurdle, she vowed to relax into the slower island lifestyle and enjoy every moment of her imperfect vacation.

The waitress delivered a fresh carafe of cream with her cup, but the ritual of stirring in the white cloud wasn't as comforting as she'd hoped.

A call to the property manager only informed her that Carter was beyond redemption. And the no-longer-in-service message she received when she dialed *his* number shocked her on one level, but should have been predictable. Tears threatened to fall, but she blinked them back. That wouldn't help.

Phone still in hand, she pulled up every travel site possible. Someone on the island had to have a place, even just a room.

Nothing.

In complete desperation, she dialed the number of her former best friend. If Bethany answered, maybe Missy could fly back and stay with her until the apartment in New York was ready. Skipping her vacation would suck but not as bad as being homeless. No answer, and the voice on the greeting was someone she didn't know.

Tears streamed down her cheeks as she choked down the cold cup of coffee.

As soon as the caffeine kicked in, she did the only thing she could. Digging through her purse, she retrieved the abandoned card. Missy dialed again.

Ned answered on the second ring. "Edward Strauss."

"Ned? It's Missy, from the plane?" She was unsure if the man honestly meant she should call, but she was out of options. If he hung up on her or couldn't help, she didn't know what she would do.

"Missy. How's the bungalow?"

She sucked in a sob, trying to keep it together.

"Are you okay? What's happened?"

After a deep breath, she answered as calmly as possible. "The rental, it's wrecked. I-I don't know what to do."

"Where are you?"

Missy told him the name of the diner and the street.

"Stay put."

A surprisingly few minutes later, Ned and Jack, freshly showered and changed into casual wear, slid into the booth. Jack's light blue t-shirt hugged his muscular frame. Ned's chin was dusted with dark stubble. Both of them stared at her intently, warriors ready to do battle on her behalf.

"What happened, sugar?" Jack asked.

"The place I rented months ago—apparently there was a big storm..."

"Yeah, the caretaker secured my house. I had some damage.

20

Nothing too major." Ned's eyes didn't leave her as the waitress placed two more coffee cups on the table.

"Well, I guess the landlord isn't the planner you are, because the rental looks like it was hit by a hurricane. Which, I guess it was."

"Didn't he contact you, or warn you, or anything?" Jack's eyes were wide, and she imagined she'd had a similar expression on her face when she was in the taxi.

"He said he did, but I never saw the letter. Or the refund." She gritted her teeth to stop the tirade of vitriol that threatened to erupt.

"The boyfriend?"

"Yes." Missy's voice was a low rasp. Beneath the anger, she was embarrassed she'd spent so much time with Carter and trusted him completely when he obviously wasn't the person she'd imagined he was. "We had an agreement. Budgeted everything. I paid the rent. He was going to cover the food and stuff while we were here. I mean, I have some savings, but..."

"How did he get the refund?" Jack's hands clenched on top of the worn Formica.

"We used his credit card, but I paid the bill." Despite promises to herself, she was crying, wasting tears over him again. Ned handed her a handkerchief from his pocket.

"Have you called him?" Ned's voice seethed with anger.

"He changed his number." She gripped the phone in her lap tighter, barely resisting the urge to sling it across the restaurant. The Shit had outdone himself. Maybe he'd assumed she would never get on the plane without him.

Ned's jaw was set as tight as hers, and he had a white-knuckled death-grip on his mug. Strangers cared more about her well-being than her ex-boyfriend did.

She wiped her eyes with the handkerchief again. "How could I be so blind?"

Jack held up a hand to stop her. "Some people aren't what they portray. They wear a mask and perform to get what they want. They don't have actual feelings. They're human parasites. That type of deception is impossible to see through. I should know."

21

Ned's eyes never left Missy as he put a hand on Jack's shoulder.

The tension left Jack's body. "Sorry, go on."

"I asked the landlord if he had anything else I could rent, and I did a search. But—"

"You're staying with us," Ned interrupted.

Missy let the comfort in his deep voice wash over her. If she went with them, it could be a huge mistake. It felt right, but she'd believed Carter was trustworthy, too. "I don't—"

"At least for tonight." Jack cut off her argument.

It was a terrible idea, but she didn't have another option. If she had to trust someone, and it might as well be Ned and Jack. "Just one night. Let me text my friend Bethany the address?"

Ned smiled and then rattled it off. She posted it to her Facebook account that she hadn't accessed in months.

MISSY GRIPPED the passenger door armrest as a fluttery dance started in her stomach. Ned parked in the open asphalt driveway at the base of a sprawling, creamy-yellow, one-story house. The huge stained-wood front door sat invitingly at the top of a flight of painted concrete stairs, contrasting with the white trim. The house hovered on a small cliff that edged the beach. Expansive windows, framed by shutters, would let in plenty of light, and the oversized, pitched metal roof provided tons of shade for a deck that seemed to surround the entire structure. Palm trees, clustered artfully around the house, ruffled in the breeze, and the orange light from the setting sun glinted off the waves. It was postcard perfect. A complete opposite of the tiny, once-turquoise wreck she'd planned to inhabit.

"Wow. *This* is your house?"

"It is. Let's get you settled," Ned replied while he and Jack helped remove her belongings from the trunk. As nice as the house was, the view of them was better. They handled her months' worth of luggage like it weighed nothing. She reminded herself that it was temporary.

One night. If she left in the morning, she wouldn't be preying on their kindness.

"You sit here." Jack patted a stool at the bar that flanked the gourmet kitchen. "We'll be right back."

As an unexpected guest, she should be the one to haul her bags, but she sat. For tonight, she would let them be in control.

"Are you hungry?" Ned asked as soon as they returned from the back of the house.

"No, I'm fine, really." She crossed her arms around her still-churning stomach.

"Nonsense. There's plenty." Ned pulled a tray of lobsters and asparagus from the stainless-steel fridge and stepped through the door that led to a back deck.

"Go with it. He wants to feed you." Jack opened a bottle of white wine and poured three glasses. He set one in front of her.

"Can I at least help?"

"Ned's grilling everything. Should only be a few minutes."

"I feel like I should be doing something. Calling someone. Looking for a place to stay." Even though she'd already done that, there had to be someone else she could call. Or something else to try.

"No rush." His lips wrapped around the edge of his wine glass, and his eyes locked with hers. Heat filled the space between them, and Missy forgot to breathe.

Damn. She had a million problems to deal with and all she could think about was how good-looking Jack was. She tasted her glass of wine. For just one night, she resolved. Decision made, she took another sip of wine.

Ned toed the back door open and set the platter of steaming red lobsters on the counter. He glanced from Jack to Missy and back again. "Everything okay?"

"Never better, partner." Jack grinned at Missy.

Ned grunted and took three plates from the cabinet. Jack handed him a glass of wine and took over plating the food.

"That smells amazing." Missy's mouth watered.

Dinner tasted even better than it smelled, but it wasn't a meal for

23

manners. They each dipped pieces of the tender meat into the lemon-and-butter sauce with their hands. Missy tried to ignore the way Jack licked his fingers. And the way Ned groaned in delight every few bites. She focused on her plate and used every bit of etiquette her grandmother had taught her. Lobster had never been served at the Winter household, but damn, it was good. After the ravenous eating slowed, Ned and Jack chatted about things to do on the island and a little bit about the businesses Jack was trying to buy out and combine. She was interested but could barely keep her eyes open.

"All right. That's the third yawn you've tried to hide." Ned stood and took her plate.

Jack followed Ned with the remaining dishes.

"I can help clean up." Missy pushed back from the dining table.

Ned came out of the kitchen. "You need to rest. I'll show you to your room."

Missy tucked her chair in and followed him. Exhaustion, emotional and physical, from the last twenty-four hours hit her hard.

Jack came out of the kitchen as they passed. "Good night, sugar pie." He kissed her cheek.

It was a sweet gesture, one her grandparents had repeated nightly when she was growing up. Warmth seeped through her at his kindness.

"This is you." Ned opened the door and stepped back with his arm out. The walls were the same creamy color as the outside of the house, with matching white trim. Bamboo flooring warmed the space. Picture windows, covered with gauzy drapes, flanked a door that led to the wraparound deck. She let her fingertips drift over the fluffy white queen bed and admired the five-star-hotel-quality linens.

"It's lovely. Thank you, Ned."

"I'm glad I could help." His eyes locked on hers. Slowly, he reached up and tucked a lock of hair behind her ear.

Frozen in his gaze, a part of her wanted it to mean more than he surely intended.

He kissed her cheek. "Get some sleep," he said gruffly before he closed the door, leaving her alone.

After she changed into sleepwear and brushed her teeth, she fell into bed. Their kisses lingered on her cheeks in contrast to the unwanted tears that ran down her face. Crying wouldn't help her decide what she could do to get beyond the latest betrayal from the Shit, but she couldn't stop. The tears ran for more than Carter; she cried for the loss of her grandparents and for the act of selfishness that had led to the death of her parents. If she hadn't stomped her eight-year-old foot and refused to go with her parents, they would have been on the earlier train as scheduled. Instead, they'd indulged her and drove her to her grandparents' farm. The later train derailed. Her parents were killed instantly. A ruined vacation was nothing less than she deserved.

Missy woke the next day a little achy yet completely rested. Yesterday's despair had receded with a full night's sleep. She stretched and went into the en suite. The gorgeous bedroom paled in comparison to the showroom bathroom. After she'd had some sleep, she could appreciate the overall effect. Glass tiles mimicked the colors of the ocean as they faded from azure at the ceiling to soft white. Sandy brown tiles covered the floor, providing contrast to the sparkly alabaster countertops. A dream bath.

Before she left, she'd try to make use of the deep soaking tub. But first, she needed food. After quickly brushing her teeth and combing the knots out of her hair, she threw her little silk kimono robe over her short pajamas and padded out to the living room.

Ned and Jack sat on stools at the kitchen bar, documents scattered across the granite. Their heads were nearly touching. Ned's bare arm wrapped around the back of Jack's chair. She wasn't sure she should interrupt, but she required coffee.

"Good morning, my heroes," she called to them across the open living area. The men spun on their barstools in unison.

"You mean 'good afternoon,' sleepyhead," Ned corrected her.

His smile zinged through her veins, making caffeine unnecessary. Jack caressed her with his crystal eyes, lingering over her bare legs.

"What time is it?" she asked.

"About twelve-thirty island time, so about nine-thirty in the morning for your internal clock. I bought bagels. Not as good as in New York, but they come close. There's coffee and juice. Make yourself at home." Ned jutted his chin toward the kitchen.

"Thank you. A bagel sounds perfect."

"What are your plans for the day?" Jack followed her into the kitchen with his empty coffee cup. "Because I'm going down to the beach later if you want to join me." He pulled a mug from the cabinet for her and put a bagel in the toaster.

"Uh, I was planning on finding some work, possibly at one of the hotels or inns that might have staff quarters." She held out her mug as Jack poured. "Maybe try to rent a bike. I read they have that sort of thing for tourists. I can't pay hourly. Hopefully, I'll find someone willing to rent an older bike for the month—"

"What are you talking about?" Ned crossed his arms, and his brow furrowed. "You're staying here."

"You guys have been so kind, but I can't impose." She stirred in the cream and took a grateful sip.

"You aren't. We have plenty of room—"

"And you would be doing us a favor," Jack cut in. "We need to have some fun while we're on the island, not just work."

"You should stay," they said in unison.

"Really, guys, I appreciate the rehearsed invite, but I can't. It wouldn't be right."

"How do you figure?" Jack's brow wrinkled.

"This is my problem. I should work it out." She couldn't accept.

"What would it take to get you to change your mind?" Jack returned to his barstool next to Ned.

It became a settlement negotiation. Both men's eyes locked on her. Her belly fluttered with arousal, which wasn't helping her brain decide. Selfishness could lead to disaster.

"With your law degree, you could help us with research and the contracts we're working on." Ned tapped the pile of papers at his side.

"Seriously? I just graduated. What could I possibly contribute to your project beyond some clerical assistance? I would get more benefit out of the real-world experience than you would get from me."

The bagel in the toaster popped, and Missy took a breath as she pulled it out. She didn't want to argue with them, and she didn't have a better place to stay. But, there had to be a compromise that didn't involve exploiting their kindness. "I'm willing to work for you. Cleaning, cooking, running errands, or whatever." The same type of job she would find on the island. "If you need that sort of thing."

"Done. Why don't you finish your breakfast and take some time to get settled in?" Ned told her.

Missy hesitated. It was too easy. Ned was clearly used to getting his way and the smug expression on his face told her he loved winning. Those two would be able to maneuver her into doing anything if she let them. Not that they were manipulating her into doing anything she didn't want to do. Who wouldn't want to stay at an idyllic island house for a little light work? She would make sure she didn't take advantage.

But first, deep soaking tub, here I come.

"Don't forget, we're leaving for the beach in two hours. There has to be some kind of swimsuit in all of that luggage we hauled in," Jack teased.

Although unaccustomed to flirting, she decided to play with him. "I might have a scrap or two tucked in a small corner." She cocked one shoulder up flirtatiously. Would her lame attempt work?

"I can't wait." His devilish smile removed all doubt.

CHAPTER 4

*N*ed led the way to his office, Jack's bare feet echoing on the wood floor behind him. The room was designed to accommodate two people comfortably. Antique wood furniture held state-of-the-art equipment. The plan had been for him and his wife to be able to be together when he had to work. She'd passed having never seen it. Until recently, he'd kept a picture of her on his desk. But he'd tucked it away in the drawer with his pain.

"You want her, too," Jack stated out of the blue.

"Who?"

"Don't play dumb with me." Jack squinted at him. "You aren't country enough to pull off that game."

Ned turned his attention to the monitor. "I'm old enough to be her father."

"You're not her father. She's twenty-six and has a law degree. How much more of a woman does she need to be?"

Ned spun around to glare at Jack. "How do you know she's twenty-six?"

"I might have peeked at her passport while she slept. I also might have had a quick background check run on her overnight."

"You *what?*" Ned barked.

"Hey, everything she said was truthful." Jack crossed his arms and widened his stance. "She's squeaky clean. But I can't risk having some clever competitor send in a plaintive spy. I had to know who she was, especially since we're fixin' to have her in our bed."

"You could've given me a heads-up. As for *we* want her in *our* bed —what are you talking about?" The heat in Jack's gaze forced Ned to look away. An image of Jack and Missy in his bed formed, and his cock stirred despite his resistance.

"You may be in full denial, but based on what I've seen, she's naturally attracted to you." Jack shook his head. "Do you even know how to flirt? You're acting like you're still married instead of a widower. It's time to get back in the saddle."

"First of all, she's a lady, not a horse." Ned crossed his arms, mirroring Jack. "There is no saddle. Second, she's a guest in my home. I will not subject her to some sexual whim I may be experiencing."

"Ah, so you admit it." Jack pointed at him.

"Of course. She's a beautiful girl, but—"

"*Woman.*" Jack sat in the desk chair and tapped the keyboard to bring the monitor back to life. In typical Jack fashion, he stopped arguing because he had acquired the information he'd been seeking.

Ned grimaced and focused on his computer. It wasn't that he didn't find Missy sexy. He did. Unbelievably sexy. What Jack failed to understand was that he was unwilling to have any relationship, much less a casual one. Casual was all Jack was interested in since his divorce. Missy was special and had an incredible future. Ned refused to toy with her for Jack's temporary amusement.

MISSY UNPACKED HER SUITCASE, hunting for her swimwear. They were both at the bottom, of course. She considered her two options, conservative or sexy. The fifties-pinup-girl style in navy with white trim was more appropriate to wear with virtual strangers. Well technically, they weren't complete strangers. And she had teased Jack with the "scraps" comment. Before she could overthink it, she dropped her robe and pulled off her pajamas. The strappy black bikini was much smaller on than it had appeared in the store. Four little triangles, with lots of open areas between all the straps that held them together. Missy checked the mirror and dragged her finger under the bottom edge of the suit, adjusting the coverage. Good thing she'd been brave and waxed before she'd left. At least her cover-up hid some skin.

There was still an hour until they were leaving for the beach. Instead of interrupting them, she could finish the steamy romance novel she'd picked up for the trip—an improbable story about an administrative assistant and a billionaire who end up having sex in the office. It was insanely hot if she overlooked the premise that would result in a massive lawsuit in real life.

Lying on the bed, she continued reading about the boss doing all kinds of kinky things to his young, horny assistant.

"I said bend over." Her boss pushed gently on her lower back, and Lily rested her chest on his desk. She was so vulnerable in this position. Had she locked the door? What if someone came in?

He was on his knees, lifting her skirt slowly. "Lily, you bad girl. Where are your panties?"

The breeze across her bare ass and slick thighs from the office air-conditioning made her shiver.

The smack of his hand on her naked cheek echoed loudly in the otherwise silent space. She gasped and got impossibly wetter. She bit her lip. Someone would hear.

"I asked you a question." He inched his hand higher and nudged her ankle so she would open up for him.

An achy, wishful heat built between Missy's legs.

Her boss's fingers teased her bare lips, sliding her intimate cream all over before he plunged them inside her demanding pussy. Lily choked back a squeal and thrust her hips out, begging for more.

Missy slid her hand under her suit and rubbed herself, spreading her own wetness around as she read. She pushed two fingers into her hot core and pumped them in the rhythm that always worked so well. Her orgasm built like a summer storm. The book fell when she reached up to pinch a hardened nipple. She squealed from the bit of pain. In her mind, two sexy, dominant men pressed her over a desk, her skirt pushed up, her naked ass on display. One slid his cock deep inside her. The other gripped her hair and filled her mouth.

The pressure between her legs peaked, and her channel spasmed around her fingers.

Over her panting and moans, she could almost hear them groaning with her. She bit down hard on her lower lip to keep from screaming their names.

JACK LIFTED his hand to knock on the closed guest room door when a cry of pain carried past the wood. Alarmed, he burst through the door. The sight on the bed had the words he'd been about to holler freeze in his throat.

Missy was splayed across the duvet, a hand thrust inside the bottoms of a tiny black swimsuit. No question where her fingers were hidden. The other hand was at her breast. Her back was arched, in the middle of a full orgasm, but her lips were clenched as tight as her eyelids.

Jack groaned. He stepped into the room and closed the door. "Oh, sugar pie, let it out."

Missy's eyes flew open. "Ah. Jack. What are you do—uhnn—ing here? Go!"

"I can't go. I have to finish watching you come." He resisted the urge to adjust his hardening cock. "It's the most outstanding orgasm I've witnessed in a very long time. And calling my name while you do it—it just doesn't get better than that. At least not from watching."

Missy blushed bright red over her entire body, and she rolled away from him, hiding her face. When she finally spoke, her voice was trembling. "I wasn't calling out your name like that, Jack. I...I didn't expect you."

Dammit. She was so sweet. The women Jack had been with in the past would have invited him to join them for round two. He needed to fix the situation or he would have to willingly let Ned kick his ass for being so stupid.

"Don't be embarrassed." Jack sat on the edge of the bed, taking care not to crush his rock-hard erection as he did. "I was coming to tell you we're ready to leave. I heard you cry out and didn't even consider anything except you were in trouble." He tentatively brushed his hand over her lower leg, hoping she would look at him. "You really are beautiful."

Missy still didn't say anything.

"If it would make it better, you can watch me get off any time you like." Jack nudged her, counting on his playful timbre to bring her back to him.

She barked out a laugh and swung her pillow at him. "I'm pretty sure you would benefit from that as well."

"Can't blame a guy for trying." He took the pillow from her hands and tossed it away.

"That naughty smile lets you get away with everything." Missy's relaxed tone eased Jack's worry that she might leave.

"Come on." He pulled her up with him to stand. "We're going soon. I'll get changed and meet you at the back door."

"Don't tell Ned."

"I won't. But I'd love to see it again. Next time, without the bikini in the way." He waggled his eyebrows.

"Go." She pointed her finger at the door, a huge grin on her face.

Thank goodness he hadn't run her off. It wasn't that he didn't respect her boundaries, he just hadn't expected her to be going downtown on the Finger-Fuck Express with an unlocked door. If there was any chance he could get her to squeal like that with him in the room, preferably naked—well, he was going to work very hard to make that happen. If he could find a way to include Ned, even better. In the meantime, he had a swimsuit to put on *after* he dealt with his raging hard-on.

CHAPTER 5

*M*issy trailed the guys down the wooden stairway. A soft breeze played with her loose hair, and the salty scent of the ocean tickled her nose. She tried not to stare at the half-naked men—still in their prime, neither one a furry man-beast in a banana hammock.

Nope, they were stylish.

Jack led the procession in navy board shorts. Ned had on some red, mid-length, designer trunks and could have been in an ad for a yacht.

"A private beach?" she asked.

"It was the main selling point of the property," Ned said over his shoulder. "Had to tear down the original house. It was falling apart."

They might as well have been on a deserted island if she ignored the boats in the distance. A hardwood forest, peppered with palm trees, covered the slope that hugged the beach on the left. To her right was a rocky field separating Ned's property from any possible intruders. The only access was the way they'd come or swimming in from the ocean. His beach was part of a tiny bay or inlet. Private, untouched, except by the shorebirds that hung out at the edge of the water, pecking away when the gentle waves rolled out.

The sand was soft under her feet, flicking up to sting her calves as she made her way across it in her flip-flops. It was browner than she'd expected. The white edges of seashells poked out here and there closer to the water.

Ned beelined for an alcove worn away in the cliff on which his house sat. The recessed area provided some protection from the afternoon breeze. He planted a huge shade umbrella while Jack arranged the beach towels.

Once their eyes were back on her, before she lost her nerve, she slowly slid her white crocheted tunic up to her hips and carefully toed off her flip-flops. Glancing up to make sure they were still focused, she raised the cover-up to just below her breasts. Jack grinned at her from over Ned's shoulder. She pulled it over her head, shook her hair loose, and revealed her barely covered body.

Ned clutched the beach bag in front of himself as he retrieved the sunscreen. Despite his efforts, Missy caught a glimpse of his erection.

He pointed to one of the towels. "Let's get you protected."

She dropped the tunic on the nearest towel and moved to where he wanted her.

"I get to help." Jack bounded to the other side of the towel across from Ned.

"Do my back. I did my front before we left." Missy lay down on her stomach.

"The drugstore stuff is crap for fair skin." Ned held out the bottle. "This is from a dermatologist, and it's waterproof."

"You noticed I'm blindingly pale?"

"You'll have a month in the sun, sugar pie. No point in getting burned on day one." Jack offered his palm for the lotion. Ned squirted some out for each of them and then rubbed his hands together.

Unable to craft an argument, she drew her hair aside and relaxed.

They gently caressed her upper back, then rubbed lotion into her arms as if the moves were choreographed. Four warm, strong hands slicking coconut-scented cream into her skin made her want to purr and arch into their touch. It was impossible to focus on one specific sensation before being distracted by another until the clasp on her bikini bra released.

"Hey." Missy secured the loose fabric across her chest with her hands and lifted her shoulder to roll over. Ned pressed her down gently.

"Don't worry." Jack's voice was playful.

Their continued strokes set her on fire, hotter than the sunbaked sand under her. No opportunity to graze the sides of her breasts was missed as they worked toward the edge of her bikini. Tingles rolled down her spine. It was a naughty fantasy, like she was a spoiled princess and they were her concubines or whatever the male equivalent was.

Someone's fingers slid under the edge of the tiny bottoms, and she frowned at Jack over her shoulder. He grinned and raised an eyebrow. She stuck her tongue out at him before returning his smile. Ned reached across her and poked Jack's shoulder. They moved to her calves. The lotion application had transformed into a massage. Missy wiggled and pressed her thighs together.

"Spread your legs a little, sweetheart," Ned instructed. "We need to cover you completely."

A breath caught in her throat. Was she going to do it, let them touch her all over? She forced herself to exhale, let her body go lax. Why not? It was her sexy adventure, no reason to waste a minute of it. As soon as she parted her thighs, their hands stroked her and worked the lotion in while kneading her muscles. Higher and higher, they rubbed her inner thighs. Wetness pooled between her lower lips. But they stopped right before they touched her where she wanted it most.

"Roll over, Missy." Ned's deep rumble broke through the dreamy erotic bliss she'd slid into.

Missy carefully held the top to her chest as she turned.

"It's a private beach. Women go topless on the island all the time. Don't worry," Jack said.

Ned and Jack waited for her to make the next move. Missy took a deep breath, lifted the fabric high in the air, and dropped it to the side.

Both men froze, their eyes glued to her chest. Arousal danced up her body from her core, and her nipples pebbled. It was a total power trip to capture *two* men with just her body. She leaned back and waited to see where they would go next.

Jack turned to Ned. Ned blinked several times and then met Jack's eyes. Slowly they descended, and, as if by silent agreement, each man took a hard, pink nipple in his mouth. Ned tongued her bud, and Jack nibbled. Her sex clenched at the contrasting sensations, but she still pushed them off, one finger on each of their foreheads, testing her control over them. "Lotion application, or we'll never make it to the water."

"We had to get a taste before those lovelies were covered. No man could resist." Jack laughed.

"What's your excuse?" Missy squinted at Ned.

"Jack started it..." Ned cleared his throat, and his cheeks were pinker.

Missy smiled at his embarrassed justification. They were irresistible, and it was her vacation—her fantasy vacation, apparently.

They coated her shoulders, breasts, and belly, hands sliding under the side straps of her bottoms. Each made sure the skin on her hips was well-protected, and their fingers teased right on the edge of her pussy. She tried unsuccessfully to breathe normally.

From her ankles to over her knees, they massaged the lotion into every part of her. When they reached her thighs, she dropped them open without thinking. Neither one declined the obvious invitation. They nudged and pressed into the tiny swim bottoms, already wet with her arousal. Through the fabric, fingers found her clit—it was too much. Unable to focus, she closed her eyes. Electric bolts shot from her spine to every muscle, and she moaned. They mastered her body and she arched her hips into their fingers as the tension built ever higher.

The sound of a wave crashing on the shore thundered through her.

"Yes, please, *yes*." Her hands gripped the towel at her side as she rode out her climax. They stroked and teased her until her muscles released. When she was finally able to focus, the blaze of desire in their eyes stunned her.

"Wow, that was unexpected." Her face heated and she panted in recovery.

"No, that was spectacular." Ned grazed his fingers down her arm.

"Oh yeah. When she comes, it's like performance art." Jack grinned. "Fucking phenomenal."

She rolled away from them, her cheeks heating. Jack had seen her come twice already. "I'm not... I don't..."

Ned's face fell, his eyes locked on hers. "Are you okay?"

"I'm not what my grandmother would call a 'floozy.'" There. She'd said it. But she closed her eyes to hide from the mortification.

Jack laughed. "Of course you're not."

Ned pushed Jack's shoulder. "She's serious."

Missy peeped up at them.

"What?" Jack's brow wrinkled, no sign of the laughter. "Why do you think—"

"I'm fooling around, outside, with two men I just met."

"No one's judging you." Jack brushed a wisp of hair off her forehead.

"I'm sorry, Missy. Things just... We'll back off. You're in charge." Ned's low voice soothed her rattled nerves. But she didn't want to stop. She was mostly embarrassed about what they must think of her. Unfortunately, she'd made what had been fun awkward. There had to be a way to fix it to get back to the erotic vibe, the sexy experience she'd hoped for when she'd booked the trip. Even if Ned and Jack hadn't been in her plans, the reality was turning out a lot better than her intention.

She shook her head. It was time she took control.

With a sultry smile, she rose to her knees and grabbed the sunscreen. "My turn."

"You don't have to return the favor," Jack responded.

"No, I get to protect your sexy bodies. Stand up."

Jack didn't disappoint. With a grin on his face, he was right back into the playful scene. Though she'd let her insecurities take over, they were going back in the proverbial box. She could get them out again after her vacation.

"Turn around." She squeezed some of the lotion in her hand. Ned reclined on his towel, his eyes never leaving them. The power that came with capturing his attention made her want to perform for him. Reassured by their support, she didn't hesitate to follow her desire.

Missy began with Jack's wide shoulders. He was a few inches taller than her, and she used the difference as an excuse to press her breasts into him as she massaged the sunscreen over his upper arms and across his back. She rubbed down each arm, enjoying the firmness of his well-defined muscles. His back was equally toned, and she gently caressed his sides. Was he ticklish?

"Brat. I know what you're doing."

"What? I'm making sure to get you everywhere."

"I'm counting on it. But it's a waste of time, sugar. I'm not that sensitive. I will, however, remember to check if you are."

After she knelt, she placed her hands on his calf and rubbed up to his thigh. She slid her hands into the leg of the loose board shorts until her knuckles grazed the underside of his sac. When she tilted her chin up, an icy fire locked her eyes to his.

Beside her, Ned groaned, breaking the spell. He pressed his hand down on his obvious erection as if he could hold it back.

Jack sucked in a breath and spread his legs farther apart. Emboldened by their reactions, she teased Jack's balls one last time before she focused on working up his other leg. The next time she came to his apex, she spent a little more time stroking the bottom of his scrotum with her knuckles. His hips thrust in response before his muscles tensed and he stilled.

When she stood, her berried nipples trailed seductively along his back. "Other side."

His muscles were still tense, but the corners of his mouth were turned up when he faced front. The outline of his hard dick trapped beneath the swimwear made her mouth water. She forced herself to ignore it and rubbed the lotion into his athletic chest. Up and over his pecs to his shoulders, she closed in so she could reach every bit of him. He grabbed her waist and tugged her to him. His erection pressed into her belly.

"No, you have to let me finish." Missy slapped at him playfully before freeing herself.

"That's exactly what I was thinking." Jack relaxed into a huge smile.

A laugh at his silliness erupted before she could choke it down. She worked her hands over his abs. They were firm and had the definition of a six-pack.

"Not bad for a guy who spends his time playing with companies," she joked.

"I'd like to show you how good these abs are for playing other, more erotic games, sugar."

"Hmm... but right now, I need to protect these fine legs." She dropped to her knees again, her face at his crotch.

Jack groaned. "Are you trying to kill me?"

"Nope, just save you from a bad burn." She covered his legs in sunscreen but didn't go under the board shorts again. She smacked his ass lightly. "Okay, all done."

Ned gripped his hard cock through his swim trunks. "What about me?"

"You two take your time. I'm going to cool off." Jack strode down the pristine beach.

Ned raised his arms above his head, giving her full access to his bare chest.

With a handful of sunscreen, she focused on his toned muscles. The desperate desire to entice him as she had Jack filled her with an unfamiliar confidence. She'd never had the opportunity to tease a man or enjoy her sexual power over him. With two to play with, she was going to enjoy every minute.

"Roll over." It would be easier to indulge her imagination if he faced away.

He flipped without a word.

She stepped across him to straddle his hips and slowly lowered herself down until her wet bikini-covered core rested lightly on the edge of his shorts at the top of his firm ass. Although she would have sworn it wasn't possible, she became wetter from the heat of his body radiating into her.

Pressing her fingertips into the muscles of his strong back, she rocked slowly forward and rubbed the lotion up his spine and across his deltoids. Damn, he had an amazing body, slightly thicker than Jack's but sexy as hell. Forward and back, she caressed his golden skin. The feel of him branded her hands with memories that would last well beyond her holiday.

"I feel your heat." He pressed his hips up into her core.

She leaned forward and whispered in his ear, "You're to blame."

"Jack caused that fire."

Sitting back, she tipped her hips to rub her clit on the top of his tailbone, getting the pressure and friction she craved. "Oh, he may have sparked it, but you have it raging into an inferno."

He rolled and gripped her waist as soon as he faced her. She perched directly on his hardened cock, their swimsuits only providing more frustration. The hard length of him parted her perfectly. The twitches and spasms built inside her, increasingly intense. Her body screamed for him to enter her. Grinding into him, her heart pounded, and she searched for that edge. When she lost the ability to coordinate her movements, he took control of her hips.

"Are you going to come?" she asked, barely able to form the words as her arousal reached an apex.

"Give me some credit. I'm old enough to wait until I'm inside you." He rocked her hips harder into his erection, and her clit sang with each thrust.

Riding his cock through the fabric was enough to send her over. She arched and cried out, the sound echoing off the curve of the cliff wall.

Her orgasm left her boneless, and she collapsed over his chest. Ned grinned like a Cheshire cat and lightly rubbed her bare back.

"Everything okay here?" Jack ran up to them, dripping wet from the waves.

"Mmmhmm," she purred.

"Yep, we're good."

"Really good." She giggled.

"Seems I can't leave you two alone for a minute. Huh, Ned?"

"Guess not." He released his hold on her.

"Tide's coming in. Let's go jump some waves." Jack pulled Missy up, tossed her over his shoulder, and smacked her ass. Missy squealed with delight and kicked her legs. Jack started across the beach as if she weighed nothing at all.

She reached out to Ned. Her eyes were glued to his still-hard cock, which he adjusted when he stood.

Ned followed Missy and Jack to the water, where the trio splashed and teased each other. Her bare breasts bounced freely on the crests of the waves, drawing their eyes more often than not.

Ned and Jack were easy to be around. She hoped neither one would push her to choose one over the other. Her plan had been to seduce her boyfriend while they were on vacation, explore more of her sexuality. Although Carter had dumped her, she'd been gifted with two wonderful men who asked her to stay with them in a beautiful island retreat. And they were both attracted to her. It was an unbelievable opportunity as long as no one got possessive. She'd get everything she could from it, leaving them, the fantasy, and her secret tryst behind at the end of the month.

CHAPTER 6

$\mathcal{M}$issy sprawled on the distressed leather couch. She'd been half-naked on the beach with two men. It was only the second day of her vacation and already she'd had more sexual variety than she'd ever experienced. A small part of her felt guilty about moving so quickly from Carter to Ned and Jack. They were practically strangers, but Carter had been a stranger, too—she just hadn't known it.

The beach house living room was cozy, with a soft rug over the bamboo floor and warm lighting. She could spend the month curled on the couch with books and wine. "Three orgasms in one day...I should be in a coma. I need to lie here until I stop vibrating."

"Three orgasms is a starting point." Jack took one of her feet and rubbed her arch. "Didn't that shitty boyfriend of yours know anything?"

Missy moaned and put her other foot in Jack's lap. "He hated anything outside the ordinary."

"Define *ordinary*." Ned waited for her response as if she were a witness on the stand.

"Um, face-to-face, twice a week."

"Foreplay?" Ned fired back.

"Does kissing count?"

"Only if it's below the neck and involves tongue." Jack licked his lips teasingly.

"Well, then no. No foreplay." She sighed. "I can't believe we're talking about this."

Jack tipped his head back and laughed. "We've done a lot more than talk, sugar."

Ned's compassionate gaze was focused on her as if she were going to break.

She gave him a half smile, trying to reassure him silently that she was far from broken. Pissed was closer to what she felt when she thought about Carter.

"You can trust us." Ned's warm, confident voice wrapped around her like a hug.

Jack rubbed her calf lightly. "I assume that's a no for oral sex, too. Unless that selfish bastard had you sucking him off."

"No, he was disgusted by the idea of his penis in my mouth."

"I find myself getting angry at a little boy I've never met," Jack drawled.

"He's my age."

"That may be true, but he sure as hell ain't a man." His sneer summed up the Shit's bedroom skills.

Jack was right—she'd been dating a boy, a selfish brat.

"You stayed with him for how long?" Ned's eyebrows knitted.

"Five years." Saying it out loud left a sour taste in her mouth. She couldn't get back the wasted time. Her fingernails dug into her palms before she forced herself to relax her fists.

"For fuck's sake, sugar, you're practically a virgin. Don't worry, we can fix that." Jack's eyes twinkled.

"How do you propose to fix my semi-virginal state?" Missy played along despite the discomfort with her lack of experience.

"A bucket list." Ned nodded, his voice low as if he were talking to himself. "A sexual bucket list—things you're interested in trying. We'll complete it while you're here."

Missy pushed herself upright, and Jack leaned forward, mouth agape. His clear shock at Ned's suggestion echoed Missy's reaction. She didn't want to seem like a complete idiot, but was a sexual bucket list even a thing?

"My wife and I did one when we found out she was sick...for travel and other experiences, not sex." Ned rubbed his palms down the legs of his shorts and gripped his knees. "I don't know, it was just a thought." He turned his head slightly, and she caught his brief glance at her.

"That's an inspired idea, sir. We should start now. No time to waste with a whole world of experiences to consider." Jack thrust Missy's feet back to the ground and got up.

Ned rose from the couch, a gleam of excitement in his eyes.

"Whoa. What exactly is going on this list?" Missy was taken aback by the idea as well as Jack's response.

"Don't panic. It's just a suggestion." Ned held his hands up like a magician proving he had nothing up his sleeve. "We can talk about the possibilities while I make dinner."

Her stomach rumbled, but she didn't have the energy to follow him. A list. Of sex things. And they were serious. It wasn't a terrible idea. But wow, if she could have predicted how her vacation would end up a week ago, it wouldn't have been in her top thousand guesses.

"Come on, we need to feed you." Ned held his hand out to Missy. "Jack, grab a yellow pad."

She allowed him to drag her from the comfy spot. Jack jogged off toward the study.

"Do you really want to make a list?" Missy sat at one of the bar stools, with her elbows on the sandy-colored granite counter.

"Are you..." Ned cleared his throat. "Interested?"

"I'm not sure." It was a total lie. "Are you?"

"You have no idea how...*interested* I am."

"But, a list?" She bit her lower lip. "I mean, how many things could we put on it?"

"With Jack here, it shouldn't be a problem." Ned paused from gathering ingredients from the stainless-steel fridge. He took her hand across the bar and locked his eyes with hers. "This is up to you. If you want to. Either way, your decision will change nothing about you staying here."

His commanding voice and quiet confidence reassured her. They had chemistry, and she felt safe with them. At the end of the month she could take her memories and experiences to her new life in New York. "Let's make that list."

Ned nodded once and released her hand. "We'll start with the light stuff and work our way up. You have the final vote, full veto power."

Jack took the seat next to her at the bar, with a pad, pen, and laptop. His naughty grin and his sparkling eyes were those of a man who'd been told he was going to an adults-only theme park.

"Are you okay?" Missy asked. His enthusiasm freaked her out a little. He was a grown man with plenty of experiences...shouldn't she be the one bouncing off the walls with excitement?

"We get to play for an entire month. And we get to plan it. Anticipation is a major part of sex and sexual satisfaction. Of course I'm excited." Jack's shoulders dropped, and he turned his entire body on the stool to face her. "Wait, you're excited, too, right? I mean...we don't have to. If you don't want to..."

Missy touched his knee that was so close to hers. "I want to."

Jack opened his mouth to speak, but her stomach rumbled loudly, interrupting anything else he might have said. He spun back to the kitchen. "We need to feed this woman, Ned."

"How about a salad and asparagus risotto?" Ned uncorked a bottle of chardonnay.

"You know how to make risotto?" Missy leaned forward on her stool.

Ned nodded and selected three wine glasses from the cherry-stained wood cabinet over the bar.

"Wow, maybe I should be taking cooking lessons instead of sex lessons."

"We could do both. I'll give you the sex lessons, and he'll provide the cooking lessons." Jack thrust his head toward Ned.

"Nice try, Jack. I won't be relegated to the kitchen."

"Don't fight." Missy ducked her head briefly and waved her hands between them. "I was teasing." Missy took the wine glass from Ned, hoping it would give her liquid courage. "But how is this going to work? I mean with both of you and only one of me."

"It works however *you* want it to." Ned partially turned away from her. "I don't have to be involved, if you don't—"

"I do. I do want you to..." The words disappeared from her mind. It was hard to talk about what she wanted. One thing she was sure of: "I don't want to hurt your friendship."

"Of course. You wouldn't do that," Jack said.

"No, I don't want to come between you. We all need to be involved or we should forget about it completely." Missy made a circle in the air with her finger then picked up her wine glass again, swirling the liquid inside. Her throat was dry and tight.

"The whole point is to ensure you do *come* between us, sugar pie." Jack's exaggerated leer almost made her laugh in spite of her nerves.

"You're so bad."

"Is that what you want, Missy?" Ned's eyes were locked on hers.

"Where do we start?" She was pleased her voice sounded more confident than she felt.

"Well, all right." Jack picked up the pen and hovered his hand over the paper.

Ned stirred some wine into the pan on the stove. "What about starting with foreplay, then positions, then exploratory? It gives us a way to make a logical list that will naturally build trust."

"Logical. Good." She gulped more of her wine. They were really going to do it.

"I don't want to spend three weeks on foreplay and never get to the good stuff." Jack slapped the pen down.

"Anything we do is going to be...more daring...because there's three of us. But we should ease into it." Ned looked pointedly at Jack before he resumed stirring.

"I'm up for whatever." Jack nudged Missy's shoulder with his.

"Seriously though, while we make the list, you have to tell us if it's something you will never be interested in or something you might try."

"Give me an example."

"Well, I'm never, ever, going to be interested in sexualizing toilet activities." Jack shuddered. "Although, I might be interested in trying anal sex as a receiver—"

Ned dropped the wooden spoon, the clatter loud enough to startle her. Ned faced the sink, his eyes huge in the reflection in the window.

"If the timing were right and it was with the right person." Jack ignored what happened in the kitchen and focused on Missy. "Get the difference?" His crystal-blue orbs were devoid of any playfulness. Seriousness had changed them into lasers. That side of him, though unexpected, comforted her. He respected her limits.

Missy nodded, keeping her eyes on his.

"You have to be honest with us, at all times." Jack's voice was strained.

"Okay. Limits. That works. 'Yes,' 'no,' or 'maybe.' Got it." She took a deep breath and wiped her sweaty hands on her shorts.

Ned returned to cooking, his face crimson. *Fascinating*—both Jack's admission and Ned's response. It was obvious both men valued and cared for each other. But Ned didn't strike her as the type to consider having any sexual contact with a man. Jack was definitely more open to it.

"Kissing, we have to start with kissing," Jack said, writing it down under foreplay.

"I've been kissing since I was sixteen," she said.

"So you're an expert kisser?" Jack raised one eyebrow. "Have you ever come or made someone come solely from kissing?"

Missy barked a laugh. "That's impossible."

"I'll take that bet. And I won't even kiss you below the waist." Jack smiled smugly at her—his playfulness was back.

"Massage," Ned said. "Specifically, sensual massage."

"Won't understand someone's body until you know how they react to your touch. Where their hot spots are. And warm oil slicked over your skin. Oh yeah." Jack wrote it down.

"Any objections so far?" Ned caught Missy's eye.

"No, but didn't we cover massage on the beach today?"

"Hell no, sugar. That would be like saying you saw a movie because you'd seen the preview. It was a taste, an appetizer." Jack shook his head.

"Can't wait for the full meal." She spoke under her breath, but Jack grinned.

"The next logical thing is shared showering or baths." Ned poured more broth into the pan and stirred.

"I always wanted to take a shower with the Shit, but he said bathrooms were private."

"The Shit?" Ned turned to Missy, eyebrows pinched together.

"That's what I call him, my ex-boyfriend, since he dumped me."

Ned nodded thoughtfully and went back to cooking.

"Well, of course, he's partially correct. Some things in the bathroom should be private. Showers or baths aren't one of them. But, taking 'the Shit' in the shower is off-limits." Jack pointed at Missy and added it to their list.

Missy nearly snorted wine out her nose.

"Sorry." Jack patted her back. "How about observed masturbation?"

"Observed?" She glanced over at Jack's lap. The bulge in his shorts had grown.

Jack ran his hand slowly over himself and then squeezed. "Kind of like what happened this afternoon before we went to the beach."

She jerked her head up as heat rose up her face, and she was sure it was a deep shade of red.

"What happened this afternoon?" Ned asked.

"I barged in on Missy doing the two-fingered two-step. It was beautiful. Only could have been better if she'd been naked and I could've seen those fingers sliding in and out of her slippery lips."

"Mmm." Ned paused and lowered his eyelids.

Ned's moan was better than any scene in a dirty book. She pressed her thighs together, trying to relieve the ache in her core.

48

"The difference is we'd all be naked and masturbating at the same time." Jack stared at Ned. "You'd be amazed what you learn watching someone get themselves off."

Missy nodded her assent and took another drink of wine. She felt a little light-headed. The heat from the stove must have been affecting her.

"How about mutual masturbation?" Ned asked.

"My answer is 'absolutely.' Missy?"

"I would love to stroke your cocks until you come. I always fantasized about jacking my boyfriend until he came all over me. I wanted to see it come out and be coated in his cum." Missy slapped her hand over her mouth. She did not just admit that out loud.

Both men stared at her, eyes bulging, mouths ajar.

"I might be a little drunk. That was too much, wasn't it?" She bit her lower lip.

"I'm just trying not to come in my shorts right now." Jack adjusted himself.

"Missy, you have a natural sexuality that has been denied for far too long. We're going to fix that. Aren't we, Jack?"

"Oh yeah. We're going to fix that as soon as possible." Jack nodded like a bobblehead doll.

"Okay, I've got another." Ned started plating the delicious-smelling food. "Non-penetrative sex."

"Non-penetrative?" Jack and Missy said together.

"Grab your glasses. Let's move to the dining room." He followed them with their plates before retrieving his own.

She sat at the far side of the white wood table. Jack sat across. The twin floor-to-ceiling windows at the narrow end of the room provided an unobstructed view of the dark ocean and a sky full of stars. Ned took his seat at the head of the table, and they ate in silence.

"So, non-penetrative?" Missy's hunger satiated somewhat, she was ready to consider the list again.

Ned sipped his wine. "Well, there are lots of ways to stimulate the genitals without intercourse. Some are more popular than others. Some were more accepted in history, but less so now."

"You're talking breasts or feet to stroke me off?" Jack waved his fork between two spots above his plate as if making a selection. "I'm all for breasts, not so much the feet."

"Breasts could be interesting." Missy nodded slowly.

"Breasts are always interesting." Jack stared at hers pointedly.

"Yes, breasts, feet, thighs, ass, without penetration." Ned's voice reminded Missy of her undergraduate history professor. "Intercrural sex was more widely practiced in history and is coming back as a safer-sex option, I've read." He paused and considered the wine in his glass before taking a drink. "Then there's frottage. The term was hijacked to refer primarily to the rubbing of two penises together, but really the term defines rubbing genitals together regardless of the gender. Some women orgasm more quickly with the penis rubbing against their clitoris directly instead of actual penetration. Like on the beach today."

"Well, thank you, Dr. Ruth, for making all those fantastic options completely clinical and dry." Jack threw up his hands and shook his head. "I'm up for boobs, ass, thighs, and rubbing. How about you, Missy?"

"All of those are a yes. Any chance I'll get to see penis-on-penis frottage? That sounds hot!"

"You pervy little minx." Jack smiled at her.

Ned stared at his plate. "Jack, did you get the non-penetrative sex on the list? Make a note we're going to need lube."

Jack finished writing and then glanced from Missy to Ned. "Fore-play's covered. What's next?"

"Oral sex?" she asked. "I mean, it's not intercourse, but it's not really foreplay in the strictest sense. There's penetration, a penis entering a mouth, a tongue entering a vagina..."

"This discussion is going to kill me," Jack groaned. "The only reason I'm not in the bathroom whacking off right now is I don't want to miss anything. Yes, we should include oral sex, absolutely."

Ned licked his upper lip. "I agree."

His deep voice reverberated through Missy's pelvis, and she shivered.

Jack sucked in a breath. His hand shook, and the pen vibrated as he noted the entry on the yellow pad next to his plate. Was he imagining his dick in her mouth, or Ned's in his?

~

"THAT WAS SO GOOD." Missy moaned and leaned back in the linen chair.

"Lemon sorbet or coffee gelato?" Ned stood up from the table.

"Lemon sorbet." She was going to have to get a run in soon if Ned kept cooking like that.

"Sit. I'll get it," Jack told Ned as he gathered the plates.

Jack came back in a few minutes with dessert for everyone. "All right, since we got the standard sex positions covered during dinner, we have one last topic. The kink, or as Ned likes to call it, 'exploratory.'"

"Is this like all that stuff in those books everyone was reading a few years ago? Those gray ones?" She took a bite of sorbet and slid the spoon slowly out of her mouth, savoring every bit of it.

"I don't know about the gray books, but anything considered unusual or extreme," Ned answered.

"Technically, the three of us having sex together in any form is kinky." Jack focused on Ned.

Ned stared at his gelato like it held the knowledge of the universe. How much of what was on the list was new to him, or was he nervous about doing things with Jack?

Missy paused mid-bite when exhibitionism occurred to her, and her stomach clenched. "Nothing in public." The last thing she needed was to become the next viral post on social media. The human resources paperwork from the firm specified employees had to maintain a respectable public image. It would be dreadful to lose her job before she even started.

"Agreed." Ned was quick with his vote.

"No more playing on the beach?" Jack's pout was exaggerated.

"My beach is private," Ned said. "But nowhere else."

51

Missy nodded. Ned had a point about his beach. If she were a celebrity, it wouldn't be enough, but she was a nobody.

"I want to add blindfolding. It would be amazing to lose one sense and enhance the others. That would be incredible. Four hands, two tongues..." She waved her spoon in the air, pointing between them.

"Done." Jack spoke over Ned's grunt. "What about a little light bondage or impact play?"

"Explain." Missy squinted at the sexy man. The shock of discussing how they were going to fuck hadn't quite evaporated. Jack was right—the anticipation was building.

"Hands and maybe feet bound to the frame of a bed. A little spanking or light flogging," Jack answered.

"Restricted movement and a little light pain greatly enhance the sexual response for some people." Ned's voice was low and husky.

"Hmm, let's put that in the maybe-yes category. I'm leaning toward yes, but I'm not convinced." She couldn't bring herself to agree to being tied up and spanked by two men she didn't know well, no matter how hard her insides clutched at the thought of it.

"Okay, I'll add a star next to each of them, and we'll talk about it when we get there. We won't do anything you aren't comfortable with, sugar pie." Jack made his notes.

"Since there are three of us, the next obvious choice is double penetration," Ned stated in his detached, professorial tone. His accelerated breathing and slight sheen of sweat revealed he was having a reaction to the discussion despite his attempts to appear calm.

"I love you, buddy. You put 'double penetration' and 'obvious choice' in the same sentence." Jack squirmed in his seat.

Missy expected Jack to cackle with glee. But it was her body they were talking about treating like a giant pincushion of pleasure. "Hold on. I need more clarification."

"Double penetration includes many combinations. We'll explore what you're comfortable with. It could include anal," Ned answered.

"Anal?" she squeaked.

"So, that's a hard no?" Jack sighed heavily.

"Um, maybe not a hard no, but a maybe no. Leaning towards no. I never considered having anal sex before. It seems like it would be really painful without much benefit. I mean, I know the guy would like it, but would it do anything for me? Have either of you ever tried anal? Receiving it, I mean?"

Ned stood up from the table and took their empty bowls to the kitchen without a word.

"Sugar, if you give me a chance, I will make it amazing for you. I promise. Let's put it as the last thing on the list. If it doesn't happen, no big deal." Jack's voice was soft.

"Okay, that's fine." Missy was uncomfortable that what she'd asked had offended Ned, yet Jack had continued on like nothing happened. Ned's footsteps echoed through the hallway. Although sad he hadn't come back, she didn't know what to say. She would talk to him tomorrow.

"We have our bucket list." Jack smacked the pen on the tablet and stood up. "I can't wait to get started. For tonight, let's limit it to a kiss? It's been a big day."

Jack kissed her gently but thoroughly. His lips were soft and firm. He teased her with his tongue, and she opened to let him explore. Damn, he tasted good, like sweet coffee and strong man. His erection pressed into her, and every instinct insisted she should take him to bed. But there was one person missing. She finished the kiss that would have gone on forever.

"Thanks for an awesome day, Jack. Tell Ned I said goodnight?" A hot bath and early night would be the safer finish to such an unusual day.

"Of course. Sleep tight, sugar pie."

JACK RESISTED the urge to slam open the study door. With all the control he could muster, he closed it gently behind him before he let loose on Ned, who was seated, curled over his desk. "What the hell was that, partner?"

"I don't have to explain myself." Ned slammed the middle drawer shut and went to the wet bar.

"We asked her to trust us, Ned. She's allowed to ask questions."

"And I'm allowed to decline to answer." He opened the lower cabinet and retrieved a half-empty bottle of scotch.

Jack leaned back against Ned's desk, his legs crossed at the ankle and his arms folded across his chest. "Which desire scared you more? My dick or your ass?"

"Fuck you, Jack." Ned's voice was harsh and forced.

"That's what made you run."

"This isn't about us. There is no *us*." Ned glared at him briefly over his shoulder.

"I'm painfully aware of that." He hated that he sounded like a wounded cow. Maybe Ned could just shoot him and put him out of his misery.

With a shaky hand, Ned poured scotch into two cut-crystal glasses. "This isn't going to work. You and Missy play with the list. I'll focus on the merger."

Jack accepted the glass that had a lot more than two fingers.

Ned walked to the window and stared out into the night.

Jack took a deep drink of the smoky liquid—let it burn away the pain of his friend's rejection. As if it could be that easy. "We convinced her to plan her sexcapades with us. Spend her vacation with us. We're in this together or not at all." Jack steeled his spine, done with being weak. "I'll pay for her to stay somewhere else."

Ned spun around. "Why should she leave because... I don't want her to leave. I just don't want her to regret anything."

"Who says she's going to?"

"Things done in the heat of the moment can lead to a lifetime of shame." Ned paused to take a drink. "It's a miracle we were on the same plane. Imagine what could have happened to such a beautiful girl alone on the island with no place to go?"

Jack smiled into his glass. Ned was in protector mode, and no way would he let Missy leave. At least the man was still capable of feeling something for someone, even if he was avoiding the thing between them. "Should I look for a rental for her in the morning?"

"No." Ned's head snapped up, and he glared into Jack's eyes.

Jack perched in the club chair near the window. "Then what?"

"We're going to have to be careful with her." Ned sat in the chair's mate.

"Of course. I don't want to hurt her any more than you do."

"What I mean is, she's putting up a brave front, but she's vulnerable. We need to be careful she doesn't regret this."

Jack relaxed into the leather seat. "We've put her in charge. She wants to play, and she knows she has control."

"All of us have the power to veto." Ned frowned at him.

"Of course." Jack could not let his joy at Ned agreeing to participate show on his face. If he'd been at a corporate negotiating table, that would have been the point where he stood up, shook hands, and left.

"I'm not sure how much she trusts us." Ned dragged his finger around the rim of his glass.

"Yeah. She hasn't told us where she's going after this. New York. New job. Fresh out of law school. Doesn't make it very easy to find her. I mean, how many law firms are there in Manhattan?"

"Far too many." Ned sniffed. "I want her to enjoy this month so that she stays in contact afterwards." He paused, his grip on the arm of the chair visibly tightened. "She doesn't have anybody in the world to care for her."

"You like her that much already?"

"I do." Ned rolled his lips closed.

"I didn't think it was possible."

"Neither did I." Ned went quiet and stared into his drink.

Ned's confession of his growing attachment to Missy was unexpected. He'd shut down when his wife was diagnosed with terminal cancer and had never shown his grief publicly. Along the way, he'd cut off all emotions.

One day with Missy had done more for his friend's well-being than anything Jack had tried. If, while playing with Missy, he got to satisfy some of his desire for Ned, well, even better. At least they were going to be naked and having sex in the same room with the same woman. His friend was likely to freak out again and possibly try to back out of the deal. There would be repercussions, but better to beg forgiveness than ask permission.

CHAPTER 7

Sunlight streamed through airy curtains. Missy rolled over
and stretched. The typical disorientation of waking in a
new place didn't hit her. After only two nights, she was comfortable,
not just with the bed, but there, in Ned's bungalow—with *them*. Anticipation energized her—would Jack make good on his boast to bring
her to orgasm with kisses? Hair and teeth brushed, she threw on tiny
white shorts and a tank top and wandered out to the kitchen.

Ned's abrupt departure still rumbled in the back of her mind. He
hadn't refused to participate in the creation of the list. In fact, he'd
suggested it. If Ned backed out, it would be impossible for her to
continue the plan with Jack. Whatever it was, she hoped they'd been
able to resolve it. To have her first and last adventure end prematurely
would stink.

Worrying about what Ned would or wouldn't do wasn't produc-
tive. Cooking breakfast was the more logical task. The guys would be
hungry, and she had agreed to help in exchange for her stay.

After the coffee maker finished, she relished the quiet that only
existed before a household awoke. She sipped the brew and prepped
veggies for an omelet, one of the few healthy things she knew how to
cook. Her grandmother had taught her plenty, like biscuits and gravy,

and how to make a pot roast. But most people didn't eat like that anymore. She paused mid-chop when bare feet slapped against the kitchen tile.

"Good morning, sugar," Jack breathed into her ear.

"Mmm. Good morning." She tilted her head and leaned into him.

He pulled her loose blond locks aside and nuzzled her neck. With the tip of his tongue, he licked the edge of her ear, and she shivered.

"So, we're starting already?" she teased.

"Oh yeah. I find a sexy woman in the kitchen with coffee made, breakfast in progress—I have to show my appreciation. And since oral is a little way down the list, you'll have to settle for kisses." Jack nipped her neck where it met her shoulder, then turned to take two mugs from the cabinet.

"Well, you told me you could make me come from kissing. If you can actually do it, that'll be thanks enough." She delivered the cheeky response over her shoulder, her gaze caught by his shirtless muscular back and strong arms. Thin sleep pants hung low on his hips and caressed his ass, making her jealous of the fabric.

"Oh, sugar pie, I love a challenge." Jack returned the coffee carafe to the machine and locked eyes with her. "You'll be screamin' later."

Liquid heat flared low in her belly. Time to change the subject. "Where's Ned?"

"In the shower. The plan is to get our business out of the way this morning, then spend the afternoon making you squirm." Jack put his hands on her hips and looked over her shoulder at the pile of chopped vegetables. "What can I do to help?"

"Toast, please. I have everything else ready to go." The nearness of his body to hers made her want to jump him right there in the kitchen.

"What are you going to do with your morning?" He dropped four pieces of bread in the toaster.

"A little tidying around here. Maybe go to the shops." She poured the eggs into the heated pan. "Are there any errands I need to run?"

"No. Ned has a delivery service for the groceries and weekly cleaning."

She glared at Jack, the spatula frozen in the air. "But I agreed to do things around here in exchange for rent. If there's nothing that needs to be done, why did he agree?"

"Because I didn't want you to run away."

Missy jumped at the unexpected sound of Ned's husky voice behind her.

"You needed to negotiate an exchange to stay." Ned poured coffee into the mug Jack had left out. "But it doesn't matter. Everything's changed."

He draped one arm around her shoulders and gave her a quick kiss on her temple. His hair was damp from the shower, and he smelled deliciously masculine from the soap he'd used. The gentle gesture and manly presence gave her a sense of safety she hadn't had in a long time. It could easily become addictive if she wasn't careful.

"I don't have another place to stay or the money to get one." She layered the vegetable onto the cooking eggs. "Nothing's changed."

"You became our lover yesterday." Ned's voice was firm and resonated in her vulnerable chest. "I don't charge my lovers rent, and I don't expect them to provide services. You're here as my *guest*, as you were from day one."

"But—"

Ned spun her around, wrapped her in his strong arms, and kissed her hard, his tongue parting her lips. She held back for a half second before melting into his possession.

Jack took the forgotten spatula from her hand. "Don't want to burn the omelet."

Ned leaned back. His arms, still clamped around her waist, prevented her collapse. All the blood in her body had rushed to her lips—and lower. If that was a preview of the month to come, her vacation would be unforgettable.

After they finished eating, Missy picked up the breakfast plates and took them to the sink.

"Let me help you." Jack reached for the sponge in her hand.

"I've got this."

"You don't have to clean up after us. I made that clear." Ned entered the kitchen, and the adequate space shrank, filled with testosterone.

"I can wash a couple of dishes. Sheesh." She flicked her hands at them, shooing them out. "I'm going to do some shopping when I'm done."

"There's a bike in the shed, or you can take the car. The key is on the hook." Ned pointed toward the back door. "The bike's easier if you don't mind riding. Parking is scarce."

"Perfect. Now refill your coffees and go."

"So bossy." Jack bumped her hip with his and then filled his mug.

Ned tugged her hair, tilting her head back, and kissed her lips. "You can have your way. For now." He left with Jack.

Missy let the butterflies settle while she tidied up. The guys were awesome but much more than she was used to. The Shit didn't kiss her randomly or talk about sex at all hours of the day. It was everything she wanted yet so different from anything she'd known. It would be good to get some time to herself.

Missy pedaled toward the port side of the island, the most active area according to her search. Ned's luxury home and private beach tempted her to spend the day lounging in his perfect world. But that wasn't *her* world. It wouldn't be wise to be dependent on him for everything. She had to be prepared if things didn't work out between the three of them. Besides, in a few short weeks, she'd be navigating the streets of one of the biggest cities in the world. Better to remember she was on her own in life.

As she got closer, people and cars jostled for space on the narrow roads. Ned hadn't been exaggerating about a lack of parking. Docking a ship would be easier than fitting a car into one of the tiny spaces. She locked up the bike as soon as she found a rack and let her feet carry her where they would.

The beach town enchanted her. Cute shops, nestled in small colorful buildings, were filled with trinkets and shells. Food trucks scented the air with mouthwatering aromas. The streets vibrated with laughter and music and the call of boats. The rhythm of the place was so different from Missouri, and Carter wasn't there to criticize every little thing. She could relax and enjoy it all without judgment.

After a couple of hours, pleased with her solo expedition, she was ready to return to the quieter estate.

She found the men still hard at work in Ned's office. "How would you feel about a picnic lunch on the beach?"

They started to rise, but she waved them off.

"Give me an hour to put something together and get changed. I'll meet you guys at the back door."

The perfect weather from the morning persisted. A light breeze flowed off the ocean. A few wispy white clouds broke up the vast expanse of blue sky like the white sails of the distant boats in the bay. Ned placed the umbrella, and Missy spread out the beach blanket. Jack dug in the bag that served as a picnic basket, murmuring about starving. He must have been hungry—he hadn't mentioned her beach attire at all. She'd foregone the top of her pinup bathing suit and instead wore the bottoms with her crocheted cover-up. Being dressed in such a risqué manner turned the heat up between her thighs.

They dined on chicken-salad croissant sandwiches, fresh fruit, and ice-cold mineral waters. Ned and Jack chatted about the status of the project, the challenges, and strategies. She listened, intrigued by their descriptions and insights. The delicious food and relaxing in the sun recharged the muscles she'd tested with the morning ride.

"That was delicious. Thank you." Ned wiped his fingers one last time before he discarded the napkin in the empty bag.

"Would you guys like some of the macarons I found at the bakery? I went with a variety. I'm sure there's a flavor you'd enjoy." Up on her knees, she reached in the picnic bag for the petite box. Their eyes were on her, and she thrust her hips out a little to exaggerate the pose.

"Maybe later. I have my mind on a different flavor," Jack answered. "Don't think I didn't notice your lack of an appropriate top."

"My top's inappropriate?" She peeped at him over her shoulder. A

61

flutter twirled through her belly. "I thought it was completely appro-priate for the day's promised activities."

"Take it off," Ned commanded.

Desire zinged up her spine.

"Well, since you asked so nicely," she sassed. She placed the pastry box back in the picnic bag before she stood and inched the top up, slowly teasing them until she fully exposed her breasts. The icy-blue stare from Jack combined with the midnight-blue focus from Ned made her shiver and her nipples harden.

"Kissing, we're only kissing today," Ned said as if to remind himself. He guided her to the blanket to lie between him and Jack. She was engulfed by two men kissing her neck, her shoulders, and the tops of her breasts but not her tight buds. Jack's light stubble rubbed her skin, making it more sensitive. Ned methodically nibbled every inch. She gripped their heads to hold them to her, aching with desire for more. More *anything*. Both of them grabbed a wrist and held her in place. Warm, strong hands planted on her hips restrained her from avoiding their teasing attentions, not that she wanted to. Pinned, she couldn't squirm or writhe as her body demanded. She closed her eyes and let the liquid heat of their mouths fill her mind. They kissed down her ribs and across her stomach. Someone tongued her belly button, and she twitched with the foreign sensation.

They worked their way back up, kissing the undersides of her breasts, nuzzling her with their noses, and leaving fire in their wake. Their breath teased her skin as much as their touch. A frustrated moan escaped, and she wrenched her hands free to grip the sides of Ned's head, dragging him back up. She licked his full, masculine lips before she opened them with her teasing tongue to taste him. His mouth made her want more than kissing. He cradled her head in one hand and stroked her face as he made love to her with his tongue.

Jack suckled on the tip of her breast, then nipped her lightly. Ned captured her squeal in his mouth.

Jack leaned into them. "I'm going to make you come so hard."

She was already on the edge.

A shiver moved through Ned's body, dancing with her own

response to Jack's sexy threat. She wriggled around, trying to clench her thighs to provide the pressure she needed on her bundle of nerves. Jack swung his leg across hers, holding her in place. It was like he knew what she was trying to do. If only his thigh were a little higher on her leg, she'd be able to make herself come. She'd curse him later when she could think straight.

"Switch." Jack's voice was lightning, and Ned moved away immediately.

The pause was too brief for Missy to regain her senses, and four hands and two mouths quickly continued to drive her insane. Ned caressed her cheek and then latched on to her right breast. Jack nibbled her neck, working his way up to her mouth, finding every tender spot along the way that made her squirm. Cream soaked her bikini bottoms. He tilted her head with his hands to face him. He barely licked her lower lip, like butterfly wings brushing her skin. Gently, he sucked it in, held it between his teeth, and stared into her eyes. His gaze burned somewhere deep inside her, and she forced herself to blink. Ned's teeth on her nipple broke the spell completely as he applied the perfect amount of pressure while flicking the tip with his tongue.

They released her at the same time. Their eyes focused on each other as if silently planning their next moves. She couldn't process all the sensations—total system overload. The sea air blew across her wet, tender breasts, causing her already taut peaks to tighten even further, all of the excess energy directed right to her sex. Jack returned to her lips with light, teasing touches, making her ache to be filled. Ned teased her breast briefly with his tongue before he worked his way back up her body.

Jack retreated to the side and stroked his straining cock through his shorts. His eyes followed Ned's movements over her body.

"Please," she begged and arched toward Jack. He leaned in and gave her the deep kiss she craved as Ned found her ear. He traced the shell of it with his tongue and sucked on her lobe. She needed to move or get her hand to her clit, but Jack prevented all of that. His leg held down both of hers, and he gripped her wrists above her head. The pressure between her legs continued to build, and she moaned a protest into his mouth.

The men shared a look and dove back to her breasts, tracing each areola with their tongues. Ned's mouth was harsh and demanding, Jack's a flickering tease. Missy was incoherent with lust and need. Words poured out of her mouth, all of them begging for them to do something to relieve the exquisite desire. Instead, they tormented her aching nubs. Deep inside her core, she tensed, squeezing the empty space that demanded to be filled. She pleaded for relief. Finally, her back arched, and she screamed as she came with her entire body. Every muscle in her pussy clenched before a river of honey slicked her thighs. They slowed their attentions while she rode out the climax.

"Your eyes look like they're on fire when you come. So beautiful." Ned's focus riveted on her.

Her heart stuttered at the compliment. She would never forget the words that rumbled from his throat.

Missy forced her breathing to slow as she stared into the two sets of unique blue eyes. The intensity threatened to overwhelm, and she wiggled in Jack's continued restraint. "You win," she said.

Jack laughed. "I think *you* won, sugar." He kissed her softly and released her hands.

"Let's get back to the house and get changed. I got a little sandy with all the thrashing she was doing." Ned stood and dusted off his tented shorts before reaching down to aid Jack.

"Fine with me, but you know there's a test on this lesson, right?" Jack asked as he accepted Ned's assistance.

"A test?" The words fought through the erotic fog that clouded her thoughts.

"Yep, you have a couple of men you need to kiss up and down—above the waist, of course—to show what you learned." They each reached out a hand for her.

"Oh, I can do *that*." She stretched languidly before letting them help her up. "It will be my pleasure. And yours."

∼

AFTER DINNER, Missy lingered at the entrance to the kitchen, heart racing in anticipation. Jack didn't realize the beast he'd unleashed by mentioning a test. She'd spent the last seven years nailing every one of her exams. Already she studied to prepare for the New York bar, the test to end all tests. If she passed, her life would be set. To say she knew how to prep for a test, even an erotic one, was an understatement. The internet search she'd done on foreplay had proven quite informative.

Ned and Jack relaxed on the couch with their drinks, chatting about business. Jack with his wind-tousled hair highlighted from the sun. Ned's cultured voice resonating with thoughtful legal insight. They were both so fucking sexy. Checking off more items with them couldn't happen soon enough.

Missy sat down between the men. Nerves at instigating the encore to their earlier beach play made her hands quiver. The conversation halted, both men eyeing her as if she were prey. Forcing herself to focus, she took Ned's idle hand in hers, brought it to her mouth, and deliberately traced his fingers with the tip of her tongue. She took her time in the valleys in between, almost thrusting the tip between them. With slow, rhythmic movement, she sucked the length of his middle finger into her mouth, imitating the motions of a blowjob. Recalling the information she'd studied helped to steady her. She released Ned's hand and removed her shirt, exposing the fact she'd once again gone braless. "I'm ready for my test now."

"Oh fuck, we're in trouble." Ned reached down to reposition his cock.

"If this is bad, who needs good?" Jack leaned back into the corner of the deep sofa and stretched out his arms in offering.

Missy straddled Jack's legs, taking the drink from his hand and placing it aside. Slowly, she unbuttoned his shirt, using her lips and tongue to explore each area as it was revealed. A hint of salt and his clean scent tickled her senses. Once she had all the buttons open, she slid the shirt off his shoulders and nuzzled his golden skin, placing baby kisses all over his muscled torso. Licking all around his flat nipples elicited a deep groan from him, motivating her even more. She eased her mouth up his hard torso while her hands explored the contours of his warm body. Where his neck and shoulders met, she gave a teasing nip. His pelvis thrust up, more proof her actions had the desired effect on him. A sense of seductive power filled her veins as she lifted her hips to prevent him pressing his hard cock further into her clit.

"You're killing me." Jack tried to yank her hips down on him.

"No." She smacked his chest playfully. "Kissing only. Above the waist." She kissed the corners of his mouth and used her lips to play with his while her bare breasts rubbed his chest. Her buds pebbled, and she pressed the evidence of her excitement into him. With the tip of her tongue, she teased him, retreating when he tried to take over. She stared into his burning eyes, which promised retribution, and raised her eyebrow in challenge. He slowly lowered his lids and relaxed back into the cushions.

Missy glanced over her shoulder and met Ned's intense stare. One corner of his mouth eased up, and he gave her a subtle nod. His approval inspired her to increase her efforts.

Returning her attention to Jack, she licked into his open mouth, barely engaging his tongue. The flavor of the scotch he'd been drinking lingered. The smoky taste could have been crafted from the fire burning between them.

Releasing his delicious mouth, she leaned over to suck his earlobe. The supple flesh was so tantalizing between her lips. Before she could stop it, he sucked her tit deep in his mouth. She nipped his earlobe in correction and sat back. He hissed, grabbed her hips, and pulled her down on his erection. She gave in and kissed him fiercely, tangling with his tongue while grinding on his lap. His engorged cock threatened to rip through the fabric keeping them apart. Jack had begun to tense up when she wrenched free and jumped off his lap.

"Did I pass?" Her hand was on her cocked hip, and she arched an eyebrow. Her nerves had transformed into confidence, and his answer didn't matter. She'd performed brilliantly.

"What?" He slowly rose from the couch, still panting. "Yes. You passed, naughty kitten." He tapped her on the nose. "You're going to have to excuse me since observed masturbation is farther down the list." He adjusted his pants. "Good luck, Ned. She's a star pupil."

Missy and Ned were alone for the first time. She stood in front of him and waited for his instructions, still confident but filled with a compulsion to please. His eyes moved from her breasts to stare into her eyes. "Come here."

He held out his arms and seated her across his lap with her legs together on one side of his legs. Her ass was planted directly on his firm bulge. She couldn't move to tease him—he was in complete control.

Ned wrapped his hand in her hair and gently tugged her head back to expose her neck to him. "It's time for an advanced lesson."

CHAPTER 8

*M*issy's pussy creamed. She'd loved having Ned watch her with Jack, but it was nothing compared to what Ned's power over her did. As if given permission to release the tight control she held on herself, she experienced her desires more deeply and emotionally, without hesitation. With his hand threaded through her hair, he held her firmly in his lap, wrapped in his arms. He wasn't letting her go, and she didn't want him to. With the occasional teasing bite, he licked and nibbled her neck. She shook with need. "Please."

"You started this, sweet girl. Now we finish it."

"I want to feel you." She toyed with the first button of his shirt.

"That's your last request. You're mine now." He relaxed his hold on her hair. Her hands trembled so badly, she struggled to release the buttons. Finally finished, she slid the two halves of the shirt away, smoothing her hands across his muscled chest. Ned clutched her close, her naked breasts pressed against him, and the warmth of his skin seared her. The connection was so right. Given a chance, she'd strip them both, removing the final barriers between them.

He owned her mouth, kissing her over and over, moving her willingly wherever he desired. Her lips were swollen and sensitive. She clung to his shoulders, desperate to find her release, but her mouth was too busy to beg. A moan unfurled from deep within her.

Ned angled her head back and nuzzled her neck as he spoke. "I can feel your heat."

The day's stubble on his chin rasped her sensitive skin. His voice, soft and low, resonated through her, intensifying the empty ache in her core. She whimpered as goosebumps rose on her arms. The ability to form words had left her.

He pulsed two rigid fingers against the top of her still-covered mound, driving flames of desire into her core. She tried to buck off his lap, but he held her and teased until she finally let go. It wasn't the screaming explosion she'd anticipated, but an engineered demolition, tearing apart her sanity thread by thread. Only his arms kept her from completely disintegrating.

Ned cradled her until the quaking stopped. As he picked her up, she wrapped an arm around his neck and let her head rest on his chest. He carried her to the guest room and placed her gently on the bed, drawing the covers out from under her. Without pause, he popped the button on her shorts open and took down the zipper. Missy lifted her hips, eager for what would come next, and he slid her shorts over her bare feet. But instead of removing her wet panties as she expected, he covered her with the sheet. A whimper of disappointment escaped her lips as she reached for him.

"Shh, no need to rush this. We have plenty of time." He ran soothing caresses down her arms until she closed her eyes. Ned kissed her forehead, and sleep took her before she could miss him.

JACK SAT on the edge of Missy's bed, watching the soft woman slumber. Morning light filtered through the curtains, highlighting her beauty. He fingered a lock of her hair, golden honey, sweet like her. It was impossible not to touch her—she had something that called to him, but he'd wait. They'd made an agreement, and he had to be patient. If there were any way he could convince her to stay after the thirty days were up, he'd do it. Jack couldn't deny that Missy was good for Ned. In a short time, his best friend had come back to life. It was a crazy dream, but maybe it could work— Ned and Missy living with him on his sprawling ranch in Texas. His hum of desire caused her to stir.

When she opened her eyes, they appeared unfocused.

"Good morning," he said.

"What time is it?" Her voice was husky, and she squinted up at him. So damn cute.

"Early. We have a conference call with the stakeholders later, so we're reworking the numbers and doing the final prep."

"Do you need help?" Missy started to rise.

"No. Rest. Smoothie ingredients in the refrigerator. All you have to do is blend. Coffee's ready to go."

"You're too good to me." She yawned and arched her back.

"Your standards are too low." Jack stroked her arm. "Any plans for today?"

"I was thinking about going for a run."

"Try the public beach. You'll see more of the island."

"Is there anything I can get while I'm out?"

"No, unless you find some massage oil you want to try. There's probably some hippie store with an herbal blend."

"What about lunch?" Missy ran a hand through her tousled hair.

"We'll be working straight through. Plan on a feast for dinner. Caveman food." He kissed her forehead. "See you later, sugar."

"'Kay" Missy mumbled, then rolled over.

He watched her from the doorway but closed it when his phone vibrated in the pocket of his shorts. As soon as he was far enough down the hall that he wouldn't disturb her, he answered the unknown number.

"Jack here."

"Andrew." The all-too-familiar voice grated across his eardrum. He barely resisted the urge to sling his phone against the wall.

"Katherine." Why the hell was his ex-wife calling him from an unknown number at the crack of dawn? "What?"

"Always so polite. I do wonder how the Texans ever got a reputation for being charming. Where are you?"

"Did you call for a reason other than to annoy me?"

"I went through some old papers and found a few things you may want."

"Send them to my attorney." Jack ended the call. Bile boiled in his gut and he marched down the hall, farther away from Missy's room. Correction—thirty days with *any* woman was plenty. Dreams of anything longer were just nightmares playing dress-up.

THE BIKE RIDE to the beach and her three-mile run had left Missy a happy, sweaty mess. The urge to shower and change was hard to resist, but she had no one to impress. She didn't have to keep up appearances for Carter, who'd insisted she always be perfectly presentable. Instead, she tightened her ponytail and went hunting for massage oil. In a little tourist trap, she finally found a small vial printed with the name of the island. When the store owner said she couldn't open and smell it, she returned it to the display.

A food market across the street drew her eye as she stepped out onto the sidewalk. Maybe she could make her own mixture. A brief search of the internet provided a recipe, and she quickly found the necessary ingredients. She strolled out of the grocery store, musing on the evening's planned activities, but jerked to a stop as a taxi screeched to the curb.

The taxi driver leaned across the passenger seat and rolled down the window.

She clutched her bag to her chest. "You scared me."

"Did you find a place to stay?"

Missy peered through the window and recognized the driver as the one from the night she'd arrived on the island. "I did."

"If you need a ride or anything, call me. I'll take you wherever you want to go." He handed her a card through the window.

She tucked the card away in her bag and retrieved her bike from the small rack at the corner.

～

THE CONCOCTION OF COCONUT OIL, vanilla bean, and a couple of pinches of red-pepper flakes—since she didn't have chili-pod seeds—simmered over a double boiler. Hopefully the substitution would work. A few more minutes and Missy could strain the mixture into the small glass container she'd already sanitized. According to the website, it would be solid when it cooled but would begin to liquefy as soon as they put it in their hands. The tiny bit of chili was supposed to provide a mild stimulating effect. Not that she'd need any more stimulation. The promise of a slow, slippery seduction with her hands all over their bodies had her hotter than the water bubbling in the pan.

The guys hadn't left the study all day as far as she could tell. Last she'd checked, they were hunched over their laptops discussing finances. They'd need a massage by the time evening came. Rather than Jack's lesson-test approach, she'd give it her best effort initially. He could always offer instruction if her skills fell short. Then, she'd give Ned the star treatment like he had for her last night. If they weren't completely wiped out after that, she might get hers. Hopefully the internet's suggestions for "how to give a massage" would be as good, or better than, the "faking an orgasm" instructions she no longer needed.

She grabbed the steaks from the fridge and set them out to come to room temperature. After opening a bottle of cabernet, she prepared a quick garden salad. The cheese in the scalloped potatoes was bubbling away, beginning to brown, when she checked the oven. Whether or not that was "caveman food" she wasn't sure, but it was one of her favorite dishes. At least someone would eat them.

"Oh my god! What do I smell?" Jack froze in the entrance of the kitchen.

"Manly dinner, as requested. The steaks need to go on the grill, and we'll be ready to eat."

Ned cranked the pepper grinder over the plated meat.

Jack tugged her hair and grunted. "Should I club you and drag you back to the bedroom by your hair to claim you?"

"Sounds kinda drastic. And you can't claim me. This is temporary." Missy poked Jack in the ribs.

"I'd keep you forever," Ned said as he carried the steaks out to the grill.

His voice was so quiet, Missy must have misheard him.

AFTER DINNER, which the men inhaled along with two bottles of wine, Missy retrieved her coconut-oil concoction from the refrigerator. In the living room, she waved the jar at them.

"Who's first?" Her confident tone belied the butterflies in her stomach. An unknown recipe, two attractive men, and her first massage ever. What could go wrong?

"What do you have there?" Ned asked.

"Something special." She swiveled her hips and shoulders in a silly shimmy, jar in one hand, two towels under her other arm. If she kept things light, her lack of experience wouldn't matter. "I want to rub you."

"What about me, do you want to rub me?" Jack jumped up from his seat and thrust his hand in the air like an eager student. Thankfully, Jack reflected the tone she'd been trying for.

Ned laughed out loud.

"I want to rub you both." She tilted her head and lowered her chin. "Thoroughly."

Ned rose from his seat and placed his hand on Jack's shoulder. He whispered something in Jack's ear before he stepped back and looked at her with fiery focus. "My bedroom."

Jack opened his mouth but quickly closed it. He blinked a couple of times before the surprise left his eyes.

Ned held out his arm, indicating she should go first.

The room was as gorgeous and elegant as the man who inhabited it. The pale silver walls reflected the soft lighting. The deep midnight-blue bed linens and drapes were the exact shade of his eyes. All the furniture was a warm gray stain, like weathered beechwood. Three large black-and-white photos of close-up elements of a sailboat hung on one wall. It became Missy's favorite room in the house.

While Ned lit a couple of unused decorative candles and dimmed the overhead light even more, Missy set the jar of oil on the night-stand and proceeded to strip naked. Jack entered the room, and Ned turned around as she dropped her bra. The men stood there, eyes glued to her body, mouths open.

"Jack? Are you ready?" She did her best to make her voice sound sexy and inviting. If they laughed, she'd pretend she'd been playing.

"I'm fixin' to be." The rough edge to his voice confirmed she'd succeeded in her attempt.

He placed the glass of water he held on a coaster, then yanked the clothes from his ripped body. Damn, he was glorious. Angles and planes were prominent in the candlelight. His body made her want to get charcoal and a sketchpad, and she wasn't even an artist. The muscles of his lower abdomen formed a perfect *V* to point at his long, stiff cock. Her mouth watered. It would be a privilege to learn to give oral with Jack.

Missy took a deep breath to regain control as she spread the towels out on the bed. "Lay down on your stomach."

Jack followed her instruction, adjusting his erection as he did. Ned backed away to sit in the distressed leather chair in the corner. His eyes were still locked on her, and he had one hand inside the edge of his shorts. If only it were her hand.

Missy knelt on the bed so that she faced Ned. She scooped up some of the homemade potion and rubbed her hands together. The white solid liquefied, slicking between her fingers, and the subtle scent of vanilla became stronger. As soon as it melted completely, she placed her palms on Jack's warm skin and pressed into his rock-hard muscles.

Up and down Jack's back, along his spine, she followed the natural lines of his body. His tension eased as she rubbed his shoulders.

"Sugar, that feels so damn good," Jack grunted into the mattress.

She dragged her nails down his sides hard enough that it wouldn't tickle and light enough that it wouldn't hurt. "You do feel good, Jack."

Damn, was that her voice? She sounded like the confident seductress she'd striven for. Using her newfound power, she nudged his legs apart and moved between them.

Jack chuckled. "I'd rather be between *your* legs."

She squirmed with need that heated her core, unable to reply. It was time to get serious and really work him, just like the internet had suggested.

Missy massaged his calf, pressing her thumbs into his athletic flesh, and repeated the process on his other leg before moving to his thighs and butt. She stroked and pulled, then scratched her short nails tenderly across his skin. Jack groaned and shifted his pelvis.

"I don't want to stop touching you," she admitted.

"I got nowhere to be. But we can't forget Ned."

Missy's eyes met Ned's across the room. She hadn't forgotten him at all. Her effort was just as much about him as it was Jack. She slowly rubbed her hands down her breasts, eyes still locked on Ned's. Then she scooped some more magic muscle relaxer out of her jar.

Jack's skin shone with the oil, but his muscles were like iron. With each stroke, she discovered more about how a man's body was so different from her own. And she wasn't going to let any part of him go unexplored.

"Roll over." She moved from between his legs so that he could comply with her demand. Her control over him was intoxicating, much better than lying there and taking whatever Carter felt like giving her.

Jack flipped over. His long cock twitched against his washboard abs.

Resisting the urge to continue with her mouth, she started as far away from the object of her desire as she could—his feet. His eyes were glued to her as he moaned his appreciation. On her way up his body, she avoided direct contact with his balls and hard-on, taking every opportunity to tease him.

"What did you put in this? It smells delicious." Jack stretched his arms overhead.

Unable to resist the invitation, Missy licked his coated chest. "Coconut oil." Then she kissed him, letting him taste. "Vanilla bean." She sat back on the mattress and traced a finger down his chest to the start of the happy trail of hair that led from his belly button to his glorious erection. "And a pinch of red pepper, simmered in a double boiler." The candlelight played over his toned muscles. His gorgeous body shimmered like the silvery walls, the oil sheen emphasizing the shadows.

Jack smiled up at her, his eyes blissed-out. "It's fantastic."

"Sweetheart, it's your turn." Ned had moved from his chair. Jack slowly stood up with a hand from Ned and stepped away from the bed.

Missy tugged Ned's hand. "No, you're next."

Jack locked his crystal-blue eyes on hers. "Let us take care of you, and then we'll get to him."

She sighed and gave in.

Ned guided her down. Jack took the space Ned indicated.

They followed the pattern she'd set. Ned had removed his shirt and used his forearms to complement talented fingers. Ned's touch was firm and forceful, Jack's tender and soothing. Together, they didn't miss an inch of her heated skin. Jack, still naked, took every opportunity to use his rock-hard erection in the massage. She was fevered and relaxed, hot and dripping wet. When she rolled over, Ned's arms interwove with Jack's, working her body in perfect synchronization without words. It was so beautiful, it took away the urge to beg for more. They were both engaged—Ned no longer the observer, Jack not poised to run away. Would she get her fantasy, a real threesome?

"Ned, you have to take your clothes off and get yours," she panted.

"Sweetheart, you don't have to massage me. I loved giving you one."

"I want to see you naked. Touch you." She reached out to him. "Please?"

"How can I deny you?" He unbuckled his belt and opened his zipper, eyes locked on Missy.

She knelt on the bed across from Jack and waited while Ned arranged himself facedown between them. They worked his body in tandem. But Ned tensed up every time Jack's hands went lower than his ribs. Missy claimed Ned's lower back and massaged him softly until he finally relaxed.

She was slippery with the massage oil, and she used the slickness to her advantage. She trailed her breasts across Ned's skin, timing her movements with Jack's so he would be bombarded with the contrasting sensations of her gentle caress and his firm, masculine grip. The incoherent noises coming from Ned spurred her determination to give him the most sensual experience.

They moved up his legs and she teased his inner thighs with her fingers. Jack worked on the thigh closest to him, staying to the outside. Missy slowly licked the part of his inner thigh she could reach, and Ned's hips pressed into the bed.

Jack guided her hand to the bottom part of Ned's sac exposed between his legs. She scored her nails lightly across his testicles.

"Oh yes, sweet girl," he groaned.

She leaned over his back, pressed her breasts to his heated skin. Her nipples pebbled against the masculine plane of strength. His scent, a smoky musk, rose over the sweetness of the oil, and her pussy gushed. With effort, she slowed her panting breath and whispered in his ear, "Do you like it? Do you want more?"

"Please." The dominant man reduced to begging.

Jack deeply massaged Ned's glutes, parting them slightly so Missy could continue to tease his most tender places. She alternated between lightly scratching his scrotum, pressing and stroking his perineum, and even using her fingertip on his asshole. Ned grunted and moaned. Power surged through her as she owned Ned's pleasure. Missy teased his private hole again, and at the same time Ned jerked his hips. Her finger penetrated him.

"Fuck!" Ned froze.

Wide-eyed, she awaited direction. Ned arched his back, lifting his hips from the bed. Jack smiled and, without releasing Ned's ass cheeks, gave her a quick nod to indicate she should keep going.

"Is this okay?" she asked Ned after a couple of shallow strokes in and out, working his body without leaving it. His anal ring clenched the tip of her finger, and it was the single most dirty, sexy thing she'd ever experienced in her life.

"Oh god." Ned's voice was raspy and tight. "I need...I need your hands on my cock."

Missy removed her finger as he rolled over. His sex was hard and purplish red. She took her other hand and rubbed lightly over it, afraid to hurt him.

"More," he groaned. "Show her."

Jack wrapped his hand around hers, taking control of the pressure and speed. Ned's hips thrust up toward her. Jack held Ned down with a hand on his thigh and helped her stroke him to completion.

Ned came hard, covering their hands and splattering his belly and chest.

"Oh, I wanted to wear it." She released his shaft and laid her body on his, wiggling until his cum coated her breasts.

Ned gripped Missy's ass, tugging her closer.

"Hey, what about me?" Jack asked. "We need to make a Missy sand-wich." He dropped to his side and embraced his two playmates. The three of them rubbed and wiggled until they all collapsed in sleep.

UGH! Why is Carter lying on me? Missy rolled, lifting an arm—a muscular, somewhat hairy arm. *Wait, what? Carter's not this built.* She sat up in the bed. The wine fog and coconut-oil haze lifted from her mind. Ned. Jack. All of them in bed together. As fun as last night had been, there was no sleeping with them like that. Her head hurt, and they suffocated her. She slid her legs out from under theirs. After she was completely disentangled, she tiptoed off the bed without waking them.

If there were a vacation lottery, she'd definitely won it. There the men lay...gorgeous, half covered in the sheets, facing each other, a picture in her mind recorded forever. Ned groaned, restless, until his arm—the one she'd freed herself from—found Jack and he tugged himself close, still asleep. Buoyant happiness for them expanded her chest. They would be fine when she left at the end of the month. They wouldn't even miss her.

CHAPTER 9

*J*ack woke up feeling damn good but confused. He was not in the bedroom he'd occupied for the last few days. With a yawn and stretch, he recalled the events of the previous evening and smiled.

It faded quickly.

Although he was alone in Ned's bed, he wasn't alone in the room. Ned had retreated to his wingback chair, wearing only a pair of sleep pants and a frown.

"Good morning," Jack said. He shifted in the rumpled bed linens, discretely trying to cover himself.

"We should talk," Ned replied in a deep monotone.

Jack's stomach curdled. The night before had been filled with the kind of intimate play he'd always desired but had never before been in the right situation to experience. He'd expected Ned would have some sort of reaction, but dang, it sucked to have to deal with his insecure, grouchy ass before his first cup of coffee.

Jack rubbed his hand over the cold sheets. He avoided Ned's gaze, staring instead at the open bathroom door. "Where's Missy?"

"She went back to her bed sometime in the night."

"So, she's fine." If he could end the conversation there, he would.

"Seems to be." Ned's voice dropped to a harsh whisper. "But I'm not."

"What's wrong?" A headache built. Jack rubbed his forehead. It was no mystery, but Ned was going to have to say it out loud.

He shifted in the chair, crossed his ankle over his knee. Then he uncrossed his legs and straightened his pajamas as if they were trousers. "I woke up with a naked man. Tangled in his limbs. Head on my pillow."

Damn, why couldn't they have woken up the same way—hard-ons ready to rock. And with a woman overseeing everything as Ned fucked his virgin ass. Jack shut down his dirty thoughts when his dick began to respond. An erection would not help his reality.

Ned's hands curled into fists. "Last night, I had a finger in my ass. I could say I hated it, but my body already betrayed that lie." His face turned a deep shade of crimson. "I can't continue with the bucket list. Not like this."

Jack's breath caught. Ned was going to quit the list after one night of fun? He sat up more and scooted back so he could lean against the headboard, making sure the sheet was over him. Outwardly, he forced himself to appear calm while inside he panicked with the potential loss. There had to be something he could say to salvage the situation. "You told me I couldn't run away last night."

"I know."

"I was ready to leave. You pointed at the bed." Jack smacked his hand on the mattress. "*This* bed." For once, Professor Ned had nothing to say. He was going to have to take a different tack. "Ned, at any time, did anyone hurt you last night?"

"No." His eyes focused on the bedroom door.

"Did anyone do anything to you against your will?"

"No."

"Did you enjoy it?"

"Yes." Ned met Jack's eyes for the first time.

The condemnation in them stabbed Jack's heart, but he couldn't go back and change what had happened. He wouldn't want to. He was done apologizing for who he was. Ned and a beautiful woman in his bed was a perfect fantasy. But perfection, even fleeting, always had a cost. "So, you're embarrassed because you enjoyed sexual play with another man?"

"Of course," Ned snapped.

Jack bit his tongue. *Of course.* Like it was obvious that what they had done was wrong and shameful. The urge to scream at Ned that he wasn't a sicko and what they were doing wasn't wrong welled up. He took a slow, deep breath, searching for the words that could patch everything back together, maybe even preserve the agreement to do the bucket list. "Did you ever consider the outcome if we did this? Did you ever wonder what *I* might want from this?"

"No. I didn't think about—everything that could happen. Especially so soon." Ned pressed his lips together tightly.

"Kate left me because of my preferences." Jack drew the sheet up further. "With this list, I could finally be myself. With you. Missy's not the only one with unexplored desires."

Ned started to speak, but Jack held up his hand. If he didn't get the words out, he'd never say them. "I want to go through with this. With *you.* Some of it might be a one-time thing. Or you could find something you can't live without." In Jack's dreams, Ned would figure out he couldn't live without him.

Ned closed his eyes.

Minutes passed until he finally opened them again.

"Ned, all of this is temporary. We can always go back to the way things were. I'm just asking you to try, partner."

"Discussing isn't the same as doing." Ned stood and crossed his arms.

"You don't get to play professor. You're a participant."

"And you're fucking naked in my bed." Ned glared at Jack. The judgment in his eyes hurt. As if Jack were trespassing.

"Your bed's off-limits?"

Ned's shoulders sagged. He slowly nodded.

"Fine. For now, your bed is out until you specifically invite *me* back."

"Agreed."

"Now, I'm going to go find our missing princess and talk her into sharing a shower with me. You're welcome to join us." He whipped back the sheet and strode naked to the bedroom door.

"Bring her in here."

Jack froze mid-stride. "What?"

"Come back here. I have the biggest shower."

"You're gonna give me whiplash," Jack grumbled as he strode into the hall.

Jack paused in his room to take care of his morning needs before going to Missy's room as if there wasn't any problem at all.

She was splayed across her bed, facedown with her arms flung out. Her hair was a tangled mess of blond curls. He started to grow hard as he yanked the covers from her body. She was still as naked as he was.

"Wha—?" She rose up on her elbows and peered around, eyes barely open.

He grabbed her, throwing her over his shoulder and smacking her bare ass once.

Missy chortled as she pushed herself up from his back. "Wait, I need to pee."

"Fine. But hurry up." He set her on her feet. "I have plans this morning, a shared shower before we start our day."

Missy shut the bathroom door, and Jack leaned against the wall. As soon as she returned, he picked her up again. There was something fun about having a naked woman over his shoulder. "Why'd you leave?" Jack wanted to make sure she wasn't having second thoughts like Ned.

"I was *sticky*. And I can't sleep with other people. Carter always kept to his side when he stayed over. No touching. You two were practically suffocating me," she said to his naked ass. She grabbed on to his hips as he marched through the house.

He pinched her ass playfully.

Missy laughed and kicked her legs.

"Waking to your lover is an underrated pleasure. At least it should be." Jack scowled as he walked into the bedroom and faced Ned.

~

NED GLANCED up from the spot on the floor where he'd locked his eyes since giving his best friend shit about something that wasn't his fault. He didn't know why Jack hadn't punched him and left. Instead, he'd agreed to come back, giving Ned another chance.

Another chance at what? To expose themselves to censure and ridicule when they were outed. When *he* was outed. It had been decades since Greg, the only man Ned had allowed himself to be intimate with, had killed himself. The professor he'd chosen over Ned had denied their relationship rather than sacrifice his career. The rejection and ultimate loss still stung. It was a long time ago and things had changed since he was in college, but prejudice persisted—it was just more subtle. He rubbed a fist over his chest. Would he do that to Jack, deny the truth, if their intimate actions were exposed?

The right thing to do would be to walk away and let Jack and Missy have their fun. But any intentions of retreating vanished when they crossed the threshold of Ned's bedroom.

The sight of Missy over Jack's shoulder—naked ass crowning her long, tan legs, and delicate toes framing his erection—made Ned's cock threaten his brain with retribution if it didn't get out of the way, while his still-frozen heart remained silent.

Ned stood and turned his back to them. Unable to find the words that would fix his friendship, he went with "I'll start the water."

Jack followed him into the bathroom and put Missy down in front of the huge tiled, open space that served as the shower. The walls were peppered with various jets, and a rain showerhead bigger than a dinner plate hung from the ceiling. A single narrow panel of glass protected the bathroom door from any unlikely overspray. The design was extravagant. Yet at the moment, Ned was glad he'd sprung for the extras.

The tension in the room was thicker than the steam wafting up to the ceiling. Missy's head swiveled between them as if she could hear their unspoken conflict. She stuck her hand under the closest jet. "The water's hot already?"

84

Her attempt to distract him and Jack was charming, though her voice was just a little too sing-songy and innocent, not the real Missy. Shit, all of them were uncomfortable. A technical explanation erupted from his mouth: "I had a secondary on-demand water heater installed in this bathroom since it's so far from the main heater."

Dammit. He couldn't have sounded more detached if he'd tried. Rather than bang his head on the counter, he grabbed the Diamond Dunes Spa bodywash, shampoo, and conditioner.

"Did you get those for me?" Her sweet voice was full of surprise, still trying to lighten the heavy mood that he and Jack—no, that wasn't fair, *he*—had created.

"I asked Ned to have the service bring them with the last delivery, sugar pie. Can't have you smelling like a man. We have enough of that in this threesome." Jack smiled gently at Ned, but he dropped his gaze, undeserving of Jack's smile or his forgiveness. Ned had to get his head out of his fucked-up past before he could be worthy of what Jack offered. Removing the stickers from the bottles became the most important job in the world.

"This shower is unbelievable." She spun in a slow circle as multiple sprays from the marble-tiled walls worked in tandem with the huge rain showerhead to slide over her body from every angle. God, she was gorgeous—a young woman willing to put her body, her sexual experience, in their hands.

Jack stepped in behind her and stroked his straining cock against her ass. "What's unbelievable is how good you look in the water. I'm like one of those guys in the pharmaceutical ads where they warn about hard-ons lasting four hours. I've had one for the last four *days.*"

Ned tracked Jack's hands as he glided them over her ribs, down her hips— and made a decision. No way was he being left behind. Even if he was a total asshole, it was his damn house.

He dropped his sleep pants and entered the shower. After putting some of the expensive bodywash into his hand, he held the bottle out for Jack. As soon as Jack took it, Ned moved his soapy hands to Missy's breasts. Her nipples were pebbled, skin silky-smooth perfection. The water washed the bubbles slowly down her body, and he wanted to follow them with his tongue.

Ned glanced at Jack. The grim look on his face was a knife to Ned's gut. He should apologize, but right then anything he said would come out wrong. At least they were in the shower together.

Jack filled his own hands with the liquid soap and rubbed them over Missy's back and around to her belly, going lower with every stroke until he grazed the cleft of her sex. Ned couldn't tear his gaze away from the way Jack's long fingers spanned so much of her creamy skin. If he wasn't so far in the doghouse, he'd tell Jack to enter her. Watch as Jack's fingers fucked in and out of Missy's hot wet heat until her legs gave out. They'd hold her up as she came all over Jack's hand. Ned would take Jack's cum-soaked digits deep into his mouth and suck them clean.

"That feels so good," she moaned, undulating under their caresses. Missy's voice penetrated Ned's fantasy, only to provide him with a better one as she writhed between them.

Ned rotated her under the rain showerhead. "Tilt your head back." He worked the water through her hair, saturating her golden mane. Jack passed him the shampoo after taking some himself.

"Wow, this smells fantastic," she said. "I could get used to this."

"You should be pampered every day." Ned kissed her cheek.

Soft, sweet Missy—Ned could fall for her. Her *and* Jack. But that wasn't reality. Only an ephemeral construct. They'd all agreed. One month. The only reason she was participating—the only reason *they* were together—was because it was temporary and private.

He knew firsthand what happened when someone was outed. Made ashamed of their sexuality. He'd promised he would never allow himself to be in that situation again. Yet, there he was. And already he'd hurt Jack. There had to be a way to give them everything they'd asked for but keep his fears and longings out of it. He had to take control.

Ned took his time massaging the tea-tree-and-peppermint potion through Missy's hair, working in tandem with Jack. She reclined her warm, wet body against his while Jack used a hand-held sprayer to rinse away the suds.

"Pass me the manly-man bodywash," she demanded.

Jack replaced the nozzle and picked up the next bottle. "You need conditioner first if we're going to comb out this mane. You had some epic bed head."

"Okay, you can rub your *cream* in my hair. But then I get to rub your entire body." Missy stuck out her tongue. She was so cute, still trying to ease the unspoken conflict.

"Damn, you're a dirty girl. My favorite kind." Jack worked the conditioner through her locks.

Ned gripped her hips, holding her in place.

A small smile at their teasing eked its way out for the first time that morning. Ned had an idea, a plan for how to apologize to Jack without meaningless words. His hand shook slightly as he picked up the bottle of soap. Reaching around Missy's body, he took her hand and tugged it to him, palm up. "The other one, too."

She cupped her hands as he instructed, and he pooled the liquid into each of them but didn't let go. After setting the container aside, he wrapped himself around her body from behind, his erection nestled in between her sweet cheeks. The shower sprays danced across his back, but it barely registered. He was on a mission to make amends.

"Come here, Jack," Ned rasped, hoping Jack would respond, averting his gaze so Jack wouldn't know how much it mattered if he did.

Jack slowly stepped forward, and the tightness in Ned's chest eased a little. He placed Missy's hands on Jack's shoulders, using them to stroke the soap down his lean, muscular body. Together they caressed his biceps, rubbed over his defined chest and down his taut abs. Ned guided her every movement, using her hands as if they were his own. Touching Jack the way he wished he was brave enough to do without Missy between them. If only he were a stronger man. Not that he didn't want Missy there—he did. But he was holding back part of himself and hating how that hurt Jack. So he did what he could, sliding Missy's hands to the outside of Jack's erect cock.

Ned pressed Missy's body forward, trapping Jack's erection against her belly. He drove her hands around Jack's hips to glide over his firm ass and up his back. They rubbed the soap across his shoulders and down his ribs as Ned ground his demanding cock against the soft skin of her ass.

"Turn around." His voice gave away what he wanted to hide.

Jack obeyed without hesitation. He moved with athletic grace, the spray fanning off his body. With forearms braced against the wall of the shower, he turned his head, and Ned caught the questioning look in Jack's crystal eyes. Doubt Ned had put there. Into the most confident man he knew.

In silent apology, Ned used Missy's hands to cover Jack's back in soothing, firm strokes, kneading his shoulders and slowly working down his spine, stopping at the crest of his buttocks. Jack twitched his hips toward the wall.

Bending his knees into Missy's legs, Ned controlled their descent. He moved her hands to Jack's ankles, and together they worked the soap up the outsides of his quivering legs, then finally over his ass, massaging deeply. Jack groaned, dropping his head to his arm. Ned's attempt at atonement was having the desired effect. The tension in Jack's back released, replacing pain with pleasure.

They stroked down his inner legs. Ned used Missy's hands to grip Jack's hips and turn him around.

Missy's face was right in front of Jack's erection, and Ned's mouth watered with the desire to taste. Instead, he focused on guiding her hands up and down Jack's legs.

"All this foreplay is making me crazy," she groaned. "The ex may have sucked in bed, but at least I was used to getting regular sex."

"It will make the experience so much better if we wait," Ned told her as he stared up into Jack's eyes.

Jack broke the connection, and Ned's heart clenched—he wasn't forgiven yet.

Ned moved her hands around Jack's thighs and hips, coming ever closer to his cock, grazing his balls. As Ned's arousal built and his cock wept with need, he pressed harder against Missy, searching for control.

Drawing one of her warm, soapy hands over Jack's cock, Ned guided her up and down, working it as if it were his own, loving the way the angry head pressed out from her fist and hid again with each stroke.

"Tease his balls," Ned instructed.

Missy cupped her hand around Jack's sac.

"You're killing me." Jack's voice was choked. Ned's own throat went tight in response. He couldn't explain, but he could show Jack, show him that he understood, that he was trying to let go of the past.

Ned pumped Jack's cock with Missy's hand, faster and harder. "Let go, Jack. Let—"

Jack exploded on Missy's chest, fucking their hands until they'd milked every last bit of his orgasm. The vision of Jack's cum splashing her breasts, marking her, grabbed Ned by the balls. He leaned back and finished jacking his own erupting cock on Missy's back and ass.

"Mmm." Missy rubbed Jack's cum into her skin. "Reality is way better than fantasy."

Her words tugged at Ned's heart. In his fantasies, there were never any bad feelings, no consequences. It was too late to back out of the list. But he was terrified about how reality might come back to bite him. It always did.

CHAPTER 10

$\mathcal{M}$issy sat down at the kitchen bar and pulled her mostly dry hair into a ponytail. She was determined to make sure Ned and Jack got past whatever had happened yesterday. After the glorious, albeit tense, shower, she'd thought they were okay. But Jack had hidden in his room all day, and Ned had retreated to his study. It wasn't like she couldn't entertain herself—quite well, actually. But, the fact they weren't talking to each other was a problem. There was no way she was going to sit through an awkwardly silent dinner again and then hide in her room reading.

Ned cracked eggs into a bowl on the other side of the counter, the sound breaking her directionless train of thought.

"So, what's the plan for today? More beach? More bucket list?" she asked. *Checking off a few more boxes would be perfect.*

"Shopping."

She couldn't have heard him right. "What?"

"I'm taking you out to dinner. I try to get over to the resort at least once a week when I'm on the island."

"The Diamond Dunes?"

"Yes, the place I told you about on the plane. They employ locals.

And the food…" Ned made a low noise in the back of his throat that made Missy shiver.

"What about Jack?" She didn't want to leave him behind even more than she didn't want to risk public exposure of their intimate connection.

"He's coming, too." Ned pulled plates from the cabinet.

She glanced out the window, searching for an excuse. "I didn't pack anything fancy."

"Which is why we're going shopping after we eat."

There had to be a way out of it. Missy would be perfectly content staying at Ned's for the month having tons of sex.

"Um, I didn't really budget that."

"Ned and I are buying." Jack wrapped his arms around her from behind and nuzzled her neck. "It will be our pleasure. Especially since I plan to clothe you from top to bottom." He patted her butt.

She wiggled on the chair, forcing herself to scowl at his antics.

Ned set a plate of food in front of her.

"You guys will spoil me."

"Good," they replied in tandem.

At least they were in sync again. But shopping and dining—in public. Neither one able to keep their hands off her. She swallowed back the sour taste of dread. It wasn't like anyone on the island knew her.

NED FOLDED himself into one of the two club chairs at the boutique. It had been years since he'd gone to an expensive little shop packed with racks of colorful fabrics, shiny baubles, and overly-polished clerks. Waiting outside the dressing room was always the worst part. There must have been a special catalog for husband chairs, as he called them. The tagline in the catalog would read, "So uncomfortable, he'll willingly pay any price to leave."

Jack fidgeted next to him, working on his phone, tapping his boot against the wood-planked floor. The saleslady had given them her undivided attention and only referred to Missy as Ned's daughter once. His glare might have scarred the woman's eyeballs, but damn, he wasn't that old—at least he didn't feel that old anymore. He flexed his arms. Still in great shape, too.

Of course, the woman made the wretched comment right after Ned had handed her a conservative dress in a coral color. Something his wife would have liked. It didn't help that Jack had gone the opposite way, finding a racy red number that looked like a toddler had cut away large chunks of fabric. The sales clerk had pointedly picked out a few more options for Missy without asking either of their opinions.

"Which dress do you think she'll pick?" Ned asked, trying to get Jack's attention.

Jack lifted one shoulder, still focused on his phone. "Doesn't matter. She's gorgeous no matter what."

Jack was right. Better than either of them deserved. And Ned was going to have to work a lot harder to get Jack to forgive him.

The clerk emerged with several items on hangers from the curtained space where Missy was still sequestered. She didn't dive back into the racks for more dresses, so maybe they could get out of there. Finally, Missy came out in her shorts and t-shirt.

"Not going to model for us, sugar?" Jack teased.

The intense need to know her and her preferences sucker punched Ned in the gut. Missy was breaking barriers he'd built so long ago that he'd forgotten they were there. And he was willing to share her with Jack. Shit. His line of thinking was too much for the middle of a ladies' clothing store. "I would love a preview of your selection."

"No, you both have to wait." Missy jumped back from Jack's grasping hands and bumped into Ned.

Before he could wrap his arms around her, she danced away.

"But the only reason I came was to get a sneak peek." Jack pouted dramatically with his hands on his hips.

"Don't worry. It'll be worth it." She smiled over her shoulder and went to the front counter, where the saleslady, who'd been whispering to the other clerk, had the dress on a rack, wrapped in an opaque store bag.

Missy'd started to take her wallet from her purse when Ned placed his hand over hers. "I've got this."

"You're already doing too much." Her amber gaze met his, and the vulnerability he saw there reinforced every desire to care for her.

"Allow me to do this." Ned's chest ached, and his testosterone surged with the pleasure of taking care of a woman again.

Jack murmured something in her ear.

"All right, but I need a pedicure, and you guys are going with me." She waved a finger from Ned to Jack. "My treat."

"Only if I get to pick the color for those delectable toes." Jack's tongue touched his upper lip.

A pedicure? Ned grimaced. So much for feeling manly, but it was a month of trying new things.

MISSY WAS SHOCKED that the men had gone along with her pedicure idea. She would never forget the look on Ned's face when the attendant had slipped bags of warm paraffin wax over his feet. You'd have thought he was being tortured. While Jack and Missy bantered, Ned drove home wordlessly. He parked the car and opened her door before she realized they were back.

They followed Ned along the deck to the side door that went into the kitchen. Rough waves crashed into the shore, and clouds scattered across the perfect blue sky. Missy's hair whipped in the salty breeze. Tension drained from her as she entered Ned's beach house, her temporary home.

"We still have a few hours before we need to get ready for dinner." Ned sat on the barstool next to her.

Jack held up the garment bag. "I'll take this to your room. Then I've got some emails to handle."

"No peeking or I'll have Ned hold you down while I paint *your* toes iridescent lavender."

Jack turned to Ned, who just cocked an eyebrow.

Missy held back a laugh at their unspoken conversation. Jack wandered down the hall muttering about traitors and unicorns.

"Would you be willing to read over some contracts?" Ned asked. "There's one the company sent and the one I drew up."

"Me?"

"Of course." Ned spun the stool to face her. "You have a law degree."

"But I don't have any experience."

"You have everything you need. An education, two eyeballs, and a big brain. Let's put them to use."

She wrinkled her brow and sighed. He didn't have to pretend she had anything to offer.

In the study, Ned unlocked a file cabinet and extracted two folders. "Here's the 'Agreement to Manufacture' the company sent for authorization. Check it over and ask me anything you think of."

Ned sat at the heavier desk next to the bar that faced the fireplace. With shaking hands, Missy placed the contracts on the more delicate desk that faced the windows. Ned was already making notes and flipping pages when she sat in the black mesh office chair.

She opened the file. It was like drinking a fifth cup of coffee, all nerves and excitement. A contract. An actual contract for a real business.

Most of her classmates wanted to be in a courtroom and considered contract law dull, but it was her passion. The rules of the game. Reviewing cases where some nuance—even as small as a comma—changed the expected outcome of a lawsuit was exhilarating.

About halfway through the bulky document, something caught her attention. She flipped back two pages. Then returned to the original clause. It had to be a mistake.

"Ned? This doesn't sound right." It was the first time she'd spoken for…she glanced at the clock—two hours? Her voice sounded craggy. She stretched her back and rolled her shoulders.

"What'd you find?" Ned rose from his desk and rolled his chair next to her.

"The payment schedule and the repayment terms are all in favor of the manufacturer."

"Explain."

"Jack has to pay for the products thirty days prior to manufacturing, and the products are considered approved after sixty days from the date of order. Past that, they can't be returned.

"But if the products are rejected during the second thirty-day window, after our company has already paid for the product, the manufacturer has ninety days to redo them." She continued to detail the contradictory and punitive payment schedule that she would never advise her client to commit to. Her voice rang with authority as she concluded her argument.

"Those terms aren't atypical," Ned observed.

"My first issue is the fact that the product could be delivered after the sixty-day approval window with no option to reject them and no way to get the money back." She smacked the back of her hand on the contract.

Ned held out his hand. "Let me see."

Missy handed him the relevant page. "Also, our company is the one that will be penalized if the products need to be remanufactured. How is that right? They screw up production, and we have to pay overages?"

"Correct. I already told them that clause was a no-go."

The approving nod he gave her was more validating than any score she'd received in college. With increased confidence, she continued to tear apart the poorly worded documents.

"Finally, let's say the order never gets made. If we pay at the time of order, thirty days goes by before they theoretically start production. Then they notify us they're canceling the contract and aren't going to manufacture anything. Maybe they have a fire or a strike or something." She shrugged. "They don't have to return our money for an additional ninety days. How are we going to absorb a—best case—four-month delay in production?"

Jack came in with food and bottles of cold water.

"Nice job turning details into scenarios," Ned said as he continued to review the paperwork.

"I love contract law. If the lawyer my grandparents hired hadn't seen some double-dealing in a bank loan, they might have lost their farm. And we'd have been homeless. My dad would've never let them sign it." And her dad should have been there. Another reason she'd chosen contracts over courtrooms.

Jack handed her a bottle of water and set a plate of food in front of her. The soft look in his eyes made it hard to keep her emotions in check. She took a deep drink and swallowed everything back down.

"She earned her keep," Ned told Jack as he took the other plate. "She caught a couple clauses that could have killed production for a third of a year."

"Well done." Jack locked his eyes on hers, silent for a moment. "Thank you, Missy."

Warmth flooded her, and she dropped her gaze to her plate, hoping the heat didn't show on her face.

Jack moved one of the club chairs to the front of Ned's desk. She, Ned, and Jack continued to discuss the nuances of the deal for the rest of the afternoon.

It was almost better than sex.

~

THE MODERN GLASS-AND-TIMBER resort and restaurant sat right on the beach. As the sun set, shades of crimson and honey painted the lingering clouds from the earlier storm. Golden light gilded the edges of the waves. Reflections of the scene on the oversized panes of the building compounded the effect. The world around Missy had become sharper since she'd met Ned and Jack. Everything was more vivid, more significant.

Although the bucket list and the sex would conclude at the end of the month, maybe there was a way they could still be friends. No one would have to know they'd been more than that. It wasn't like they could be her boyfriends, because having two *simultaneous* lovers would surely be seen as a violation of the conduct clause in her employment contract. Besides, the word *commit* would give Jack a rash. But friends could work.

"You okay?" Ned put his hand at her lower back.

Jack was at the restaurant entrance staring back at them, hand over the handle of the door.

"It's such a beautiful night. I was taking a mental picture."

"I was doing the same thing." Ned pointedly looked from her face down to her shoes and back up.

Missy smoothed the front of her silk sheath. A small laugh escaped her lips.

Jack was suddenly in front of her, his fingers gently lifting her chin until her eyes met his. "Ned's right. You're beautiful."

"It's the dress." The periwinkle, sleeveless garment was perfect for the occasion. The stunning embroidery in navy, lilac, and silver at the neck and the hem showed off the notched V-neck that made her modest chest appear ampler than it was. A side slit framed her leg up to mid-thigh. She'd added some classic silver jewelry as the final touch.

"It's you," Ned and Jack said at the same time.

Ned leaned in and kissed her cheek. "Come on, let's eat so we can play later." Ned moved his hand from her back to caress her shoulder down the length of her arm, then held his own out at an angle.

She took the offering and allowed him to lead her into the restaurant while Jack held the door. The quick pat on her ass wasn't Ned's hand. Over her shoulder, she flashed Jack a saucy grin. One he mirrored with eyes that promised more. As much as she wanted to enjoy dinner, she couldn't wait to get them back to the beach house, naked.

They were seated at the best table, right against wood-framed windows overlooking the ocean. It wasn't completely secluded, but with the low lighting and tall accent plants, it felt private.

"Did I tell you how gorgeous you look tonight?" Jack asked, leaning toward Missy.

"Yes." She laughed. "At least three times. Since we got here. But thank you, again. You both set quite a high bar." She ran her eyes up and down the men, taking in every detail. Jack wore dark slacks and had foregone his boots for traditional dress shoes. His jade shirt made his eyes shine. Her hands itched to trace every line of the muscles underneath the expensive fabric.

Ned was decked out for the island in khaki linen pants with a loose white shirt in a thin weave. Relaxed, confident, and sexy, he could have modeled for a travel poster. A slight shadow of stubble on his face tempted her to find out if the stories she'd read about chafed inner thighs were telling the truth. She pressed her knees together and tried to focus on the menu.

Ned ordered a bottle of wine and a mixed seafood appetizer. He and Jack chatted about the calls they would make in the next couple of days to move the merger along. She listened with only half an ear because the view outside the windows captivated her. It was as if they were sitting on the water. It couldn't be her life, but it was a memory she would always cherish.

The waiter returned, but Missy still hadn't decided what to eat.

"Miss?" The server's raised eyebrows finished the question. She quickly scanned the names of the unfamiliar dishes.

"The braised rabbit loin is superb." Ned placed his menu on a bare spot on the table.

"Really?" She wasn't sure about eating the Easter Bunny.

"It tastes like chicken." Jack nudged her shoulder with his. "Try it. If you hate it, you can always order the quail, which also tastes like chicken."

It was a month for new experiences, so she agreed to Ned's recommendation.

Another server soon appeared with the appetizer and opened their bottle of wine. Ned held up his glass to make a toast.

"Andrew?"

Jack's eyes went wide, and he snapped his head around toward the source of the voice.

A woman approached the table, and Missy's confidence in her own appearance shriveled. The woman might have stepped off a fashion runway. Tanned skin and legs for days were set off by a short white dress. Her honey locks were in a perfect up-do, and she wore enough diamonds to purchase the restaurant, if not the entire island. Five-inch stiletto sandals and pristine French mani-pedis finished her impeccable look.

Jack stood. "Katherine." His tone was devoid of emotion. He didn't reach for the woman or touch her in any way as she air-kissed his cheeks.

"Babysitting?" she asked him, gazing down her patrician nose at Missy.

"No." He glanced at the older gentleman who stood off to the side. "Volunteering with the senior center?"

Missy felt like she was watching a tennis match. If the ball had razors.

"Funny, darling. Does the little virgin know you can't get it up without another man in the room? Or have you got it all taken care of with Ned here?"

After the last volley, she turned to Ned. His jaw clenched tight, and he signaled to the maître d'. Hunger disappeared, squeezed from her roiling stomach.

"Did Daddy sign your permission slip for this field trip?" Jack snarled as he moved between Katherine and Missy, blocking her line of sight to the vicious bitch, but not before Missy saw the murderous look in the woman's eyes.

The manager arrived at the table. "Please have this woman escorted out," Ned said.

"I don't need an escort." She spat out the words like an angry cat. "We were just leaving. Enjoy your sick games, Jack."

"Please, be a stranger." He picked up his napkin from the chair and sat down. He appeared calm, but his knuckles were white as he gripped the fabric.

Missy wanted to crawl under the table and sneak out of the restaurant. How many of the other patrons had overheard the venomous comments? If they left right then, maybe no one would recognize or remember her. A painful silence hovered over them until Missy quietly asked, "Who was that?"

Ned cleared his throat. "Jack's ex-wife. Her father's a partner at my firm. She must be using the company condo."

"It's obvious why you divorced her."

"We should go," Jack said. Missy nodded her support.

Despite the way Missy's grandmother had raised her, a small thread of hate wormed through her veins. There was no way Katherine could have known they were intimate. Either she'd guessed or didn't care if it was true as long as she could hurt Jack. But since the woman's father was a partner with Ned, she could hurt him, too. Missy lifted her chin to look at him.

An internal war played out on Ned's face. He took a large swallow of wine and thumped the glass on the table. "No. She will not ruin this. We've ordered and we're going to have dinner as planned."

She picked at her meal, much like Ned and Jack. The conversation faltered, and a gray haze settled over everything that had been shiny and bright only an hour ago. Once back at the house, they went to their separate bedrooms without a word.

CHAPTER 11

The next morning, Missy shuffled into the kitchen. It had the air of an abandoned playground at midnight.

Instead of teasing and playing, Jack sipped from his mug like a zombie. Ned was physically at the kitchen bar, but he could have been a mannequin if not for the subtle rise and fall of his chest. Missy set her jaw. They couldn't let that vile woman ruin another minute of their limited time together.

"So, when do I get to masturbate for you two?" she asked as she stirred cream into her cup.

Jack's coffee erupted from his mouth all over the kitchen counter.

"Yes, I imagine it would look something like that when you perform for me." She picked up a towel and wiped up the mess as Jack coughed and sputtered.

Ned laughed so hard he had to grip the counter to keep his seat on the barstool. "What's the matter, Jack?"

"Nothing, nothing at all. Just wasn't expecting discussions about petting the kitty first thing this morning."

"Petting the kitty?" Missy arched an eyebrow at him.

"Okay, tickling the taco."

"Oh my god, that's worse." She slapped at his chest.

The twinkle in his eye was back. The fear of no more fun, sexy times released its painful grip on her heart and she could breathe. Sad Jack was something she didn't want to see again.

Ned shook his head, laughter lingering on his lips. "We have a couple calls and such that we have to take care of. But we can wrap up early and do show-and-tell after lunch."

"Mmm, show-and-tell. That sounds much better."

"I expect you to show me what you like and do what I tell you." Ned could have been dead serious except for the corners of his mouth twitching upward.

"That gives me a couple of hours to prepare my presentation." She put her hand on her hip and smiled saucily. "I want to make a good impression, after all."

Jack crossed his arms, eyebrow cocked. "You expect me to work while thinking about her preparing her, ah, presentation? All I'm going to be thinking about is how soon I can start my own performance."

"Okay, guys. You get to work. I'll make lunch in a few hours and gather up the supplies we'll need."

"Supplies?" Jack asked, excitement obvious in his voice.

"Yeah—lube, tissues, you know. Any favorite toys lying around you'd like me to bring?" she teased.

"No, sounds like you have it well in hand." He wiggled his fingers at her.

She kissed him on the cheek and breathed in the clean scent that was all him. "Not yet, but I will."

Their groans filled the air, and Missy laughed as she walked away.

AFTER LUNCH, they sat at the table, no one daring to speak first. Missy plucked at her lightweight cotton sundress. The only other item she wore was panties, having decided to leave her hair loose and her breasts unconfined. Waiting for one of the men to make the first move, she squirmed in the chair. It was so much easier to be bold in her sexuality if she followed their leads.

Ned stood and held out his hand to her. "Let's go sit in the living room."

Relieved, she took his hand. Jack quickly followed. Ned seated her on the couch and sat in one of the two chairs that faced it. Jack dropped into the other.

"I understand you prepared a presentation for us." Ned took command, giving her a way to start.

"I did." After the last three years, her presentation mode was familiar and almost relaxing—even if that particular type of presentation would never have occurred in a college classroom.

She took a deep breath and began, keeping her voice low and husky. "A woman's body is a complex instrument. There are many methods of playing it. And every woman has her own particular preferences when it comes to her instrument of pleasure."

With trembling hands, she clasped her dress and inched it up, tantalizing them with the promised view. She stopped before her panties were exposed. Jack tugged at his pant legs, and Ned crossed one ankle over his knee, clearing his throat. Her plan was working.

Wetting her lips, she continued, "Not only does each woman have her preferences, there is often a pattern that works well for her, such as starting with ancillary areas." She stroked her hands over her breasts and tweaked her nipples through the thin cloth, then slowly moved down her body, not losing contact and making sure their eyes followed. Both hands met over her still-covered mound.

"Some prefer a concentrated effort." She rubbed her hands hard over herself and arched her hips to provide more pressure.

"Others split their focus." Raising her hand back to her breast, she pulled and pinched the peak, and with the other continued rubbing at the apex of her thighs. It wasn't solely the activity making her squirm and pant, it was their penetrating stares following her every move. The appeal of exhibitionism finally made sense to her.

"Take off the dress," Ned said. "I need to see you."

She stood to remove it. Naked before them except for her wet panties, she asked, "Is this more to your liking, sir?"

Fire lit his eyes when she addressed him. "Almost. Get rid of that scrap of silk. It's blocking my view."

"I could give you a hand," Jack said.

So focused on Ned, Missy had almost forgotten him. She took a mental snapshot of him she'd never forget. His pants were unzipped, and he gripped himself with a relaxed hand, moving leisurely up and down.

"It looks like you already have your hands full." She slid off the panties and sat on the couch, legs splayed wide, making sure Jack had as good a view as Ned.

Jack grabbed the length of his cock, then slowly stroked down each mouthwatering inch. As she moved her hand back to her open sex, she saw liquid bead on his tip. In a flash, he squeezed his purple head tight and hissed out a breath. He looked up to the ceiling before dropping his fiery gaze back to her. She rolled her lips in between her teeth to hide her smile. He'd almost lost control. Because of her. An unfamiliar confidence filled her—sexual power. And she liked it, a lot.

"Shall I continue?" she asked Ned, who had yet to participate other than verbally.

"Fuck yes," Jack said before Ned could get a word out.

"Well, I will if Ned joins us. I think he needs to let that huge cock out and show us what he likes, too. Isn't this the observed masturbation session from the bucket list?" She knew they'd already crossed into the action with their previous games, but the lines were blurry. She didn't care about following the list strictly, she just wanted to savor every second she had with them. Because when the month came to an end, she would leave it all behind like it had never happened.

In her experience, every time she'd given in to indulgent desires, there had been a cost. And an exorbitant one. But she'd done nothing to deserve what Carter did to her. He was the one who'd left her, who'd put her in such a precarious position. Not that she was in a bad position—no, every position was going to be awesome. And they'd already been outed publicly by Jack's ex, so she was owed some selfishness and misbehavior.

"Eyes on me, Missy." Ned undid the button on his shorts while she continued to finger herself leisurely.

Thoughts of punishment and Carter evaporated. She expected Ned to be uneasy, but he didn't falter under their attention. Jack's hand was frozen mid-stroke, his body angled to face Ned, and his gaze locked on Ned's hand.

He slid down his zipper, one tooth at a time and freed his rigid length. "There, now, where were you?" Ned's voice was heavy with unspoken commands.

His thick cock filled his large hand as he wrapped it around the base. The urge to drop to her knees and beg him to use her mouth was hard to ignore, but she was on a mission and oral sex would be coming up soon.

It was time to make them as needful as she was. "I believe I was right...here."

Missy took her left hand and spread open her puffy lips, showing the men exactly how ready for sex their shared exhibition made her. She put two fingers of her right hand in her mouth and sucked them, tasting herself. Although there was no need for additional lubrication, it would tease them to think about what she might taste like and what else she could be putting in her mouth.

She rubbed slickened fingers at the top of her slit, over her clitoris, gently swirling, making everything warmer and wetter. They followed her pace, slowly working themselves, using the pre-cum to ease their strokes. Both of them completely focused on what she was doing. Her pussy was sopping, but she wanted it to last.

"Show me how swollen your clit is, Missy." Ned's voice was like a firm caress over her skin.

She slid back the hood on her little pearl.

"Nice. You like this, too," Jack said.

"Pinch it," Ned said.

Pinch her clit? Instead of following his command, she rubbed a little circle again.

Ned expressed his irritation with a guttural huff.

"Trust him." Jack picked up the bottle of lube from the side table where she'd placed it earlier and squeezed some into his hand before passing it to Ned. She moved her fingers inside her cleft, pulsing them in and out with increasing speed. The only thing that would have been better was one of their cocks filling her up. Jack and Ned stroked faster, both flushed and grunting, ready to explode.

Their cocks moved through the channels of their hands. Wet sounds of flesh on flesh pulsed on her nerves. They handled themselves roughly. Groans of pleasure, the smell of arousal, filled the room—it was sex like she'd dreamed of. Raw and real.

Thrusting her fingers in and out of her clenching pussy as fast and deep as she could, the men matched her rhythm.

"Now, Missy. Do it," Ned insisted through clenched teeth.

Reluctantly, she complied with Ned's command and pinched her bud. The pain pushed her arousal over the edge spectacularly. A screaming orgasm barreled through her, and her pussy gushed out her pleasure. They followed, covering their hands in sticky streams of cum.

Nobody said anything. Panting was all they could do.

Jack recovered first. "Oh fuck. That was so much better than I thought it would be."

As Missy tottered down the hall to get stuff to clean up, sundress in one hand and her sweet ass calling to his cock, Ned wished he could recover as fast as he had in his twenties.

"I need to touch her," Jack said.

"Tonight." Ned gripped his spent length. "I know we aren't ready for intercourse, as far as the list. But if she can make herself come that hard, imagine what we can do. Take her right into the stratosphere."

"I like the way you think, sir," Jack's voice was husky, and his crystal-blue gaze burned.

The respectful address caused tightness in Ned's chest, and his balls twitched. Jack was teasing him with that shit, but it fucking worked.

"Good boy," Ned kept his tone light. But he couldn't help the smugness when Jack's cock started to stiffen again.

Missy returned, her clothes back in place, and handed them each a warm, wet towel. Ned and Jack quickly took care of cleaning themselves up and closing their pants.

"So, what are we doing with the rest of our day? Seems too pretty to waste it inside, but I'm still kind of loopy." Her eyes were focused on the view of the ocean.

Jack stood and went to Missy's back, wrapping his arms around her. Part of Ned loved the image, the sexy blond couple framed in his picture window with a sea of boats beyond. But part of him, a part he wasn't proud of, was a tiny bit jealous.

Jack turned his head and spoke to Ned over his shoulder. "We could go laze on the beach. Remember, we're supposed to have down time, too."

Ned swallowed his juvenile emotions. "Excellent plan. Get changed, and I'll load the cooler."

Jack left, following Ned's instruction, but Missy remained.

"Can we have a small fire?" she asked so quietly that Ned wasn't sure he'd heard her correctly.

"You want a fire on the beach?" He reached out to caress her cheek, pleased when she leaned into his touch.

"Well, not right now. Later. I noticed you have some hot dogs and s'mores fixings."

"I do?" The woman who stocked his kitchen always surprised him.

"Yeah, fancy hot dogs, probably more like sausages, and the chocolate is twenty dollars a pound at least, I'm sure. But summer vacation requires cooking food on a stick, over an open flame." Her hands were on her hips as if she expected him to argue.

"Then we'll have a fire." Ned tapped her nose. "And food on a stick."

He loved that she was a brilliant woman who brought a childlike joy to his empty house. She was fresh air to his smog-filled lungs.

~

JACK SAUNTERED over to Ned who was on his knees in the sand scraping a sizable circular depression. "Whatcha doing? Putting in underground parking for your sand castle?"

"Missy wants a campfire." Ned didn't look up as he continued to form a pit.

"What can I do?"

Missy stepped off the last wooden stair a few yards away. "We're starting already?"

"If we do the prep now, we won't be struggling in the dark." Ned paused his digging and focused his attention on Jack. "Gather some wood. There's a canvas bag over there." Ned indicated with a head nod.

"On it." Jack stepped away from the perfect fire pit Ned had formed.

"I can help," Missy offered and followed Jack down the beach.

"You don't want to do that, sugar. You'll mess up your soft hands." Jack didn't slow his pace. She was only offering to be sweet. No woman wanted to drag around in the forest picking up rough, dead wood.

"Jack, despite how you two treat me, I'm not a princess." Missy pushed at his shoulder. "I grew up on a farm."

"Well, alrighty then." Jack led her into the shaded green canopy. It was cool under the protective limbs of the trees, and the dirt was rich with decaying leaves and bark. The smell wasn't quite like the forests he'd hunted in with his family in his youth—too much ocean. But he was instantly at peace.

Katherine wouldn't have considered joining him. Manual labor was beneath her. She'd hated the ranch. Horses and stalls. Dirt and chores. He'd have to take Missy to his place in Texas someday.

"What happened?" Missy asked quietly, handing him another handful of dried branches.

"What happened when, sugar?"

"Between you and your wife."

The question caught Jack by surprise. His first instinct was to make a joke about marrying the before-unknown wicked witch of the North. But he wouldn't hide from Missy.

"Ah. I married her young. She was so captivating. Big-city fancy. It was like she shone and all the radiance was focused on me. But I wasn't honest with her." Jack's heart tugged. It was his greatest failure. "I wasn't honest with myself. I thought I could be what she needed."

"She didn't know you were bisexual?"

Missy's insightful, piercing statement was like a slap. "No. I thought it wouldn't matter."

"But it did."

"After a few years with her, I realized I wasn't happy and tried to get her to explore some of my other desires. She hated it. Left me." Jack lifted one shoulder. "I deserved it. But at the time, I felt betrayed."

"I wondered. There's still a huge amount of passion between you two. Just all negative."

"I'm sorry you had to see that."

"I'm sorry it has to be that way. One decision can cost so much."

The wistful tone in her voice made Jack pause. He could ask her what her decision had been, but things were too heavy already.

"I think we have enough wood for a bonfire, and we only need a campfire, sugar."

Missy turned slowly. "How do we get out of here?"

"You've never been in the forest?"

"There were always trails. I didn't realize how far in we walked."

"Don't worry. I learned how to navigate on my cousins' land in Arkansas. I'll have you back on the beach working on your tan in a moment." Jack held out his hand, and Missy instantly dropped hers into it. The trust she gave him, without hesitation or question, made his chest constrict and warmth flooded his veins. Her beauty was so much more than blond hair and long legs.

∼

Missy was sticky from eating s'mores. Cleaning her hands at the sink, she let nostalgia wash over her. The afternoon on the beach had been perfect. They'd played in the water and cooked food over a little beach fire. Peaceful contentment that had been missing since she'd left her grandparents for college washed over her. Like she belonged there. But that was crazy. It was one moment in time. A step away from her reality until she returned and resumed her regularly scheduled life plan, following all the rules and keeping her promises. Her chest hurt and a tear escaped before she forced herself to stop being so emotional. It was just hot dogs.

"Let's go to bed." Ned came from behind and wrapped his arms around her.

"Yeah, I'm ready to chill. It was a perfect day. Thank you." She took his offered hand. "Coming, Jack?"

He stood up and followed them down the hall. "Not yet, but soon. I hope."

"What are we doing?" she asked when they went to Ned's bedroom instead of her own.

"We're accelerating the plan. Observed masturbation was fun, but mutual masturbation is more fun. We'll show you."

"That sounds even better than roasted marshmallows," she sassed as giddy bubbles of anticipation zinged through her bloodstream.

"Wait until you see how it feels." Jack put his hands on her hips and pressed his steely erection against her bottom.

"Mmm, feels promising." She slipped off her t-shirt and shorts, capturing her underwear at the same time.

Ned took her hand again and guided her to the bed. "Get in the middle, sweetheart. It's time to make a Missy s'more." The naughty grin on his face was the best thing she'd seen all day.

With her legs parted, she slowly began to circle her clit in a clear invitation. They stared at her, frozen. The power she held over them was a potent aphrodisiac. As if by some unspoken cue, they reanimated and removed their clothes in a rush. She patted her hands on the bed, inviting the men to join her.

Jack flopped next to her with a bounce. Laughter erupted at his playfulness. She dragged her leg up his while she reached for his erection, trying to resume her seduction. He leaned back and put his arms behind his head. "Stroke me, baby."

"You want me to handle you?" She tried to grip him the way Ned had guided her in the shower, but there was too much friction. Thinking quickly, she dipped her fingers into her pussy and gathered the juices. When she put her wetness over his cock, he thrust his hips, fucking her hand. His cock was warm chenille over iron. Sexual energy flowed from him through her entire body, kicking up her own desire.

"Oh fuck. Yes. Just like that." His balls filled her other hand. The weight and the texture of the skin fascinated her. She pressed her fingers against his perineum, and his sac started to swell. Once again, the internet was her best friend.

Ned embraced her from behind. His warm hand caressed down her side and over her thigh, leaving a trail of fire. He reached between her legs and parted her lips. Ned tickled and teased her, distracting her from Jack's hot cock sliding through her fist.

Jack gripped her knee and lifted her leg higher, opening her up even more. Missy did her best to keep stroking Jack while she reached back for Ned. Both hands full of hard cock, she moaned and worked them as well as she could, wanting their hot cum all over her body.

Jack's hand joined Ned's at her opening. She couldn't tell who was caressing and who was penetrating, but they'd better not stop. Another hand dragged through her wetness and back to her ass, and she froze.

"Trust me, sweetheart," Ned whispered in her ear. He didn't press his fingers inside but rubbed the outside, making those nerves tingle in an unfamiliar but delightfully naughty way. Jack pulled and pinched her nipples, alternately rubbing out the delicious sting. An overload of sensations built inside her. Velvet skin over rock-hard cores, thick stroking fingers in her pussy, Ned's fingers teasing her ass, Jack's muscular leg hot against the inside of her thigh, him tweaking her breasts. Everything coalesced into a supernova that exploded out of her in a giant gush, stealing her vision and breath.

Her body was left on the bed while she soared through the stars, then snapped back to a heaving boneless puddle of pleasure. All of her nerves quaked as they tried to reconnect.

Jack groaned and arched, coming all over her hand. She wasn't sure how he'd managed since she'd lost any focus she had on stroking them, but it didn't matter because Ned followed with his own hot cum coating the side of her body.

"Wow," she said when she could finally take a breath.

Jack leaned in and kissed her, pressing his wet body against her. He parted her lips with his tongue and tangled with hers. "That was unbelievable. I've heard women could squirt, but I've never seen it. Beautiful, sugar."

Ned rolled her toward him and kissed her long and hard. Jack, who had slipped out of bed, returned to the kissing couple with a warm, wet towel and cleaned her body. She was grateful—there was no way she would be able to stand long enough to take a shower.

Ned reached for the towel and rose from the bed. When he got to the side where Jack lay next to Missy, he leaned down and she heard him whisper "Stay here tonight, Jack. All night. You. Missy. And me."

Ned brushed Jack's ear with his lips. Jack shuddered. She rubbed his arm, and he wrapped himself tighter around her. She hoped Ned didn't change his mind or regret his decision. It would kill his best friend.

CHAPTER 12

$\mathcal{J}$ack woke up in Ned's bed. Ned was gone, again. But Jack wasn't alone—a blond goddess with sleepy, unfocused eyes lay naked next to him. He stroked a hand over her cheek. "Good morning, sugar."

"Morning." Missy blinked and tried to smooth her hair.

Jack grinned. He'd never been with anyone who had come as hard as she had last night. He kissed her soft lips.

She stretched her arms overhead and arched her back with a soft moan. It had only been a week, but if he let himself, he could already be attached to her. It would be a mistake, a beautiful, horrible mistake.

"I'm going to go find Ned. Why don't you take a hot shower?" Hopefully their host was in as good a mood as he was.

"I'll use the one in my room." She rose from the bed, showing no sign of embarrassment at her undressed state.

Jack followed her to the hall. A quick stop in his room for a t-shirt and sweats, then he'd start breakfast if Ned wasn't already on it.

"Well, I guess I don't have to wonder who's fucking who now." The bitter, cold voice of his ex carried down the hall.

Missy, who was several steps ahead of him, squeaked and bounded into her room. The door slammed behind her. At least she was out of the line of fire.

His eyes burned with the unwelcome vision of Katherine. Immaculately dressed as always. "Who the hell let you in?"

"Upgrading to a new model doesn't make you cool, Jack." Her icy gaze and rigid stance was a vivid reminder of why he was divorced.

"She might resemble you on some...shallow level...but she's nothing like you. Thankfully."

Something that might have been pain flashed through her eyes, but before Jack could confirm and possibly apologize, Katherine tipped her face to the ceiling and tapped her stiletto. "Jack, put on some pants. I grew tired of seeing your limp dick long before we got divorced."

He didn't care that he was naked, only that Katherine was interrupting his morning. "It's only you who has that effect on it. Where's Ned?"

"I believe he's in his study looking over the firm's documents I delivered."

"What's going on?"

"Nothing that's any of *your* business." She finally met his eyes with an icy glare. "Get dressed, Jack."

"Leave, Kate. You've done your little courier chore for Daddy." He patted his hands around his ass, checking non-existent pockets. "Do you need a tip? I don't seem to have my wallet on me."

"Screw you, Jack."

"No, thanks. Been there, don't miss it. Now, run along." Jack shooed her off. "Go find someone else to pester."

Katherine spun on her spiked heels and strutted down the hallway in no particular hurry. "By the way, Jack, I never remembered it being so small. You might want to see a doctor. They can do wonders for old men these days."

"You would know," he called after her.

The clack of her heels stuttered, and Jack took a step toward her, but she recovered instantly, and, to his relief, kept walking.

He knocked on Missy's door, but there was no answer. When he

114

tried the handle, it swung open. The shower was running, and the thought of Missy with water cascading over her body wiped away all traces of his ex-wife.

Jack poked his head in the bathroom and called over the splashing, "Can I come in?"

Missy peeked out, wet hair plastered to her head. "Is she gone?"

"Yes, she flew away on her broom."

"I can't believe she saw us like that."

It was cute the way her cheeks turned pink. "There's nothing to be embarrassed about. If she has a problem with it, it's her problem."

And Katherine *did* have a problem. With *him*. She'd divorced him after one small taste of what he liked. He'd begged her to talk to him after a single, relatively tame experience. Instead, Katherine had been on a plane back to Daddy before he could explain or compromise.

Missy, on the other hand, was boldly exploring all the sexual things on their list. He'd had more honest conversations with her than he'd ever had with Katherine. Part of that was on him, but Katherine wasn't a deep-conversation woman. She was all about perfect veneers and keeping up appearances. Missy got sweaty running on a public beach and made massage oil and gathered wood. And she understood his attraction to Ned. Encouraged it, even. She was *actual* perfection.

Jack focused on the woman hidden behind the opaque curtain. Stirrings of desire roused his cock. "Now, can I come in and scrub your back?"

Missy dropped her chin. For a second, he worried she might deny him. Instead, she pulled the fabric back and made room for him.

NED TURNED on the barstool as footsteps echoed down the hallway. "I wondered when you two were going to appear." Warmth ballooned in his chest at the sight of Jack and Missy shoulder to shoulder, exactly as he'd left them in his bed. If only his phone hadn't started pinging so early, he could have woken up with them. "I had lox and bagels delivered. The coffee's fresh."

"In the future, a little warning if you're going to let a rabid dog loose in the house." Jack grabbed the coffee carafe and filled the two mugs on the counter.

The biting tone chilled Ned instantly. "What are you talking about?"

"We got caught in the hallway in our birthday suits by Kate."

"Are you serious?" Ned's gaze traveled from Jack to Missy. Her skin flamed. It was true.

A lump formed in his throat. He'd let that vicious cat loose in his house.

"I was escorting her out when she asked to use the restroom." Ned looked over his shoulder at the door to the small guest bathroom near the front entry. "Another call came in and—"

"She's not good with boundaries."

"I'm sorry." Ned hated that he'd left them vulnerable.

Jack handed Missy a mug. "What'd she bring?"

"Board paperwork. Her father decided it would be more secure than trying to get them to me by mail."

"Why the hell didn't she deliver them two days ago?"

"It doesn't really matter." Ned rubbed his forehead. Maybe he needed to do more than *semi*-retire from the firm. His personal life held far more appeal than being a lawyer ever had.

"What's going on?" Jack's voice was tight, and his brow furrowed. Ned turned to avoid his piercing gaze.

"Board stuff." Ned patted the seat next to him, wanting Missy near. "I need to fly back to New York for a couple of days, attend a mandatory meeting. But I want you two to stay here and relax."

"You have to go?" Missy plopped into the chair and dropped her chin into her hands, elbows braced on the counter.

"I don't like it either." Ned wrapped his arm around the back of the barstool. "But I need to be there in person. I leave Sunday morning. The meeting is on Monday, and I'll be back by Tuesday night." He gritted his teeth. "If it were the usual bullshit, I'd give one of the other members my proxy. But there's something…questionable going on."

Jack silently placed a plate with a bagel and all the fixings in front of Missy.

"I understand." Missy's gentle acceptance made Ned's gut clench. His wife would have called him out on abandoning a vacation for work—and *had* many times. Here he was doing it again when they only had a short time left together. Apparently, he'd learned nothing from the guilt that had tormented him since his wife's passing, because he was getting on the plane. Again.

"I'll make it up to you when I get back, and we still have tonight and tomorrow." He put his hand under her chin, forcing her to meet his eyes. Ned kissed her lips lightly before releasing her.

"How'd you book the flights so quickly?" Jack's tone hadn't eased at all.

"They're sending the jet."

"Wow. Nice," Missy said.

Ned swallowed past the bitter taste that rose in his throat. "Just a way to keep the partners on a shorter leash."

"Pretty fancy leash."

Being yanked around sucked—no matter how shiny the tether. Ned opened his mouth to argue. But Missy wasn't the person he should be confronting. In fact, he wasn't sure *who* that should be. Most likely, himself. He wiped his hand down his face. At least he'd made arrangements for some fun before he had to head out.

"So." Jack clapped his hands together.

Ned startled at the sudden noise that brought his attention back where it should be.

"What are we going to do today?" If only Jack's eyes held the same sparkle as he put in his voice. Ned stood up, put his arm around Jack and gave him a quick squeeze.

"We need to be at the marina by noon." It wouldn't make up for leaving, but his plan might provide some excitement and distraction.

"What are we doing?" Missy gazed at the men with wide eyes.

"It's a surprise. I think you'll like it."

∾

MISSY WASN'T sure what she should be wearing, but not a skimpy pair of shorts and a t-shirt tossed over her pinup bathing suit with a pair of flip-flops. Ned had assured her it was a casual event. There was nothing casual about the huge shiny boat he'd pointed out when they'd piled out of the car.

She took Ned's hand as he assisted her onto the polished deck. Jack was close behind and steadied her other elbow. The thing was obviously built for speed, and there was an open hatch at the back. A sunshade covered the area where the steering wheel, or whatever it was called, was.

A table with a white linen tablecloth, blue umbrella, and three wooden chairs was set up in the lower part of the boat. As soon as the waiter saw them, he poured wine into crystal goblets at each of the settings. She wasn't sure if she was shaking from the movement of the water or the unexpected extravagance.

"What's all this?" she asked as Ned held out a chair for her.

"Lunch. After we eat, the caterers will take this away, and we can go out for your surprise."

Ned seated himself in the last chair and held up his glass. His eyes sparkled more than the wine. "To adventures. Of all kinds."

Missy clinked her glass with his. "Adventures," she echoed and took a small sip.

It reminded her that she wasn't misbehaving, she was having an adventure. Something outrageous she would recall fondly when she resumed her normal, regular life.

After a meal of seared scallops over an arugula salad, she was the perfect amount of full and ready for whatever Ned had planned. A team of people whisked away the al fresco setup while she sat on the built-in bench next to Jack. Ned dropped down next to her and put his arm around her shoulders.

"Happy?" he asked.

"Of course. This vacation is so much more than I ever planned."

Ned nodded slowly. "Vacation."

Missy caught the lines that had formed on his forehead before he turned his face away.

"The list is the best plan *ever*," Jack said.

The boat puttered out of the harbor, cruising through the no-wake zone. An offshore breeze carried the scents of salt and fresh ocean to her upturned face. The one glass of champagne had left her relaxed but not tipsy.

"Where are we going?" she asked.

"Parasailing."

"What?" She whipped around to stare at Ned.

"Parasailing. You know, they hook you up to a parachute, and you float in the air behind the boat. It's like water skiing, only much better. You can see for miles."

Missy's lunch rose in her throat, and she shook her head.

Ned's shoulders sagged, but she didn't care. Parasailing wasn't an adventure. It was a death wish.

"Hell yeah!" Jack exclaimed. "I've always wanted to do that. Can we go tandem?"

"I'm not...I can't...I don't think I can go."

"What's a matter, sugar pie?" Jack asked.

"I don't do heights." Missy trembled all over. "I got on a plane for the first time in my life a week ago. I'm not ready for parasailing."

"It's perfectly safe. We would never put you in danger. Try it. If you hate it, we'll bring you right back down." Ned ran his hands up and down her arms. It should have been comforting, but it only emphasized how chilled she was. "Jack can go first. You'll see, it's fun."

"I don't know." She was still hesitant but didn't want to disappoint Ned. He'd been so wonderful.

"If you do it, I'll be your sex slave the entire time Ned's gone," Jack whispered in her ear. "I'll even go back to the damn salon for another pedicure. With polish. Anything you want."

"Anything?" Missy weighed if having Jack as her slave for three days might be worth peeing her pants in public while hanging in the air.

"*Anything.*" He nuzzled her neck and flicked his tongue over her skin.

One of the two crew members occupied with prepping the gear flicked a glance at her.

She pushed Jack off her playfully. "I'll think about it. You first."

After a safety lecture and donning lots of straps around his body, Jack went up, and the canopy of the sail opened in brilliant yellow, red, and white, framed by a perfect blue sky. His gleeful howls were audible despite the long length of cable that attached him to the boat. He pointed at things as if they could see what he saw. Missy wished he'd hold the harness with two hands.

"Don't they need to bring him in?" Missy asked Ned.

"It's only been twenty minutes." He chuckled.

Her gaze was locked on the crazy man in the sky, lifting his feet and leaning back. Then Jack waved at the boat captain, indicating he wanted to stay up there. "Won't they run out of gas?"

"They can take fifteen passengers out. There's no danger of running out of gas."

"You rented this thing for the three of us?"

Ned shrugged and turned his attention back to Jack.

Still unsure, she let Ned go next. It looked like fun, but what if she was the accident that broke the parasailing company's ten-year safety record? Ned whooped with delight at the end of the tether. Although he was noisy, probably to prove to her how great it was, she was relieved he kept both hands on the harness.

"He's fine." Jack poured a small shot of vodka from the mini fridge. "Here, drink this."

Missy held up the glass of clear liquor and peered through it.

"Liquid courage. Swallow it in one go."

She downed the shot and almost choked. "Are you trying to kill me before I get up there?"

"Nope. I'm trying to make sure you don't chicken out of having a great time." Jack wrapped his arms around her from behind and pulled her close to him. The solidness of his body grounded her—the tension in her chest seeped away. "You're going up. You'll regret it forever if you don't."

Ned came down and unstrapped the gear with help from the crew.

"Okay, it's your turn, sugar." Jack let her go. "Let me help you into the harness. God, I love saying that." That grin was so Jack, playfully naughty and contagious. "Ned, we need to get a harness for the house so I can tell her to get in the harness again."

Missy focused on getting her legs in the correct holes. The captain rechecked every point of her gear and snugged it tighter while she held out her arms. "I can't believe I'm doing this."

"Sexual slavery," Jack replied in a low, dark tone, his hooded eyes locked on hers.

"You better be worth it."

"I promise, I will be." Jack touched the straps as if to reassure himself she was safe.

"You're making it so I don't want to leave at all," Ned complained.

"I wish you didn't have to," Missy and Jack replied at the same time.

"Okay." Jack patted her ass. "You're ready."

"You're going to love it." Ned kissed her hard.

If she weren't so panicked about being flown like a kite behind a speedboat, she would have been upset with their public displays. The crew member appeared to be wholly engrossed in his task, and the captain had his back to them. Hopefully, they hadn't noticed. In the next moment, any worries about being outed disappeared as she worried for her life.

She sat on the deck as instructed while the operator held the gear. After a quick check, he released the harness, and Missy grabbed the straps so hard they bit into her hands. Going up was fast. Her stomach dropped and then rushed into her throat. It was unlike anything she'd done before. Even the Ferris wheel at the fair was no comparison. She'd never been brave enough for the roller coasters. Once the line fully extended, everything settled into a peaceful lull, and she was floating as if she was a cloud.

Weightless and flying above the world, some of the surrounding islands were visible in the distance. The ocean that had looked blue-green from the boat was a portrait of color, lighter where the water was shallow and darker in the deep. Greener tides of algae were clearly outlined. Little white boats peppered the view like stars. It was so quiet. Magical. Having faced her fear, confidence surged through her, like she could do anything.

Although she waved the captain off once, too soon she was reeled back onto the boat, cheeks sore from smiling. "I did it," she yelled at Ned and Jack, who were standing with her, removing the harness. "That was awesome. I want to go again. Can we do this again before I leave? I can't believe I was flying."

Jack hugged her and spun her around. "You won the bet. I'm yours now."

"I don't even care." She laughed and threw her arms out. "I want to fly again."

"You've created a monster," Jack told Ned.

JACK CLOSED HIS EYES, leaning back into the living room chair. Ned occupied its twin. Missy had insisted on doing the cleanup after dinner, and he was too tired to argue. If it were up to him, the dishes would wait until morning. He'd almost dozed off when the crash of shattered glass followed by a high-pitched scream spiked his adrenaline. Jack met Ned's panicked eyes, and they bolted for the kitchen.

Missy stood at the counter, her hands held in the sink below his line of sight. In front of her, the jagged remains the kitchen window didn't make sense to Jack. "What the fuck?"

"What happened?" Ned asked at the same time.

"I don't know." Missy turned toward them, her eyes wide with shock. "I was washing the dishes. The window...it just...exploded." Missy looked down at her hands.

Seeing Missy's blood gutted Jack. They'd failed to keep her safe, even if it was a freak accident. The most important thing he could do right then was calm her down and care for her. Jack swung her into his arms. "It doesn't look too bad, but we should get those cuts cleaned."

"I'll go check outside," Ned said over his shoulder, already on his way out the kitchen door.

Jack took Missy into Ned's bathroom and set her gently on the counter before searching the cabinets for first-aid supplies. The nicks were tiny, but he wasn't taking any chances with her.

"It's not terrible." She turned her hands all around.

In the back of the bottom drawer, he found a mostly empty box of bandages and some antibiotic ointment. None of her injuries needed stitches, thank goodness. Jack kissed her forehead. "We'll have you patched in no time."

He helped her wash her hands and then tended to each of her cuts.

"Do they all need a bandage?" she asked, eyeing the circles pressed all over her hands.

"You look cute all polka-dotted."

"Funny." She squinted and frowned at him.

"Jack?" Ned's voice echoed through the hall.

"In here," Jack called back.

Ned stuck his head in the bathroom, holding on to the door frame.

"Just finished," Jack said. "Nothing major."

"Good. I need you for something."

Jack helped Missy off the counter and hugged her.

She yawned. "I can help, too."

"Why don't you rest here, and we'll join you when we're done. Shouldn't be long."

Missy nodded and moved to the bed.

As soon as Jack met Ned on the deck outside the kitchen, Ned said, "Take a look at this." He held a large rock with the word *whore* scrawled in black marker on it. Someone had thrown a rock at Missy.

"What the hell?" Jack asked. "Who would do this?"

"I don't know. But I don't like the idea of leaving the two of you alone here for three days." Ned stared toward the open area of his driveway.

It was secluded, surrounded by palm trees and native vegetation, and the gate to the drive had always been unlocked when Jack had visited in the past.

123

"I can take care of her." Jack gripped his friend's shoulder, drawing the man back to him.

"I know you can, but we were both here and look what happened." Ned dropped the rock in a metal canister half full of ashes.

The back of Jack's neck prickled. "Do you know anyone who can provide security?"

"Already made a call."

"To who?"

"My buddy's son, Nick. Works for a private security firm. He'll have a team on the jet arriving tomorrow."

"A team? That seems like overkill." Jack crossed his arms. A twinge of insecurity blinked through him.

Ned paced over to the railing at the edge of the deck that bordered the cliff. "These guys will help you and give me peace of mind while I'm gone," he said as he stared into the inky night at the ocean.

Maybe they were blowing it all out of proportion. "It was only a rock."

"With a filthy word. Thrown directly at her."

Jack gazed into the broken window, able to see the lit kitchen in perfect detail. Missy would have been framed like a picture for the attacker. "Why would anyone...? Missy couldn't offend someone if she tried."

"Maybe it isn't about her. The three of us haven't exactly hidden our...relationship. Not to mention Katherine's scene at the restaurant."

"Katherine isn't violent." Jack couldn't stand his ex-wife, but he couldn't see her doing something like that. She liked to slice and dice with words. A rock might break her nail.

"I don't want to wait for it to escalate."

Jack conceded that Ned might have a point.

"How do you even know guys like this?" Jack had friends in Texas, but not the kind who could get a team on a plane in a matter of hours.

"I did legal work for Nick's parents. We're just lucky the team was in between jobs and could jump when I called." Ned continued to scan the unlit property, the wrinkles at the corners of his eyes more pronounced.

"When did she become so important to us?" Jack asked out loud, although he was mainly asking himself.

Ned turned and looked him in the eye. "I don't know, but she is."

"I don't think I'll be able to give her up." Jack was surprised by his own admission. It was true, but he wasn't happy about it.

Ned clamped his jaw shut, his focus once again on the unseen threat.

Jack pulled out his cell phone and jabbed at the screen as he walked into the house. As unlikely as it was, he had to check.

"Andrew?" God, his ex-wife's voice was like razors on his eardrums. "Why are you calling so late?"

"Where are you?"

"In New York. I had to get back for the board meeting." She sniffed as if he should have known her plans. It was like they were still married.

"Right. I didn't realize you would be returning for it."

"Of course I would. Some of us honor our responsibilities."

He ended the call. He hated talking to her, but he'd needed to be sure it wasn't her. Who would throw a rock at Missy with such a filthy word? No one on the island could know her well enough to form such a strong opinion. Nobody knew she was with both men. They'd gone a couple of places as a trio, but it wasn't like they were *that* obvious. He couldn't figure it out just then. He needed to check on Missy, make sure she was okay.

CHAPTER 13

*M*issy sat in the living room, staring out the window at a peaceful ocean. Her stomach roiled as sunlight sparkled on the tiny waves, at total odds with her emotional turmoil. She hated that she was losing three days with Ned.

A large man in khaki cargo pants and a white polo marched across her view. She popped out of her chair. More movement in her peripheral vision. She spun around and squealed before she recognized him. Jack.

"Don't sneak up on me like that!" She gripped her shirt over her racing heart.

He held up his hands as if she had a weapon. "I was coming to tell you the security team Ned hired will be hanging around for the next few days."

"Security team?"

"You shouldn't notice them after today. They're getting the lay of the land. Checking everything over and noting any issues. I should've told you earlier."

"Seems like overkill for an accident."

"Ned and I didn't want to scare you, but... it wasn't a bird. It was a rock."

"Kids?"

"Unlikely." Jack looked away. "Not with the word that was on it."

"Word?" Missy whispered. Her blood ran cold.

"It's not important."

Missy glared at him. He was going to tell her what word had been written on a rock that was thrown at her or she was going to...well, she wasn't sure.

"*Whore.*" The word crossed his lips in a harsh whisper.

"Excuse me?"

Jack looked like he was going to vomit. Everything she'd dreaded was coming true.

"You're not. That rock doesn't mean anything. Just some sicko. But we have security. Ned will be back. And—"

"You weren't going to tell me." Her stomach dropped. They'd lied to her.

"I didn't want to." Jack slumped into the nearby chair. "I didn't want to hurt you."

Missy crossed her arms but didn't take her eyes off him. The damage to her reputation was done. It had only been a matter of time. The sick flavor of failure rose in her throat. Her job. She might already have lost it.

She pulled out her phone. No email or text notifications. Bad news traveled fast, but maybe no one who mattered knew. "I'm not a child. I should know when there's a problem."

"You're right." Jack cleared his throat.

If she was going to remain there for the rest of her vacation, she had to have their honesty. "If you don't want to hurt me, don't *ever* lie to me.

"It won't happen again." He opened his arms in invitation to join him in the chair.

She shook her head. Sitting in Jack's lap, being comforted like a little girl? No.

Jack stood and held out his arms again. "I'm sorry."

Missy leaned into him and accepted his hug while standing on her own two feet. Her racing heart slowed. She huffed out a breath. "No more secrets."

"Promise." Jack held her, and she let him. He wasn't Carter. Neither was Ned. She'd accept Jack's apology and Ned's security and hope nothing worse happened. She took a deep breath and pulled out of Jack's embrace, but he held on to her shoulders.

"What should we do today?" he asked with a fake lightness to his voice.

Hanging around the bungalow while security investigated every nook and cranny held no appeal. She forced a smile to match his. "Have a picnic at the lighthouse?"

"Sounds good. Let's hit the market on the way out and get a split of wine. I can loosen you up and have my way with you." Jack waggled his eyebrows at her.

"You don't have to liquor me up for that." She sashayed her hips dramatically as she left to get changed. She didn't want Jack to think she was holding a grudge. He'd fessed up easily enough, abandoning his misguided attempt to protect her. Besides, it would be fun having a day alone with Jack. She was sorry Ned wasn't with them, but his absence would make being in public easier.

JACK GATHERED the blanket and the kitted-out picnic basket to put in the car. Both Missy's anger over their secrecy and her quick forgiveness shocked him. All the rules he'd learned in his marriage about what a woman expected in a relationship didn't apply to her. Katherine hadn't wanted the details. Jack was supposed to take care of anything difficult. He found Missy's strength and independence fascinating.

It would be nice to have her alone on a date. He loved Ned and wanted to have more of an intimate relationship with him, but the man was hard work. With Missy, it was easy. She wasn't high-maintenance and judgmental like his ex-wife. If he could marry Missy, keep her *and* Ned, he would.

Whoa. Jack froze with his hand on the car door handle. *Where the hell did that come from?*

He swore he'd never marry again. In addition to the heart-crushing rejection, there'd been some very negative financial consequences. Was he really considering a long-term relationship with her? And with Ned? Maybe Ned should marry her, then he could live with them as their permanent boytoy sex slave. Jack grinned at the vision of him on his knees in front of Ned in some skimpy leather bondage outfit. It could work.

"What's so funny?" Missy asked, interrupting his salacious thoughts.

"Just thinking about being Ned's sex slave."

She laughed out loud. "He would be a natural master. At least, as I understand *that* concept." She opened the car door and got in, buckling her seatbelt as Jack did the same.

"Yeah, he has no idea how dominant he is in the bedroom. In fact, if you told him he was bossy, I'd bet he'd deny it."

"He'd probably deny a lot of things." She adjusted her sunglasses and stared out the window.

"What do you mean?" Jack was no longer laughing. His relationship with Ned mattered a great deal.

"I mean he's uncomfortable with the fact that he loves you, that he's sexually attracted to you."

"He freaked out when you left in the middle of the night and he woke up with just me in his bed." He turned sideways to face her. "Ned doesn't want to think of his sexuality including a man."

"Exactly." She slapped the narrow armrest between them.

Jack had known it was going to be a challenge to seduce Ned. In some ways, it was a lot like the disapproval he'd received from Kate. All fine and dandy in the moment and a total shit show afterward when their embarrassment or guilt or whatever took over.

"How long have you two been friends?"

"Years. I knew him before I got married. He was my lawyer. I met Kate while visiting his office."

"Were you always attracted to him?"

"Yeah. But he was married. And I was trying to go traditional." Jack shrugged.

"There's never been anything before now?" Shock resonated through her voice.

"Nothing more than some heated looks and double entendres after several whiskeys." Jack had always believed he was reading too much into it. Seeing what he wanted to see. But he couldn't let it go.

"I think he's confused." Missy touched his shoulder. "I don't think it will resolve itself while I'm here. What are you going to do when I leave?"

"I don't know." Jack gripped the wheel and focused on the road. "But I don't want to think about it today. It's too beautiful, and I'm with a gorgeous woman whose time is precious to me."

She leaned against the seat and tilted her face to the warmth streaming through the open sunroof, eyes closed and a contented sigh on her lips.

Jack forced a smile to hide his turmoil. He didn't want to be married again. Ned didn't want to be with him without a woman involved. Missy had her own life and plans that didn't include them. Besides, it was likely going to be Ned who would win her heart. Ned was stable. He provided the dominance she naturally craved. And they were both lawyers. Jack didn't want to be left out, but if he were, he would understand. Until then, he was going to enjoy every minute she was there, particularly when Ned returned. She was Jack's ideal—independent and open to sexual exploration—and Ned's intellectually equal submissive. Without Missy, they wouldn't find the balance to be lovers.

It was time to rein in his thoughts. With a swipe of his thumb, he turned up the music on the radio. He wasn't going to ruin their day together with harsh realities.

MISSY SAT in Ned's chair in the living room. Jack was in his usual spot, nose deep in the latest thriller novel. The erotic romance she was reading on her phone wasn't distracting her from the sexy man in front of her. His shirt was partially unbuttoned, loose over the top of his shorts, and his feet were bare. It was impossible to look away.

Would he be willing to proceed with the items on their bucket list with Ned gone? She loved being with both of them, but she didn't want to stop her sexual exploration.

"Jack?"

"Hmm?"

She took a sip of water to wash away the dust of self-doubt that had dried her throat. "Thanks for today." That wasn't what she'd meant to say.

He didn't look up from his book. "Sure. My pleasure."

The corner of the room, where her gaze was locked, didn't have a magic teleprompter. She forced herself to ask for what she wanted.

"You know what would be *my* pleasure?" She purposely made her voice a little husky.

He stopped reading and met her eyes. "What?"

She released her bottom lip from between her teeth. "I want to learn how to give a blow job."

"You do?" His eyes widened.

She nodded. "I've never given one before and, well, we're at oral sex on the bucket list."

"I believe you're correct." He put the book down and stood. "And I seem to recall you've never received oral."

"No." Her face heated.

"First, I'm going to make you come on my tongue and lick you clean." He held out his hand. "After that, we'll see if you still want a lesson."

She let him lead her down the hallway to his bedroom. Butterflies danced through her insides. Something she'd only Googled was finally going to happen.

Jack's room was beachy elegance. A hint of his clean scent lingered in the air. Crisp white cotton bedding contrasted with a reclaimed wood poster bed and suede accent wall. The jute rug surprised her with its softness against her bare feet.

Across from the bed, a floor-to-ceiling mirror with a weathered frame leaned against the wall. She wasn't sure about getting naked in front of it. It was one thing to be nude; it was another to be so exposed.

"Like it?" Jack leaned against the doorway.

"I don't know." She crossed her arms, and he went to her. "It's a little intimidating to be honest."

"You'll love it. You'll be able to see everything." He reached around her waist and positioned her in front of him, facing their reflection.

Damn, the man was fine. His fair hair and blue eyes contrasted with her slightly darker hair and amber eyes.

"We look good together," he said, as if reading her thoughts.

He slid her t-shirt up, slow and deliberate, exposing her abdomen. His slightly rough hands stroked her ivory skin while he continued to gather the fabric against his arms. She caught his gaze in the mirror, unable to look away. His eyes burned as brightly as hers with erotic fire.

He skimmed her shirt off. "Beautiful," he whispered. "Let me show you how gorgeous you are when you come."

Her pale skin reddened, and she raised her hands to cover herself, but he captured her wrists to stop her from hiding. Letting her embarrassment go, she relaxed against him and met his eyes in the glass. He released her and stroked his fingertips gently over her breasts, treating her like she was the most beautiful woman in the world. Palming the pair from below, he brought them together and massaged them. His fingers grazed over her nipples, then he pinched them gently, rolling and pulling. His eyes never left hers. She sucked in a breath. The rest of her body wanted his attention desperately.

"Jack," she panted.

He nuzzled her neck, and she followed the reflections of his hands as they moved slowly down her sides, coming together at her waistband to continue undressing her. She reached back and gripped his legs through his khaki shorts. She wanted his naked body against hers. "Take off your clothes," she ordered.

"This is about you."

"I need to feel you." More than his hands—she needed to be wrapped in his body. No barriers.

Jack broke off from removing her shorts to finish unbuttoning his shirt and letting it fall to the floor. With a quick flick of his fingers, his shorts dropped, too. He pressed his warm chest to her back, and heat seeped deep into her, igniting her core. His cock, covered by thin black boxer briefs, nestled against her ass. She tried to step aside so she could see him in the mirror, but he held her in place. Slowly, he lowered the zipper on her shorts and slipped them down her legs.

"Step out."

Missy extracted herself from the crumpled fabric, and he kicked her shorts to the side. She was wet and needy. Anticipating what was coming next, she reached for the band of her white lace panties.

"No." Jack guided her hands away and placed them against the back of his neck, making her back arch. "Keep them there. You're mine. For now."

The control he provided in Ned's absence was all at once surprising and familiar. She smiled and didn't move. His tanned, muscular arms held her tight. The pose he'd placed her in was sensual and feminine, more so contrasted against his rugged male physique. Whatever he was going to do, she'd love it. But she wished he'd do it faster.

He caressed her skin and rubbed over the hard tips of her breasts. Her focus followed his hands. She was the sculpture, he the artist. They glided down her body, along the outside of her hips, then he finally dragged his fingers between her thighs and across the wet silk covering her core. She shuddered, and her empty pussy clenched, begging to have him inside her.

"You're soaked."

"I need more. I need you. Please."

He pulled the sodden lace and silk down her legs, letting it fall to the floor. She stepped out of her panties and toed them away.

Her eyes locked on his, arms draped around his neck. Jack nudged her legs farther apart for his perusal. Her thighs glistened in the reflection. A flicker of embarrassment passed like a shadow across her mind, but he made her feel too beautiful to hesitate.

He reached down to part her lower lips, opening her. Her inner pink petals were on display for them both. "Look at you. Look how pretty every part of you is," he murmured in her ear. He slid strong fingers through her folds, moving her wetness all over her sex. He rubbed a little circle on her clit, and her hips moved in the same motion against his hard cock. They both moaned.

Jack thrust two thick fingers into her, fully penetrating her. His thrusts left no part untouched. It was wicked and wonderful. The teasing dance was nothing she'd known before, and she wanted more. As soon as she started to rock against his hand, he withdrew.

She whimpered in protest, but her breath caught when he put his fingers all the way in his mouth and sucked her essence off them. "Delicious."

"Holy—" Missy trembled, unable to believe he'd licked off her juices or that her mouth watered at the thought of tasting him.

Jack dragged his fingers through her pussy again and brought them to her mouth. A musky flavor that hinted of sweetness flooded her senses. She purred over his fingers, using her tongue to tease him. It was so naughty. She gushed more.

"I'm going to eat you now."

Missy shivered as he dropped to his knees in front of her.

"You're going to watch in the mirror while I lick up every delicious drop. I'm going to lick you and eat you and finger-fuck you until you come hard all over my face."

Oh my god. It wouldn't take long because his dirty talk already had her on the verge of coming. Before she could form words, he lifted her leg onto his shoulder. He gripped her hips and brought her close. Crying out, she grabbed on to his head as his hot tongue delved deeper into her.

"You like that." He stared up at her from between her legs.

There were no words. She pushed her hips closer.

"Hold on to the bed. Don't close your eyes. Watch me eat your sweet pussy."

She clung to the bedpost. Her legs shook, and her entire body thrummed. Jack buried his head between her legs. His fingers pistoned in and out of her. His tongue lashed her clit when he wasn't sucking on it, covering it in his warm, wet mouth. She alternated between staring down at him and at the reflection of his body kneeling before her, a seductive picture. Her full-grown sex god on his knees, consuming her like it was the best thing he'd ever tasted. It was ecstasy.

Her heart pounded and both of them were moaning. The vibration fluttered her swollen lips. He moved his tongue into her opening as his fingers moved farther back to press at her anus, stimulating every nerve she had. Her legs wobbled as the last of her control slipped away.

She released a guttural cry as she came.

But he didn't retreat as she expected. Instead, he pressed in harder and licked her more thoroughly than before. Unable to hold herself up any longer, she collapsed backward onto the mattress.

"Hey, I wasn't done," Jack protested.

"I am," she sighed. "Completely and totally done. You killed me."

He crawled up her body and kissed her, teasing her with his tongue as he had down below. She could taste herself on his mouth. Fuck, he was so nasty in such a good way. How would she ever return to the real world, where jobs demanded your days and boyfriends couldn't get you off?

CHAPTER 14

*I*t was the best dream Jack had experienced in a long time. There was a woman, skin so warm. Her naked body pressed against his, her hair on his chest, but her face was turned away. She started to retreat, so he wrapped his arms around her, holding her in place.

"Are you awake?" A soft, melodic voice whispered to him.

He opened his eyes. Missy.

Her silky hand was wrapped tight around his steely morning wood. "Mmmhmm," he murmured.

"I want to give you head, but I'm not sure what I'm doing. You're kind of huge."

"Relax. There is no such thing as a bad blow job." Her touch already felt so good, he could come just from the wisp of her breath. "But no biting."

Would she like the taste of him? Would she enjoy giving him head as much as he'd enjoyed going down on her last night? All thoughts ceased as her mouth wrapped around his mushroom head and she swirled her wet tongue around it. God, she was a fucking natural. With a firm hold of the shaft in her elegant fingers, she stroked him.

Up and down. Her lesson with Ned was well-learned. He groaned at his mind bringing Ned into the action, where he should be.

She licked up his length while caressing his balls. Her tongue was heaven, her touch satin on his sensitive sac. How long had it been since someone had treated him with such tenderness, was so entirely focused on his pleasure? He stroked her cheek.

She lifted her head. "Is this okay?"

"Sugar, you're going to make me come." No, not come—explode.

"Good." She took him deep into her mouth once again.

Jack's heart squeezed. A rush of overwhelming adoration threatened to make him say something ridiculous. She hollowed her cheeks, sucking him deeper into her mouth.

He closed his eyes and forced himself to focus on her physical attentions and not what it might mean. Trying to hold back even though she'd made her intention clear, he clenched internally. Missy, so innocent, but completely committed. Her hand on his shaft moved faster, up and down, as if she could sense exactly what it would take to push him over. Then, she ran her fingers across his perineum and pressed.

Like she'd pushed a magic button, an electric current raced down his spine and his balls pulled up tight to meet it. A lightning strike couldn't have hit him harder.

"Fuck," he groaned as he came, jerking and shooting cum down her throat. She swallowed, her throat massaging the head of his cock, causing him to ejaculate even more. "Holy..."

Every muscle in his body went slack. His mind soared away as the pleasure of release rippled through him.

Missy trailed her fingers along the line of hair on his lower abdomen, a gentle caress that brought him back to his body. "Mmm, you taste good," she purred.

"I'm glad you enjoyed it, 'cause I fucking loved it." He pulled her toward him and encircled her in his arms. "Thank you."

"It was the least I could do since I passed out on you last night. I think you tongue-fucked me into a coma."

"Happy to do it again," he said as he rolled on top of her naked body. Then he kissed her, reveling in the fact she tasted like him.

Missy stopped the kiss. "We can't spend all day in bed. Plus, aren't the security guys out there? I don't want them to hear us."

"They've been out there all night; I think that horse has left the barn."

Missy groaned and pulled the pillow over her head.

He laughed and took it away. "Since you won't let me keep you screaming in bed all day, what are we going to do?"

"How do you feel about snorkeling?"

"Absolutely." He released her and rolled to the side. "I'll call a tour operator while you get ready."

~

"WHY DOES he have to come with us?" Missy whispered in Jack's ear, trying not to insult the behemoth sitting next to them on the boat.

"Ned insisted they have eyes on us at all times."

"But they didn't go with us to the lighthouse yesterday," she said, peeved her time with Jack was being observed. Nick seemed like a nice enough guy. But Jack had chartered the entire tour so they would have the boat to themselves and could snorkel without the interference of others, so why would he let the guard go with them? What was the big deal?

"Actually, they did go with us yesterday—in another vehicle. It wasn't practical to book two boats." He winked at her.

"It's not funny." She tried pouting, but Jack was too cute and the day was too nice.

After some cursory training from the instructor, they snorkeled and played in the water. Yellow and orange corals peeped out from the crevasses of piles of rocks scattered across the ocean floor. It was so clear, like she could reach out and touch the sandy bottom when it was at least thirty feet deep. Colorful fish swam nearby, and occasionally a school of silvery fish swirled under her.

Jack pulled her to him in the water, and Missy laughed, sure she

138

must look ridiculous with the goggles and big tube coming out of her mouth. He spat his free; it was still attached to the side of the goggles. "Are you hungry? They prepared lunch for us."

She pulled the snorkel out of her mouth. "Is it that late already? I feel like we just got here."

"You've been in the water for two hours. We should go in. Get hydrated and reapply sunscreen before we play some more."

Missy liked the care Jack showed her. If only Ned were there, too, the day would be perfect. The more time she spent alone with Jack, the more she missed the two of them together.

NED RESISTED the urge to sneer at the security camera when he entered the private wood-paneled elevator that would dump him out on the firm's floor. It was increasingly difficult to drag himself into the New York office. There was always some avoidable drama waiting for him. And it didn't help that the first person he saw was Katherine.

As always, she was perfectly dressed. The navy sheath she wore was appropriately conservative, while still showing enough leg to entice a man who didn't know better. "Ned, so good to see you. I was afraid you'd decide not to come."

"I *am* semi-retired." As much as he wanted to castigate her about her recent behavior, it was neither the time nor the place.

"*Semi*-retired." She smirked. "And so *busy* on the island."

The acidic tone went straight to his gut. "It certainly is compelling company."

A tight smile formed on her face. "I'm glad you're finally coming out of mourning."

Her words surprised him. It was true—a new energy had filled him after just days with Missy. And Jack. Was it that evident?

Katherine put a hand on his arm. It was all Ned could do not to flinch. "Have you met Charles Simmons?"

Ned scanned the open space in front of the cube farm where partners and wannabe partners in suits milled around. There were several people he didn't recognize. "No, is he here?"

"Yes, Daddy thought it might be good to meet the man who started the firm we're planning to acquire."

Ned arched an eyebrow. "Planning to acquire? This meeting was supposed to be a discussion of the pros and cons of the deal. Am I wasting my time?"

"Of course not. This is the exploration phase. The final vote won't happen until the due diligence is complete. But Daddy felt it was important to meet a man who would essentially be a new partner sooner rather than later, don't you agree?"

"You don't care whether I agree or not." Ned shoved his hands in his pockets to hide his fists.

Kate laughed and waved two men over. One was older, one much younger.

How far into the deal was "Daddy"? Katherine's father, Richard Wallace, was known for acting like the firm was his personal toy instead of belonging to all the partners. Ned was done playing with snakes. In his short time working on Jack's deal and having their unusual relationship with Missy, he'd lived more life and had more fun than he'd had in a decade. But he wasn't going to let Wallace piss away his investment to stroke his ego.

"Kate. Looking good." The older man moved right up against Katherine and stared down her cleavage.

Katherine gave a fake smile and took a step back. "I have someone you need to meet." She linked her arm in Ned's, and he allowed her to cling to him in the presence of such a jerk. "Ned, this is Charles Simmons. He owns the firm in St. Louis we're considering acquiring. Charles, this is Edward Strauss. He's a senior equity partner and member of the board."

"Acquiring? More like merging. I'm bringing a lot to the table. Your firm has no presence in the Mid-west and, let's face it, New York *used* to be the only place to be. It's well past time for this firm to expand to new frontiers. Don't want to get stale." Simmons clapped Ned on the shoulder.

Ned resisted the immediate urge to deck the guy.

Katherine turned her body toward the younger man, and it had the welcome effect of moving Ned away from the creep. "This is Charles's son, Carter. He's the newest member of their firm and a recent graduate from Washington University."

Ned nodded at the man, who was a younger clone of his father, then extracted his arm from her. "Katherine, I'll see you in the conference room. Please excuse me." He moved quickly, but the asshole's voice pursued him across the room.

"I take it he's one of the old guard keeping this place down?" Charles asked with snark in his voice.

"He's a critical vote and a respected member of the board. You would do well to try to cultivate him rather than offend him."

"What? What did I say?"

Ned took his seat in the boardroom. He needed the farce to end so he could get back to the island.

THE LEATHER SEAT on the jet cradled Ned's exhausted body. Maybe after they were in the air and he'd downed a scotch he'd find the sleep that had eluded him last night. The meeting played through his mind like a film. That preening dick, Simmons, acted like he was doing them a favor while avoiding the fact his firm was tanking. They were in deep debt, although a strange cash infusion had come a few weeks ago from a silent investor. Simmons hinted that another, much larger one, would come in ninety days.

According to him, the investor wasn't getting any ownership or legal services—it was a gift to the firm in appreciation for past work. Ned smelled serious bullshit. The son had flinched each time the "gift" was discussed. It was one of many red flags on the deal.

As soon as possible, he'd run the financials by Jack. The man could sniff out shady accounting tactics better than anyone he knew.

Wallace had requested his proxy on the vote. A request Ned denied without a moment's hesitation. Even if he had to fly back every week.

"Mr. Strauss?" The flight attendant brought his attention back to the present. "Can I get you a beverage, sir?"

"Macallan. Neat."

"Right away." Her eyes traveled down his body before she turned away. Ned recoiled despite the brunette's leggy beauty. Before, he wouldn't have noticed the flirtation. It wasn't welcome.

What had Jack and Missy been up to while he was gone? He hadn't called. He didn't want to interrupt, but that may have been the wrong decision. What if Jack fucked her while he was gone? What if they formed a bond that didn't include him?

"Your scotch, sir." The woman held on a moment too long when Ned reached for the glass.

He gave her a cold stare.

She loosened her grip. "Uh...can I...is there anything else?"

"No. Thank you." He sipped the expensive liquor. Maybe its fire would cut through the loneliness in his veins.

Ned rubbed his chest with his fist. Being away from Jack and Missy numbed him to the point of pain. He was dead on the inside when they were apart, exactly like the past three years. Dead.

Desperation punched him in the gut. Two weeks. Only two short weeks to figure out how to keep them. Jack would be easier to convince than Missy, but Ned couldn't embrace being a gay man. A twinge in his throat had him swallowing down the familiar lie. A lie that was becoming harder to believe.

The problem wasn't being gay, it was that he'd failed. The first and only man he'd ever loved had chosen death rather than come back to him. No matter how much he'd begged. But with Missy, it would be different. Her loving presence could help him create the life he wanted. The two of them, with Jack. His eyelids flickered as the possibilities flooded his mind.

He would do anything. Entice Jack to leave Texas somehow. His house in New York stood empty except for the few rooms he inhabited. They could have children if Missy wanted them. Ned got a little hard thinking about her swollen with child. Although he was past the age to be starting a family, he'd always wanted to have children. He and his wife hadn't been able to conceive. Was it possible? Could the three of them find a way? He couldn't imagine himself without both of them, but did they feel the same?

He tilted his wrist. The amber liquid in his glass was the same shade as Missy's eyes. The last time he'd had a scotch, Jack had been seated in the chair next to him. Fear and longing swirled in his gut.

He shouldn't have traveled to New York. It was nice to get the income and to take the occasional mentoring role on a case, but all he'd learned on his trip was that Jack and Missy—their happiness, their safety—mattered most to him. The firm was no longer his primary concern. How had that happened in two short weeks? It was ridiculous but true. Ned sipped his scotch and schemed about how to keep his two lovers in their place—his life.

CHAPTER 15

*N*ed dropped his bag in the doorway of his room, the sound booming in the vacant space. The entire plane ride, he'd had an image of them wrapped up in his bed. Waiting for him. But a perfectly made, empty mattress greeted him instead.

A sick, gnawing need chewed at the hollowness inside him.

Ned walked back into the hall and paused at Jack's door. If he found Missy in Jack's room, what was he supposed to do? Leave them be? Join them? The door slid open on silent hinges. Jack was face-down, asleep. Alone. Where was Missy? Why *wasn't* she with Jack? He knelt on the bed and nudged Jack awake.

"Wha—what's wrong?" Jack rolled over, blinking rapidly.

"Why aren't you with Missy? Why aren't you both in my bed?"

Jack slid up the mattress and stared at him as if he'd sprouted horns. Ned's five o'clock shadow was seven hours old, and his clothes were past rumpled. But some things were more important than his appearance.

"Hello to you, too." Jack rubbed his eyes and yawned. "I thought you got back tomorrow evening."

"Jack, where is she?"

"In her bed."

144

"Oh." Ned sat heavily, relieved she was okay.

"Don't get me wrong. I tried everything to get her in here with me."

"So, *nothing* happened while I was gone?" Ned didn't believe that was possible. If they'd been together, was there still room for him?

"We fooled around a little last night, and she stayed with me. But she said it wasn't the same and it made her miss you more. Insisted we wait to sleep in the same room until you got back."

The ache was gone, replaced with a warm glow. Ned let a triumphant smile slide onto his face. "Good. What about you?"

"What about me?" Jack's brow wrinkled.

"Did you miss me?"

"Of course."

Ned leaned over his lover and pressed his lips to Jack's, giving in to the desire he'd repressed for too long. It wasn't at all like he remembered. Jack wasn't a college-aged boy. He was a man. The stubble on his lip rasped against Ned's. The smell of Jack's sleepy musk teased him, tempting him to go further. He forced himself to lean back.

Jack blinked at him. "You—you kissed me."

"Come to bed."

"I'm in bed."

"Not the right bed." Ned folded back the covers. "I'll get Missy and meet you there. I'm not sleeping another night without you both."

Jack didn't move. "You sure you want me there?"

Instead of explaining, Ned stood and took Jack's hand. He didn't have the words or the energy to discuss every revelation he'd had on the plane. Life was too short, and he didn't want to keep living with the same rules he'd always followed.

Jack trailed behind him, bare feet slowly padding down the hallway. "I'm dreamin'."

Ned smiled. Jack would figure it out soon enough.

He paused at Missy's open door to appreciate the gorgeous woman who was sprawled out, bare except for her panties. Without a word, he moved toward her, Jack close behind. Ned leaned down and kissed her cheek. "I'm taking you to my room."

He rolled her over. Her unfocused gaze fell on him before she closed her eyes with a sigh. He picked her up in his arms. With a soft mewl, she wrapped her arms around him and tucked her face in his neck.

Jack's presence at his side reassured him as he took Missy to his bedroom. He needed them both. Jack drew back the covers, and Ned settled her in the center of his bed. *Their* bed.

"Jack," Ned said and opened his arms to the man. After a brief hesitation, Jack relaxed into his embrace. "I missed you." Ned kissed him again. "Let's get you out of these." Ned released the tie on Jack's sleep pants. "I plan on keeping both of you in bed all day tomorrow."

"What are you doing?" Jack's eyebrows drew together, and he stared at Ned as if seeing him for the first time.

"Undressing you."

"But..." He shook his head. As Ned slid the loose pants down Jack's legs, his body reacted, cock pressing against Ned's fingers through the fabric of his briefs.

Jack folded the discarded pajamas and set them on the low dresser. Ned skimmed his own shirt over his head. Never taking his eyes from Jack, he slipped off his shoes and pants. He sat on the edge of the bed and took off his socks, leaving everything in a pile.

It hadn't occurred to him how difficult it would be to find the words that would define his new perspective. He never expected to have to spell it out. Faced with his arrogance, he was a bit embarrassed.

"Being away clarified things for me." It wasn't much of an explanation for his changed behavior, but it would have to do.

Jack started to say something but closed his mouth. Ned got into bed beside Missy, moved as close as possible, and then patted the other side of the bed. Jack slid under the covers, positioned right against her back. Ned reached his arms around them both, pulling them closer. She wiggled before relaxing again in his embrace.

Ned kissed her temple, then gazed into Jack's eyes. "Sleep. You'll need it." Ned rolled to turn off the light, then reached for Jack again in the dark. Ned lifted Jack's hand and pressed it to his heart as if Jack's fingers could read what was there.

∼

Missy woke with two men wrapped around her. A hint of peaty alcohol teased her nose. Ned. He was back.

She grazed her fingers over the dusting of hair on his chest. Tension she didn't know she held released. Their hands were stroking her softly. She reached back for Jack, finding his hip. He pressed into her back. Ned leaned down and kissed her, licking at her lips until she opened. His taste was so recognizable on her tongue, scotch and man. The men moved as one when they maneuvered her to her back and stripped her out of her panties. Neither commented on her eagerness when she lifted her hips to help.

Jack caressed her, his firm touch running over her thigh, between her legs. Ned lightly palmed her breast, teasing the tip with his thumb. It was perfect, everything she'd missed while he was gone.

Jack was wonderful, but both men together again—there were no words for how right it felt. She parted her legs and arched her back, pressing into both of them. Taking her invitation, they teased her with their fingers, slicking her juices over her clit, dipping inside, finding that hidden spot that would send her flying. Wrapped in a cocoon of pleasure, she relaxed into the sultry caresses instead of chasing the explosion. The crest would come like waves building, slowly, rhythmically. She was in no rush.

She moved her hand to Jack's cock, but he was still in his underwear. Ned was covered, too. Half asleep and quickly falling into a lusty haze, she couldn't figure out how to get past the barriers. She rubbed them over the fabric. "Take them off," she breathed.

"Patience," Ned murmured.

"Not yet, sugar." Jack's soft words brushed her ear.

Ned teased his tongue into her mouth in the same motion as he moved his fingers, and she quickly lost track of what she'd been doing. Jack treated her clit with the perfect amount of friction and pressure. Ned's hands, long and elegant, played her like an instrument. Jack's coarser skin and rancher strength provided the perfect rough edge. Each one's touch, exactly what she needed. She peaked, and Ned captured her cry in his mouth.

"I need you." His breath on her ear made her tremble. She needed him, too. He'd freed his cock and pressed the searing hard length against her bare skin.

Ned rustled the condom box on the nightstand. He opened the packet and covered his erection, stroking and squeezing the head.

"I want to be inside you." His voice rasped over her nerves, and her emptiness clenched with desire.

"Yes," she whispered, not that there was any question that her body was begging for his. She parted her legs.

Ned lowered himself over her, one arm to her side, the other hand on the bed between her body and Jack's, his cockhead poised at the entrance to her wet pussy. He kissed her, taking his time, making her crazy with want. She bent her knees, opening herself more and hiding nothing. Why wasn't he inside her already? Tilting her pelvis to glide her wet heat across him, she tried to entice him closer. Instead of coming inside, he resisted.

"Are you ready, sugar? Are you ready for Ned's big cock to fill you?" Jack had one hand on his own straining erection, the other holding her arm above her head, fingers laced with hers.

"God, yes," she whined. Her heart throbbed, the muscles in her hips tight, poised to receive what he was denying her.

Ned pressed in with restraint, just the tip. Her body invited him in, but he remained in place. Perfect pleasure and total torture.

"More," she begged.

"Slow, sweetheart. I won't last."

She pleaded and rubbed her legs against his. The hair tickled her thighs

He entered her a little further and paused as he lifted her breast and bent to take her nipple into his mouth. Jack took the other one in his. Fire shot through her veins.

She gasped. And in one fluid motion, Ned was inside, and both men were sucking on her. It was too much and not enough all at once. She wrapped her legs around Ned's hips and thrust up to meet him. He relented, letting her take him deep inside her hot, wet channel, stretching her so good. Jack nipped the tip of her breast almost to the point of pain. Already she was so close to coming again. It had been so long.

No, that wasn't right—it had never been like that.

It was her first time, again.

Ned thrust his hips. Too slow at first, each inch tormenting her. Then finally gaining momentum.

Jack's hand slid between them. He worked her clit while still teasing her breast. "I'm— I'm...ahhh." She flew, her muscles squeezing the orgasm out of Ned. He stiffened and thrust several times with no rhythm at all, pushing himself into the space she'd gone where there was only pleasure. She clenched her thighs to keep him there. Slowly returned to her body.

Jack released her and sucked his fingers clean. "My turn?" he asked.

"Yes." She smiled up at him and relaxed as Ned rolled off her and the bed with a groan.

"Wait for me before you start." He leaned down to kiss her before disappearing into the bathroom.

Jack stared at her as he dragged his hand slowly up and down her torso. She put her hand on his chest. "I want you, Jack."

"I want you, too. With him."

Missy kissed him. The answer filled her with a different pleasure, of rightness and belonging.

Ned returned and took another packet from the box. Jack reached out his hand for it, but Ned ignored him. "Lay back."

Jack did as instructed. Ned took control of Jack's erection and lifted it to point straight up. It was sexy as hell, Jack's erection wrapped in Ned's hand. Her own palm twitched with the memories of it. Ned uncoiled the condom over Jack's throbbing head. "Missy, slide it down."

Eager to participate, she worked with precision and delicacy,

149

treating him like fine china. Ned held the tip but released Jack's shaft as she covered him.

"Is this right? I've never put a condom on anyone." Missy didn't want to rely on her experience with a banana in high school health class.

Ned stroked down Jack's cock slowly.

Jack groaned, the sound filled with painful desire.

Ned paused at the base. "Perfect."

Yes, it was. Jack didn't even have to penetrate her—they could all just masturbate each other and she'd be satisfied. It would ruin the mood to ask what had changed Ned's mind about touching Jack directly, but it was clear something had.

Ned knelt on the bed, parting Jack's legs and draping them over his thighs as he moved in close. His recovering cock was not quite touching Jack's balls. It was an image she'd never forget. "Missy, I want you to straddle him."

"Saddle up, sugar." They hadn't even started and Jack already had a husky satisfaction in his voice.

She allowed Ned to guide her as she spread her thighs wide to get them on either side of Jack, her legs tucked back against Ned's. His strong hands assisted her as she prepared to ride Jack—she was in control, but under Ned's command. With her hands braced on Jack's chest, she adjusted herself over his prone body. Jack caressed her thighs, his eyelids half-closed.

Ned held her until she was steady. She was up on her knees, back supported by Ned's chest, and Jack stared between her legs. With one hand still on her hip, Ned worked the length of Jack's cock in long, slow strokes, his hand brushing between her thighs, teasing her with every move. Jack clenched her legs in his grip. Their tight coupling, or tripling, was a secret bubble of sex. Ned held her securely. Jack wanted her. And she wanted them, more each time they were together.

Ned put Jack's crown at her begging entrance. "Come down slowly." His low command ran down her spine, and she arched her back. "Take him."

"Take me," Jack echoed as he slid inside her tender opening. Ned released his grasp. Jack's length touched her in the deepest part of her core.

"So full. I..." She moaned with need, but she didn't know for what.

Ned's hot cock was underneath her, touching where she and Jack met. Ned's hands were back on her, owning her rhythm and the depth of the ride. There was nothing she needed to do but experience it all. She reached back and wrapped her arms around Ned's neck. He held her down when Jack was fully sheathed. Missy sucked in a breath— she hadn't believed he could be deeper, but he was.

Gazing over her shoulder, Jack gave Ned a slight nod. When Ned lifted her, Jack rubbed her clit with tiny circles, then pressed it hard. Her inner muscles squeezed Jack's cock.

"I'm so close," she panted.

Ned's pelvis moved as if choreographed to the rhythm he'd set. Air filled her lungs, but she was light-headed, overwhelmed by the sensations and Ned's control. If he wasn't holding her down, she could have floated away.

"*Come.*" Ned's voice penetrated her brain, hard and hot, like Jack's cock.

Missy's insides clenched tight at his command, which set off the chain reaction. Jack shouted incoherently, thrusting his hips into Missy's clutching pussy while Ned held her in place. Ned's shaft throbbed underneath her as he released his cum all over them in hot, sticky streams. They collapsed into a panting mess.

"That was..." Jack shook his head.

"Unbelievable." Missy still quaked.

Ned guided her to Jack's side. He lay down on Jack's other side, not saying anything, just holding him.

"Perfect," Jack finished.

Missy relaxed back into sleep, dreaming of a world where they never had to part.

CHAPTER 16

*N*ed hurried through his morning routine. He'd been so eager to get Jack and Missy back in his bed last night, he'd forgotten to follow up with security. Outside, near the fence at the back of the property, he found Nick. The war vet had aged so much since Ned had seen him a few years back. Silver streaked his sandy hair, and shadowed lines edged his eyes. The guy looked like a clone of his father, except for the chiseled physique.

"All quiet?" Ned asked.

"Last logged event was your cab just past midnight."

"I didn't want to bother anyone. Wasn't sure when I'd get back."

"We were alerted when your phone left the Manhattan airspace," Nick said.

"Right." They'd insisted on installing the tracker software on all of their phones, not just Missy's.

"Your zone has been reset to the home perimeter." The man continued to scan the estate while he spoke. "We escorted two outings."

The reports had come in while Ned traveled. Jack and Missy didn't have to be cooped up in the house, but a board meeting in New York rankled in comparison to a picnic and snorkeling. And the fact that

Nick had gone with them only made it more difficult. It should have been him accompanying his lovers.

"Did I overreact, Nick? Do you think the attack was a mistake or a one-time thing?"

"A projectile through a window with a message while the perp could see the target—" Nick pierced Ned with his intense gaze. "That's intentional."

Ned's hands clenched. He forced himself to relax. "Any way to prevent it from happening again?"

"Your property is secluded but open. Impossible to keep out someone determined to come in. Not without serious investment."

A headache teased at Ned's temple. He'd selected the place for its location, not its defensibility. "I can't tell you how much I appreciate you doing this for me."

"Glad I can help, but I'm about done playing soldier. I start teaching in the fall."

"Teaching." A smile teased at the edges of Ned's lips. "That's different."

"Time to do something meaningful with my life that doesn't involve shooting people."

"Well, you're saving my ass here." Ned held out his hand.

Nick took it in a firm clasp. "You've saved my parents from so many frivolous lawsuits. Least I can do is return the favor. Last hurrah and all that."

"I don't want to be wasting your time."

"You're not." Nick crossed his thick arms. Each muscle stood out in stark definition. "Ned. Whoever did it will likely escalate."

Ned worked to slow his breathing. "I hope you're wrong."

"Me too."

It stabbed Ned like a knife to the gut that he couldn't keep Jack and Missy safe on his own, but they were more important than his ego. He'd keep security in place.

"All right, I'll leave you to it. Contact me if *anything* comes up, no matter how small."

"Yes, sir," Nick supplied before he resumed his patrol.

Putting his churning thoughts on hold, Ned walked down to the beach to join his lovers. After that conversation, he could use a little relaxation.

~

MISSY WAS LATHERING her hair for the second time when the shower door opened. Both men were already naked. Her hands froze in her hair, and she sucked in a shivering breath. *Gorgeous.* She stepped back in invitation. "At least you've got multiple heads in this thing."

Jack laughed. "Not the only thing that's going to have multiple heads in it, sugar." He wrapped her tight in his arms from behind. His warmth and strength perfectly complemented the playful teasing.

Ned chuckled as he took over the job of rinsing the ocean from her sudsy hair. Jack followed his lead, using a cloth foaming with bodywash to carefully tend every single inch of her skin. Almost as wet inside as out when they finished, Missy pressed her back against the cool tile. A welcome break from their intense heat. The men scrubbed themselves, hands dragging the soap across the planes of their hard bodies. She could watch their private show every single day. Based on their growing erections, they were enjoying themselves as well.

Ned took charge after they left the shower. "Jack, sit on the bed."

Jack dropped his towel and didn't hesitate. His cock stood firm. Her mouth watered.

"Missy, Jack needs a blow job."

The commanding tone resonated through her, and she stepped between Jack's legs with a low hum. Ready to kneel, she stopped when Ned's hands hauled her hips up and out. Clearly his plan didn't include her being on her knees. Knowing Ned, it was the next item on the bucket list. The man didn't miss a detail.

The telltale rip of a condom packet provided the only explanation she required. With a quick shimmy, she gripped Jack's thighs, bent at the waist, and took him in her mouth. Ned ran his warm hand down her spine. The tip of his hard-on pressed into her wet folds. Then he pulled away.

Why? She needed him inside her, desperately. He stroked two fingers into her instead and slicked the hot cream from her center all around her lips. God, couldn't he see how ready she was? Finally, holding her hips tightly, he thrust inside her as she swallowed more of Jack.

Yes! Unable to speak, she pushed her backside toward Ned, silently begging for more, even as she went down on Jack. *Deeper. Harder.*

Stuffed with two dicks at the same time. It was so...*dirty.* The thought of it made her brain foggy with pleasure. Her legs wobbled, but Ned had a tight grip on her. He wouldn't let her fall. His momentum drove the blow job she gave Jack, taking him farther in her throat with every thrust. Sexual power shimmered over her skin. Two men wanted to share her.

"Sugar. So good," Jack groaned.

The obscenely wet sounds of her mouth and pussy harmonized with their grunts. With one hand anchored on Jack's cock and the other braced on his thigh, she worked to relax her throat, to take him as far as she could each time Ned impaled her. The man's thrusts targeted her G-spot. His fingertips dug in almost to the point of bruising.

Jack tweaked her swaying tits. Ned released her hip to tease her clit while his huge dick stretched her perfectly with every stroke. Pleasure and pain mingled with being taken while giving, spiraling in her brain, a perfect storm of sensation.

Her orgasm exploded, and she wailed around Jack's cock before he shot his own release into her throat. She swallowed greedily. Ned grabbed her hips again before she collapsed. He thrust hard several more times, then his powerful eruption nearly set her off again. They fell onto the bed with her wrapped in their arms.

After a brief rest, Ned rose and made his way to the bathroom. A shout brought Missy out of her fog and into high alert. Jack raced ahead of her.

"Blood." Ned clung to the counter, skin sheet-white. His frantic gaze locked onto Missy. "I hurt you."

"What are you talking about?"

Jack cast a worried look at Missy. His eyes widened when he stopped at her thighs.

"Oh." Missy folded over to peer between her own legs. "*Shit.*"

"I was too rough. I didn't think I could—" Ned barreled toward where she stood in the bathroom doorway. "I'm so sorry. Do you need a doctor?"

Jack lifted his arm to block Ned. "Partner. Slow down."

"No, it's...I got my period." Heat rushed over her body and up her neck. "It...it shouldn't happen, they said." Missy forced the words past her embarrassment. "I'm on the shot. I mean, I didn't get one after the last round." How soon could she get them out of the bathroom? She needed to clean up, then figure out how to get supplies.

"You're okay?" Ned stroked his hand down her arm as he took a deep breath.

"Do you have stuff in your room, sugar?" Jack leaned against the sinks, perfectly calm and relaxed.

Could the earth please open up and swallow me now?

"I'm fine. This is just...unexpected." And completely awkward. Their presence was almost smothering. "I need a few minutes. Alone."

"Of course." Ned backed up two steps.

"I'll go get your things," Jack offered.

"No." She closed her eyes and took a slow, deep breath. And the cramps started because the universe had a sense of humor. "I didn't pack anything."

"Not a problem, sugar. I'll run to the store. Any preferences?"

She blinked, dumbfounded.

Carter didn't discuss her periods, much less buy her tampons. One of the reasons she'd switched to the shot was the lack of periods. Or at least they would be light. What a crock.

"Regular tampons?" Jack asked. "Do you need pads or medicine or anything else?"

"Yeah, all that." Missy forced herself to lift her eyes. "Ibuprofen. And chocolate."

Jack nodded and left. Ned still stood there. "Ned. I'm fine, but I need a minute."

He started. "Right. I'll, ah, I'll get the heating pad."

In the time it took Missy to clean up and take a quick shower, Jack returned with enough supplies for a harem. Two sizes of tampons, three kinds of pads, Midol, Advil, and Tylenol, along with what must have been a sample of every kind of chocolate the store had.

"Do you need anything else, sugar?" he asked when she came out of the bathroom dressed in the pajamas Ned had retrieved from her room.

"Twelve other women to help me use all of this up."

"Do it once and do it right," he said with a grin.

Ned pulled back the sheet—the same one from earlier. No sign of a stain, thank goodness. "Come here."

Missy hesitated. "I can go back to my room."

"Heating pad is already plugged in." Ned patted the mattress.

Jack tilted his head toward the bed.

With a sigh, she climbed in, wincing as another wave of cramps punched through her. Maybe it was a sign. Their relationship, no matter how wonderful and how much she felt for them, would end. Soon. A few days away from the list might help her rein in her heart.

MISSY ROLLED over into empty space. Jack wasn't there, but he couldn't have been gone long. His side of the bed still radiated heat.

Insects chirped. The sun had set while they napped.

Ned snored lightly. So far, she'd thought of him as sexy or commanding, but deep in satiated sleep, he was cute. He would deny it if she told him so. She resisted the urge to kiss his relaxed lips, reminding herself that he wasn't her boyfriend. Instead, she turned off the heating pad and slipped out of bed to find Jack.

"Hey, sleepyhead," he said when she wrapped her arms around him from behind. He stirred something that smelled delicious in a saucepan.

"Whatcha making?" She nuzzled his neck and nipped him playfully.

"Nothing, if you keep that up." He laughed.

"I hope it's something. I'm starving."

"I figured you would be, between the swimming and the sex and everything."

Heat flooded her cheeks. She released him, going to the refrigerator for a drink and to cool off.

"Feeling better?"

"Yeah, the meds kicked in."

Before she released the awkward apologies forming on her tongue, Jack asked, "Where's Ned?"

"Still sleeping." Missy selected a bottle of water.

"We could let him rest, but he'd hate that."

"Not as much as he hates waking up to an empty bed," Ned said as he entered the kitchen.

Missy yelped. "You scared the bejeezus out of me."

"Bejeezus?" Jack hooted.

She propped a fist on her hip. "It's a perfectly normal word."

"You really are from the Midwest, aren't you?" Ned chuckled.

"There's nothing wrong with the way I speak."

"I like it just fine, sugar." Jack grinned at her.

Ned came up behind Jack, pressing close to his back and peering over his shoulder. "Looks good."

"Fettuccine Alfredo."

"Perfect. I'll open a white." He selected a bottle for their dinner from the wine refrigerator.

Missy loved how close the two men were getting. It would make it easier to leave, knowing they would still have each other. An ache flashed through her heart. She might be alone, but they would be fine.

As they sat down to dinner, the doorbell rang. Ned dropped his napkin in his chair. "Eat. I'll see what this is about."

A few minutes later, he returned. "How about a movie after dinner?"

"Who was at the door?" Jack asked.

"Nick. Silly mix-up." Ned took his seat and picked up his fork. "Movie?"

"Sure. What should we watch, Missy?"

She finished the bite of creamy pasta and took a sip of wine. "Have you seen *Auntie Mame?*"

"The old Technicolor with Rosalind Russell?" Jack asked, surprised.

"Yes. I love it— the sets, the characters." There wasn't anything she wanted more than to curl up between those two and watch her mom's favorite film.

Two and a half hours later, the last visual feast flashed on the screen. The New York penthouse that the woman constantly redecorated was fun but had made no sense to a Missouri farm girl. But finally, Missy understood the message: Don't starve yourself when life is serving you a banquet.

She was done fighting her feelings. She'd come on an island adventure and fallen in love with Ned and Jack. She would still leave, but her adventure deserved to be savored for all it was worth. Then she would move on with no regrets.

"I'm going to brush my teeth. I'm exhausted," she said, standing. She began the trek to her room.

"I'll expect you in our bed in five minutes," Ned said.

She paused, already halfway down the hall. "Are you sure?"

"Yes, five minutes," Ned repeated.

"I can sleep in the guest bed," she said over her shoulder. The Shit never shared a bed with her during her time of the month.

"*Four* minutes."

"Hurry, sugar," Jack called out.

Missy squeaked with fake fear before a huge smile stretched her cheeks.

∽

THREE DAYS. Three long damn days and it was finally over. The guys had been awesome, catering to her every whim. Sitting on the beach with cocktails in the afternoon. Showering her with attention and kisses and caresses. But a ball of sexual frustration burned in her gut worse than the muscle spasms. The list taunted her. Abstinence hadn't helped tame her feelings for Ned and Jack—it made her crave them more. Finally, it was time to resume their plan. As much as she tried to ignore it, they were running out of time.

Ned and Jack waited for her in the bedroom, unaware of what she intended. Hoping the effort she'd made wasn't wasted, she paused in the doorway, her back slightly arched and breasts lifted high. She wore a sheer babydoll nighty that glazed her body like a fine layer of frost.

Jack recovered first. "Oh my god, woman. You're trying to kill me."

Ned walked over to where she'd posed. "I assumed you'd be tired and we would sleep for the night." He tweaked one of her puckered nipples. "Obviously, I was wrong."

She gasped. "I bought this for the vacation. I'd hate for it to go to waste."

"It's not wasted." Jack suckled her other bud through the gossamer fabric.

Both men were naked and erect.

"Are those for me?" she asked, tilting her head as she reached for them. Her hands itched with the need to touch.

"Not yet." Ned grabbed her wrists. He drew her close, then spun her and pressed her back into Jack's front. Ned put her hands over his shoulders. "Hold on."

He lifted her by the thighs like she weighed nothing. Damn, he was strong.

"Jack, get the condoms." Then he spoke softly in her ear, "Are you ready for us?"

"God, yes."

Jack reached over to the nightstand drawer. A moment later, she heard the rip of the packets.

"Put it on for me." Ned lifted Missy, and Jack reached underneath her to cover him.

Missy nuzzled Ned's neck. His scent intoxicated her almost as much as what they were doing. Jack sheathed himself and stepped in tighter, his skin warm against her back. After a moment, he guided them back using her hips and leaned against the wall. "We're going to need more support for where you're going with this," Jack told Ned over her shoulder.

They kissed her neck, sending shivers of anticipation down her spine. Ned released one thigh, but she was still held tight by Jack and Ned's other hand. He tucked her nighty out of the way of her pussy and slid his fingers between her lips. "You're wet."

"Of course I'm wet," she said. "It's been *days*. Jack's cock is practically in my ass, and I'm floating in your arms. I'm a *puddle*."

Ned's lips twitched into a teasing grin before he plunged his shaft into her, slapping her thigh and knocking Jack into the wall. "Sassy brat. Keep that up, you'll get your ass spanked."

Her insides clenched and gushed around him at his words.

"You *like* that idea. Want me to turn your ass red?" He pumped deep while Missy and Jack moaned in unison.

He smacked her thigh again. The delicious sting went straight to her core. Each thrust grew in magnitude. She arched her back to meet him. He reached between them and pressed her clit forcefully, wrenching the orgasm from her. Stars filled her vision, and every muscle in her body went rigid. Ned was right there with her, slamming into her with no rhythm, grunting incomprehensibly.

She was limp when he pulled out of her, cream coating her thighs. He leaned back and reached between them to guide Jack's aching cock into her. "Fuck her, Jack. Give her more of what she needs."

"It's going to be quick. I'm barely hanging on."

"Do it," she moaned. "Ned's got me."

Ned's grip tightened on her thighs, and he pressed her lower body closer into Jack.

She loved that he knew exactly what she wanted, what she needed. And could give it to her.

161

"I can't move. I need more space," Jack said.

Ned spun them to take Jack's place at the wall and made sure her head was cradled between his shoulder and neck. Unable to resist, she licked his skin, his salt tangy on her tongue.

Jack tilted her hips back, and Ned moved his hands down her thighs, closer to her knees to accommodate the new position. Then Jack thrust his hips and slammed into her drenched core. God, he filled her up so perfectly.

"Yes," Missy cried out. "It feels so good. Please, Jack. Please."

"You don't have to beg, sugar. I'm going to give you everything."

And he did.

Jack moved faster and deeper with each stroke. Using his thumbs, he spread her ass cheeks. The air on her ass gave a naughty sensation of being completely exposed.

"His cock is fucking you so good, Missy."

Ned's dirty talk combined with Jack's pounding did it. Missy exploded again, crying Jack's name. He came, too, as her pussy milked his shaft, getting every drop out of him.

Her body went limp, and the trio barely made it to the bed. Ned recovered first, removing the filled condoms and tenderly wiping down Jack and himself with a cloth from the bathroom. A second warm cloth was laid over her tender bits. Ned finished caring for her and fell back into his spot at her side.

Sometime in the night, they rearranged themselves, cuddling each other. Jack spooned Missy, and Ned held them both to his chest. The moonlight from the gaping curtain danced across their skin, illuminating the sated lovers and shimmering off the silver walls.

But the man who peeked in the window didn't recognize or appreciate the love and magic filling the room.

CHAPTER 17

$\mathcal{N}$ ed woke nestled between Missy's legs, filled with urgent need. They hadn't slept long, but he had to have her. Again. He'd been in the desert, and she was his water. They were lying side by side. He pulled her leg over his hip to open her and then slid his cock between her thighs. He thrust gently again, staying outside where he truly wanted to be. Her eyes flickered open, and a whisper of desire escaped her lips. Ned kissed her and savored her softness until it wasn't enough.

"I need you." He didn't care that he was begging. He'd beg for her every day if she wanted him to.

Her eyes gazed into his with such warmth, his heart clenched.

"Yes," she whispered.

There was no sense of urgency other than to be with her, inside of her, and connected in that timeless way. Jack's hands moved up and down her arms and shoulders, his lips at her neck. Earlier had been fucking. Their loving movement spoke the truth Ned was apprehensive to disclose in any other way.

He stroked Jack's hair, drawing his attention. Retreating from the warm, wet embrace of Missy, he locked his eyes to Jack's. "We need you."

Jack sucked in a harsh breath and, after a moment, thrust his hips a couple of times before pulling out. Ned took the obvious invitation and entered Missy's sweet channel, alternating with Jack to pleasure their precious woman. Missy followed their rhythm, tilting her hips toward him and then to Jack when he paused. It was almost like he was making love to both of them, being right where Jack had been moments before. The walls of her pussy rubbed him with Jack's essence. Soft moans and the sounds of slick flesh coming together were the only break in the sacred silence of the bedroom.

They transitioned faster and faster. The head of one cock poised at her entrance as the other moved inside. Alternating with each thrust, Missy's slick cream eased the way.

Her cooing and moaning became keening. Her voice gripped Ned's balls as if she were using her hand. She held Ned tighter with her thighs—her nails dug into his shoulders. He reached between them and carefully pressed her clit.

Their tandem efforts continued until her body went taut and she wailed. Jack pulled out, and Ned reclaimed his place to finish what he'd started. His orgasm quickly followed, his hips pumping into the heaven of her body as Jack exploded between their legs. Ned held them close, not letting either one move. After taking his time to savor the feeling of being wrapped in love, he went to get a washcloth.

In the cold light of the bathroom, the missing condom was obvious.

Dread chilled him.

How would Missy react?

The odds were extremely slim he'd impregnated her. It wasn't the only concern. They would all have to have a frank discussion. But it could wait for a few hours.

The deed was done.

～

THE MORNING LIGHT streamed through the crack between the drapes. Ned lay there, aware Jack and Missy were awake. It felt wrong to break the silence, but he had to address the issue.

"We need to talk." He stared at the ceiling, unable to meet their eyes.

"About what?" Jack asked.

Ned winced at the defensiveness in Jack's tone, but he deserved it. "Us. What happened last night."

"I *love* what happened last night." Missy caressed his arm, her touch like silk. "Although, I am a little sore."

"I love what happened, too, but we had a bit of an oversight the second time. We didn't use condoms." Her hand froze on his arm. Ned waited for her reaction.

"Oh." Her voice was low, no longer playful. She wiggled out from between the two men and climbed down the center of the bed until she got to the floor. "It's going to have to wait a sec."

After the bathroom door shut, Jack asked, "Are you worried about STDs?"

"Not really. By my reasoning, Missy and I are clean, and you're probably the most careful." Ned leaned against the headboard, watching the bathroom door.

"I had a physical three months ago, and I hadn't been with anyone for months before or since. No worries."

"Chance of pregnancy is nearly nil." Ned ran his fingers roughly through his hair.

Jack folded his arms behind his head and closed his eyes, the corners of his lips turning up. "It wouldn't be the worst thing."

"Not for us. But what about her?"

"What about me?"

Ned's eyes snapped to the beautiful woman in the doorway. Her jaw was clenched tight, arms wrapped around her middle.

"Get back in bed. This conversation requires cuddling." Jack held is arms open to her.

She dropped back into her spot with a heavy sigh. "I've never had sex without a condom."

"We're clean," Ned said. "What about pregnancy?"

"Even if I didn't get the shot, I *just* finished my period," she replied.

"I'm sorry." Ned tucked an arm around her shoulders.

She leaned into him, but her body was stiff. "About not having a baby or not using a condom?"

"Both," he answered seriously.

Missy blinked at him. Was that fear in her eyes or anger? He couldn't tell.

"If something did happen, I'm not sure I could be sad about it." Ned squeezed tighter. "And I would—"

"Correction," Jack interrupted. "*We* would be there for you and want to help you raise our child."

Ned followed Jack's fingers as they traced down Missy's arm. His stomach roiled. He'd violated Missy's trust and nearly shut out Jack. They were going to hate him if he didn't get his head out of his ass.

"Of course I meant *we*. It would be too much for one person. And we both care about you. It takes a village and all that." Ned forced himself to close his mouth before he dug any deeper.

"Babies are a *long* way off in my future. There are things I need to accomplish. Promises I made." She squeezed Ned's arm and patted Jack's hand. "I'm going to shower—in my room. My lady parts need a rest."

Ned stared at Missy's retreating figure until she disappeared, a tight ache in his chest.

"That went well." Jack's voice was anything but happy.

"Better than I imagined," Ned lied.

MISSY SLIPPED OUTSIDE and pedaled her borrowed bike down the drive once the patrolling security had passed. The door to the office was closed when she'd left. She told herself it was polite to leave Ned and Jack undisturbed.

Unlike how they'd left her that morning.

Her legs shook a bit and she tried to pull her thoughts from what they'd done last night. What she'd let them do. Unprotected sex.

If her high school health teacher could see her, she'd likely fail Missy retroactively. And she deserved it. No excuses. No blame. It was her fault. She pumped her legs faster, as if she could escape the consequences of her poor decisions. Bucket list of sex? Sure. Two men? Of course. What could *possibly* be the risk in that?

Did other people have the same problems, or did they resist the selfish impulses that seemed to define her life? The only problem with being on a bike was a lack of flat surfaces on which to bang her head.

She turned away from the port, the bustling town. In her mood, she had no desire to be around people. The day was warm, but the breeze felt cool on her sweat-dampened skin. She biked on and on, away from her bad choices. The unfamiliar terrain morphed, and she found herself recognizing landmarks from the day she arrived. A right turn and a short distance up the road she spied the bungalow.

Missy parked the bike on the side of the road. The windows had been installed, along with what looked like new shutters. The outside didn't seem to be so cratered, but it still needed paint. That was where she would have been. With Carter. Safe. Bored. Bile bubbled at the back of her throat.

As angry as she was with herself, no part of her missed Carter. He'd proven to be more toxic than anything that might have resulted from what she'd done. She mounted the bike and rode in the direction of the little café where, just weeks ago, she'd waited for Ned and Jack to save her.

Save her.

Right.

Time to do some research.

At the café, she slid into a different booth, facing away from the door. The view was toward the forested hills instead of the water. If she didn't focus too carefully, she could imagine she was back in her small town in Missouri. If only.

Hunger gnawed at her, a reminder she hadn't bothered to eat before she'd left. She ordered a plate of food and coffee and opened the browser on her phone. A few searches and page reads later and she confirmed that pregnancy was unlikely. *Thank goodness*. She couldn't imagine studying for the bar or working her new eighty-hour-a-week job would be conducive to growing a little one.

That morning, when Ned had said he wouldn't be sad and Jack jumped in with vows to help, she'd had to bite back a scream, masking her emotions as she'd practiced in law school. Ned wouldn't be sad if she wasted her education. Jack would help—what? Change diapers? Pay for day care? He wasn't going to be gaining weight, puking every morning, going through invasive examinations—not to mention labor and delivery. It would be fine when she was ready for all those things. But not yet.

Her phone chirped. Two text messages came in simultaneously.

Jack: *Sugar, everything ok?*

Ned: *Where are you?*

Missy's thumb hovered over the phone. How should she respond? With a sigh, she held down the power button. She wasn't ready to talk, even electronically.

The waitress delivered her food and refilled her coffee.

Missy scarfed down her meal. With something in her stomach, her thoughts cleared. The internet wouldn't contain any information she didn't already know. Perhaps that's why she'd avoided the search. While not as immediate as a pregnancy, an infection could be just as life-altering.

Sexually transmitted disease.

She couldn't think of a less erotic phrase. It was a layer of gray slime over everything. The food threatened to reappear, and she swallowed down some water and forced herself to breath. They'd both sworn they were clean. But how could she know for sure? As soon as she got back to the States, she'd visit a clinic and get tested. For everything.

The strength in her spine left her, and it was all she could do to not lie on the table and sob. Who should she be mad at? Carter for leaving her? Ned and Jack for failing her?

All of it was her fault, and the universe was delivering its lesson as usual. She was going to break her word to her grandparents. The promise she'd made to use her inheritance to build a life her parents would be proud of was crumbling before her.

Missy stared out the windows and sipped coffee until the sun was low in the sky. She had to go back. The restaurant didn't rent rooms.

She powered on her phone and checked the time. Ouch, much later than she'd thought, and a dozen calls from Jack and Ned. She'd deal with them in person. After paying the bill and using the restroom to wash away the remnants of stray tears from her face, she left the café. A cab appeared from nowhere at the curb.

"Missy!"

The sound of her name rose above the rumble of the aging vehicle. A loud voice she didn't recognize. She turned in the direction it seemed to have come from. Nick was running toward her.

What was he doing there? Had something happened to the guys? Oh no. She'd been so self-centered when she'd turned off her phone. Never once considered they might need her.

"I can take you," the taxi driver called through the open back door.

Nick took her arm in his hand. "Ned sent me. We've been searching for you."

The taxi sped off.

"We have to get back. Now." Nick escorted her to Ned's car and assisted her into the back seat.

"What about the bike?"

"I'll send someone for it." Nick shut the door and climbed into the driver's seat.

～

"WHERE HAVE YOU BEEN?" Ned stood in the living room, facing the front door, his arms crossed and a scowl on his face. Nerves fluttered through Missy's stomach and she considered turning around and leaving. But no, she couldn't avoid them any longer.

"I needed some air." She didn't want to explain how she was second-guessing the entire vacation.

"All day? We had no idea where you were. Your phone was off. You didn't take security. You need to have someone with you. What if something happened?" Ned's voice echoed off the walls and she cringed inside.

"Why would I need a guard?"

"You need to be protected," Ned said like it was the most obvious answer in the world.

"Like you protected me last night?" As soon as the words passed her lips, she regretted them. Ned's face crumbled. He visibly shrank in his clothes.

"Is that what this was about, sugar?" Jack moved to Ned and rested a hand on his shoulder.

"No." Missy folded her arms around herself. "Maybe. I don't know."

"You have every right to be upset. But why didn't you come to us?" Ned's gaze didn't meet her eyes.

"I have come to you. Since this entire debacle of a vacation started. I've turned to you for everything. I've excused myself from any of my rules. I've indulged every desire. Yours. Mine. Jack's. *Ours.*" She flung her arms out wide and let them drop heavily. "It's all been fun and games. Even though there is always a cost. I've been here for weeks. And now I know what's going to happen. I'm going to end up with an unwanted pregnancy—or worse, some disease that will never go away. And I'll lose my job."

"But—"

"How am I going to study for the bar and pass it when I have all of this hanging over my head? I completely abandoned reality. Well, reality came back to bite me in the butt. And the worst part is, I deserve it." She slapped a hand to her chest, beating at the dread. "I deserve everything that's coming to me. I knew it when we started this. I *should* be punished for my selfishness."

Her mouth went dry, and she was unable to form any more words to convey to them exactly how predictable the pattern of her life was. She sucked back a sob, tears streaming down her face.

"You need to be punished?" Jack asked, his voice barely above a whisper.

His words cut through the chaos of her thoughts, and her body jerked like she'd been shocked. For once, the noise in her head went quiet. *Yes.*

CHAPTER 18

"*M*issy?"

Ned's voice sounded as though he was on the other side of the planet from her instead of across the room.

He locked his eyes with hers, and Missy nodded despite her inability to answer out loud. Maybe she could choose her punishment. She hadn't been spanked since she was a little girl, when she'd run in the street after her father had told her not to. It had been the worst experience of her life. But the sick feeling she'd had from disobeying him disappeared. And she'd never doubted how much her father cared. Would it work again?

"We need the words, Missy." Jack crossed the room and gripped her shoulders.

She tilted her chin up and swallowed down any hesitation. "Spank me."

"What you're suggesting, Jack…it's one thing in the middle of sex." Ned dropped into one of the chairs. "I don't think I can."

"Hell, your palm's been itching all afternoon. Every time you sent a text, checked your phone for a response, or had Nick update you. Don't lie," Jack drawled over his shoulder.

"Please, Ned."

The words erupted from her throat without ever passing through her brain. Compulsion swirled up her spine. She needed it. From him. Didn't he understand? How could he? She didn't even understand why Jack's suggestion had resonated so deeply within her. Driving her to beg for something she'd never considered.

"You're going to have a safe word. You'll be in control, at all times." Jack appeared to be talking to her, but he'd turned so that the three of them could see each other.

"What word?" she asked.

Ned's jaw seemed to relax a bit.

"Let's use *mandarin*," Jack suggested.

"Why *mandarin*? Why not the basic stoplight?" Ned asked.

"Because those little canned oranges remind me of her. So sweet and tender. Almost addictive." His teasing smile didn't affect her like it usually did. She wasn't playing.

Something must have shown on her face, because Jack went quiet and his gaze dropped.

"Fine." Ned stood. "Mandarin," he repeated with the solemnity of a vow. Without taking his eyes from hers, he took a slow, deep breath. "Strip."

"I...I need a minute. To shower." And to compose herself. "I'm sweaty from the bike ride."

"Ten minutes. Or I'll assume you changed your mind."

Eight minutes later, Missy stood clean and naked but for her plain cotton panties. She tried not to shake from fear. Or was it anticipation?

Ned moved to the couch. Jack ran his rough hands over her shoulders. He guided her to stand so close to Ned, the fabric of his shorts brushed against her. Jack sat then pulled her chest down over his lap. Her breasts touched the cold leather of the sofa, and she flinched. Ned lifted her legs over his. Warmth from Jack's jean-clad thighs infused her belly.

Something about that position made it real, and the constant tension, the running commentary that echoed incessantly through her mind, quieted. Submission. In a few moments, it would be clear if that was who she truly was, deep down.

Ned ran his hand in slow circles over each cheek down her thigh and back again. Caressing her.

Missy sighed out a breath, and her muscles went slack.

Ned lifted his hand and smacked her ass.

Damn, that stung. *Mandarin.* The word was on the tip of her tongue, but she clamped her teeth closed.

He smacked the other cheek.

The tightness in her chest loosened, and her hips lifted in anticipation.

Jack held her hands in one of his—she couldn't rub the burn away. His other arm wrapped around her waist, preventing her from launching off their laps. If she ran, it wouldn't be from them or the spanking. It would be from herself. The side she'd denied existed.

The next impact made her core clench tightly, as if it needed something inside. He connected twice more, and she imagined him fucking her hard as he paddled her ass. His cock sliding in and out as his hand came down on her skin. The image changed to Ned working his dick into Jack's ass as she lay tied to the bed beneath them, only able to watch. Wetness seeped from her pussy.

Two more sharp swats brought her back from her fantasy. Prickling pain nibbled between her legs.

Ned spanked her again. A moan escaped. Jack reached down and caressed her breast, then tugged and pinched her nipple. Pain and pleasure melded like the horizon where ocean and sky blurred into one. Ned slapped his hand down again.

"Fuck!" she cried as her body released more cream.

He dragged the white cotton covering off her ass, leaving it bunched at her knees. She must look ridiculous, laid out naked over two fully dressed men with her underwear wrapped around her legs. Her ass was probably quite pink. Two more jolts had her squirming to get away no matter how happy her pussy was.

"Oh no, we're just getting started. You worried us for hours. We lo—care about you." Ned's breath teased over her bare skin.

"But it *hurts.*" *And I don't want you to know how much I like it.*

Smack. Smack. "I want you to think about this any time you're doing *anything* that puts you in an unsafe situation."

"And this isn't about unsafe sex, sugar." Jack pulled her hair back from her face. "This is about you running. Hiding. Not coming to us."

Ned reached his hand between her legs, fingers sliding through her copious fluids. "Besides, I think you're enjoying it."

Damn. But she wasn't the only one. Their erections pressed into her thighs and belly.

Jack kneaded and pulled her other breast. "You have something to say?"

She pressed her lips closed—no way was she saying the word that would end her sexy torment. Ned's legs tightened under her hips. Several moments passed. The constriction in her chest built—the voice in her head started to speak. She wiggled, and they both strengthened their holds.

Ned fired off a quick series of whacks. He was hitting spots he hadn't before and going much lower on her ass, almost to her legs. It burned. It electrified. Jack tormented her breasts. *Could they fuck me right now, please?*

"Feel her, Jack," Ned instructed. Missy strained against their tight hold. If only she could touch their cocks.

Jack released his grip on her side and slid his hand between her legs. He pumped fingers into her sopping slit again and again. "You're soaking, sugar. Have you forgiven yourself?"

The slick sucking sound as he pulsed into her wet passage revealed her truth. Being spanked erased her guilt and lit her erotic fire.

"Yes. Please?" she begged.

He withdrew his hand. She ached to come but had no more fight left in her. She slumped bonelessly over their legs, entirely at their mercy. Entirely safe. Entirely in their care. Her body burned, but her mind floated.

Ned tormented her backside four more times in quick succession. The orgasm that had been flitting around, teasing her, was right there. He stopped. Released her. *No,* she nearly screamed but bit her tongue.

175

They helped her to her feet, fabric still trapped at her wobbling knees. Her ass throbbed.

"Go wait for us on the bed. I want you on your hands and knees so I see your cherry ass when I come in the room," Ned commanded. His tone made her insides flutter.

"Hold on," Jack said. He knelt at her feet and helped her step out of her panties.

She drifted her fingers through his golden locks.

He stood and kissed her forehead, then patted her behind, making her suck in a breath. "Go. Do what Ned asked."

All she could think about was the fucking she was about to get. Her inner thighs were slick with desire. She needed them. Somewhere deep inside, she craved the bite of pain and Ned's control. If she were honest, she hadn't felt so cared for, so cherished, in far too long. Heat pulsed along the back of her thighs and over her ass. But she refused to rub out the sting. She embraced it as she took her position on the bed and waited. There was no fear of judgement.

NED GLANCED DOWN THE HALL, anxious to get to Missy. He had to let her anticipation build.

"She's fine. How are you doing?" Jack asked.

His voice drew Ned's attention back. "What do you mean?"

"You were nervous, but it was perfect." Jack laid his hand on Ned's knee.

Ned swallowed hard. "Not sure I'd use that word for spanking a woman I'm coming to care for."

"She needed it. You needed it. It broke the tension, wiped the slate clean."

Ned stood, putting space between them. "You were angrier than I was. What about for you?"

"What about me, Ned?" Jack stood up and pressed against his back. His words husked into Ned's ear. "Do I need your dominance? Would you be able to do that for me?"

"You want me to spank your ass?" Ned turned to face Jack. So close, their chests were touching.

"I want you to do *something* to my ass."

Ned snorted and took a step back. "I was talking about Missy. How are you going to get over the fact she left?"

"She ran. Hid, really. It was a mistake. I can forgive. Once."

Ned raised his gaze and faced the beautiful man he kept pushing away. "What about me? Can you forgive me?"

"You haven't run. Shied a bit." Jack blessed him with a dazzling grin. "I'm working on taming you."

"So, I'm your horse now?"

"You're hung like one."

Ned laughed. "Let's go get our girl."

"You lead...sir." Jack held out his hand toward the hall.

Ned stuffed his hands in his pockets to hide his reaction. Another thing he loved about the man. As strong as Jack was, he understood Ned's compulsion to be in charge, to lead, especially in the bedroom.

Ned froze on the threshold. Jack pressed against his back. Missy posed, ass bright red, pussy swollen and glistening, on her hands and knees as instructed. Her blond hair cascaded down her back. She stole his breath, a fantasy come to life. Ned's sense of power and possessiveness zoomed off the charts. The urge to tie her up and fuck her, and get Jack to fuck her, to own them both, threatened to overwhelm. He took a deep breath and waited until he regained control of himself. Jack remained still. Ned stepped into the room and kicked off his shoes. "Thank you, Missy."

Missy peered over her shoulder. "Thank you?"

"For doing as I asked."

"You're welcome, sir." She grinned and lowered her chest, pushing her backside up in the air a little more and exposing her sex further. The pose was like a seductive caress over his balls and down his stiff length. He couldn't sink into her heat fast enough.

"Nice." Jack ripped his shirt off and unbuttoned his pants.

"What *shall* we do with her now?" Ned asked Jack, as if they both didn't already know. Something about their ménage relationship removed all the barriers to express his desires. He had to make sure he didn't ruin things by going too far. It suddenly dawned on him—that's why the three of them worked. Jack had a way of escalating to the next level without overwhelming her. Jack could convince her, while he would command her. They created the perfect balance.

Jack continued to strip. It was the only thing that could have drawn Ned's gaze away from Missy. Jack's long cock was hard and ready for him. For them. Ned's palm itched with the urge to stroke Jack until he came. Instead, Ned finished taking his clothes off and followed as Jack moved to the naked woman on their bed. A mischievous grin lit his face.

"I think this sweet, cherry ass needs some more attention." Jack palmed her punished cheeks, pressing the flesh in with his fingers, and then pulling them apart to expose more of her wetness and her tight little asshole. His tanned hands contrasted with Missy's reddened flesh. Those strong hands…one could wrap around his cock and guide it into Missy. Ned's balls tightened with the erotic vision.

Jack's gaze turned to Ned—his normally icy eyes were like flames, melting away more of Ned's inhibitions.

Ned dragged his fingers through Missy's swollen, waiting lips, grazing her clit. She whined in protest and wiggled her hips. He savored the power that ran up his arm and did it again. Boundaries disappeared, and there was only the three of them and their connection. He gathered her dew and held his soaked digits out to Jack.

Jack opened his mouth. Ned dragged Missy's essence down Jack's tongue. Jack hummed in pleasure.

Ned retrieved more of her sexy fluids. This time he swirled them around on her pucker. "Relax," he instructed. "We're going to take such good care of you." *For as long as you let us.*

MISSY LET her fears slip away. Trust gave her the courage to let Ned and Jack guide her in the fantasy. One she never would've been brave enough to admit she had. There was no question where it would lead, and she welcomed it. Just one time. She'd return to reality in a couple of weeks, and she'd never wonder again.

Ned pressed his fingers against her back passage a little more, massaging with added pressure but not penetrating her. Tingles ran down her legs, through her pussy and up her spine, forbidden and exciting. How much more thrilling would the real thing be?

Jack kneaded her cheeks, holding her open. Ned lowered his face to her upturned bottom and, starting with her clit, licked and sucked all the way up to her little hole. The tip of his tongue pressed the edges and then circled. *Fuck*. That was so dirty. And hot.

"Relax." Jack rubbed a hand down her back.

"What's your word?" Ned asked.

"Mandarin," she whispered.

"Do you want to use it?" Ned's gravel-heavy voice ground through her insides.

"No. Don't...I don't want you to stop. It feels..." Her words faded into a moan as he returned his tongue to the taboo place and added a finger. She was empty and full at the same time. Overwhelmed with foreign sensations and the urge to beg for more.

Jack's hand rubbed her pearl, and her pussy gushed. In and out he stroked her. In and out Ned worked his finger in her ass. Missy turned her head to peer at Jack over her shoulder. He stared at Ned, not even blinking. Was he aware his erection was bumping into Ned's side? Jack licked his bottom lip and thrust his fingers into her faster and deeper. She lost all focus and dropped her head as ecstasy washed over her.

Ned lifted his lips from her ass and pushed his thumb in deep. Stretched and stuffed, and it wasn't even his dick. Her core muscles clenched, and her hips twitched in time with his ministrations. Jack removed his fingers from her channel and squeezed her clit between his fingertips. She burst like a comet hitting the atmosphere, exploding in orgasm and flooding her cream all over his hand. Her arms collapsed, and her entire body shivered.

"You liked that, sugar. Tell me you didn't," Jack drawled. As if she could form any words, much less a lie.

179

Ned left her body, and the sound of running water a few moments later told her he was in the bathroom. Jack reclined next to her, petting her skin softly and murmuring praise as if she were a sex goddess worthy of worship.

"How's our girl doing?" Ned dropped a towel, lube, and condoms on the mattress next to her.

"I'm so good," she purred.

Jack reached past her, and the next thing she knew, her hips were lifted, and a pillow was positioned under her. "Ready for more?"

She arched her back and murmured her assent.

Jack picked up the bottle of lube, and she heard the telltale click of it opening. The gel was unexpectedly cold when he touched her heated skin but quickly warmed as Jack rubbed his fingers over her opening. One finger slid in, different from Ned's thumb, not as thick. Then he worked in a second finger, stretching her. She whimpered and rocked into his hand.

"I'm gonna make this so good for you." Jack's other hand moved between her wet lips and teased inside, but Ned's warm grip on her ass reminded her who was really in charge. Another drop of cold lube hit her pucker, and Jack pressed a third finger into her hole. Pain. Pleasure. Filled completely. Nothing else existed but their hands.

"You doing okay?" Jack asked

Missy shook her head no, but mouthed yes, expressing the war of reticence and pleasure. No intention of stopping it with her safe word.

"Ned? She's ready."

"I'm going to take over from Jack, sweetheart," Ned said quietly as he leaned over her. "I'm going to fuck my hard dick into your ass."

"Oh yes."

Jack withdrew his hands from her body. A sense of loss had her turning her head to find him.

With the telltale rattle of the condom box, the ache of absence turned to anticipation. Ned added even more lube directly to her hole and worked it in with his strong fingers. "Okay, sweet girl, we're going to take this nice and slow. If anything hurts you or you don't like it, you need to tell me. Understand?"

She pushed her ass toward Ned.

Ned pressed the head of his cock at her entrance. He blew a hot, panting breath across her skin.

"Hold on, sweetheart, or I'm going to come before I get in." He went slow, applied gentle pressure, then just when she was convinced it wouldn't fit, the head of his dick was inside. Full and stretched, it was more startling than the first time she'd had sex.

Jack's face came into view. "Sugar?"

"More," she grunted.

Ned pushed in a little farther. He groaned and squeezed deeper inside her body. His strong hands gripped her hips hard and held her in place. She huffed out little breaths, trying to adjust to his claiming. The scent of their bodies was musky and carnal. He pressed again and slid all the way into her, his balls slapping up against her hungry lips.

And it was so much better than she'd imagined, but different, too. Unlike regular sex. The sensations were harsher, the pleasure unfamiliar but so good. "Fuck me, Ned."

Ned blew out another breath. "I forgot—I can't control—"

Jack's fingers found her clit and teased her. Finally, Ned retreated almost completely before he thrust back in, making Missy gasp. Jack's hands no longer held her attention. Only Ned's cock existed, fucking her with increasing speed. He spoke in the rhythm of his movement. "Fuck. So good, Missy."

"Yes, Ned. Please." She didn't know what more he could give her, but the threat of something huge flickered at the edge of her awareness.

Jack fingered her pussy, toying with her bundle of nerves.

Ned drove harder and deeper. "Tell me. When she's ready."

Faster and faster, they danced inside her until she was screaming mindlessly. Ned exploded, shuddering against her hips.

Jack withdrew his cum-soaked hand, a huge smile aimed at her. Ned curled his sweat-dampened body around hers, and they collapsed on the bed together. Her breath sawed in and out of her lungs as she floated.

"Beautiful." Jack swept her hair back from her face.

Ned pulled out of her carefully and went into the bathroom. Jack continued to croon praises to her as he petted her arms and back. The shower kicked on, the sound of the spray muffling Jack's low drawl.

Ned called from the door, "Bring her in here."

Jack helped her up and guided her to Ned. Together they washed her, lathering her like fine crystal with gentle touches over her entire body. She hummed her pleasure, reviving under the steamy water.

Missy stole the soapy scrubby from Jack's hands. She ministered to Ned with the same care he'd shown her. She washed his cock and balls and down his legs. As she worked her way back up, she moved behind him. She took her soapy hand between his cheeks and stroked his asshole. There was no pressure in her touch—she was just feeling him.

Ned met her eyes over his shoulder. He picked up a second scrubby and added soap before applying it to Jack's chest. She shifted to follow Ned's lead and ran the cloth down Jack's spine, giving him the same personal treatment. Unlike Ned, Jack pushed his ass out for her to get him completely clean. She laughed and washed his inner thighs, his sac, and finally, reached between his legs to wash his stiff cock, stroking him until he thrust.

"Wait. Not here," Ned told her. He lifted her to her feet and rinsed her thoroughly before he shut off the water and handed each of them a towel.

CHAPTER 19

After drying off and returning to the bedroom, Jack hesitated. Missy would be exhausted, but he was ravenous for more. Finally, he had what he'd always dreamed of: his sexy best friend and an adventurous, smart, loving woman.

At the same time.

It wouldn't last.

On some level, he was aware of the fragility of their dynamic. Hell, he was amazed Missy was back. Part of him had figured, after she'd been gone so long, she'd left them. When Nick had called and said they were on their way, the relief had nearly brought him to his knees.

Not only had she returned, but she'd been willing to trust them again. When he'd blurted out the word "punishment," he'd been thinking only of when he'd been in trouble. The atonement he felt after a whupping or a lecture when he was younger—he'd wanted her to have that relief. And Missy had agreed to it. Damn, just thinking about her draped over his lap while Ned spanked her had his cock coming back to life. He paused at the edge of the bed, wary of exceeding her limits.

Missy looked at him, or rather a specific part of him, and licked her lips. Maybe his sweet woman was just as eager.

"You want to keep playing, sugar?" Jack asked, trying not to sound like he was begging.

She lifted her amber eyes to his and nodded. "But I want to give, too, not just receive."

"I'll play with you any way you want." Jack smiled and held out his hand. She took his offering, and he pulled her in close so he could nuzzle her hair and kiss her plump lips. Sparks of energy bounced through him.

Ned cleared his throat. Jack paused mid-kiss when Ned's hand gripped the back of his neck, dominant and strong. A shiver shot up Jack's spine, and he leaned back into Ned. The man's muscular arm wrapped around him in a moment of possession. Jack would willingly be claimed by him. Ned's commanding voice brushed hot against his ear. "Jack, bend over the bed."

Ned released him, his hand tracing from his neck down his back. A tremor of yearning raced up. Jack let go of the soft woman in his arms and moved into position as instructed.

"Missy, I want you to do everything to Jack that we did to you to get you ready."

Ready registered like a brand in his brain.

Ready for what, Ned? What I've dreamed of since the day we met?

"You have to tell me what to do." She sounded unsure but eager. "I want to make him feel as good as you made me feel."

"Get on your knees behind him, sweetheart," Ned instructed. "Jack, spread your legs."

He moved his legs apart. Missy's hands glided against his thighs as she dropped. Her warm breath whispered across his ass while they waited for what came next.

Ned said nothing.

And then she moved. She licked slowly up his inner thigh almost to his scrotum, pulled away, and did the same up the other leg. Her tongue grazed the bottom of his sac. She applied pressure to his perineum. His balls filled, and tension built at the base of his spine.

She laved him again, teasing the crease of his ass.

Jack's cock strained, begging to be allowed into that delectable mouth. The image from a few days ago, when she'd prepared to suck him off, formed like a photograph behind his eyes. He pinched the head hard so he didn't come all over the bed. "Holy shit."

A rough hand gripped his ass and pulled him open. Cool air hit his asshole, and he couldn't decide if he should clench or push back. Before he could move, Ned slicked a finger over it, leaving a thick coat of lube behind. The edible one Jack had bought right before their trip —hoping.

"Lick him," Ned said as if he was sharing a delicious morsel.

Will she do it? Jack counted the seconds.

Heat from her gentle breaths warmed the area as she lowered into him. Her tongue flicked over his hole. Circled. Then again, slower. And again.

Low moans escaped from deep in his chest, reverberating off the walls, echoing in his ears. His arms started shaking as he tried to keep from coming, struggling not to faceplant into the bed.

She licked him and fondled his balls, not letting him come down.

Ned placed a towel over the bed in front of him. "Come when you're ready," he said. "Don't worry, we'll get you hard again."

But he didn't want to come yet. Not until Ned—

Ned's chest hair tickled the outside of his thigh as he knelt down beside Missy. "Stroke him."

Missy went to his side and gripped his needy cock with a slicked hand. Up and down she stroked. Too slow to get him off, but it was fucking heaven. And then a thick, strong finger —*Ned*—slid into Jack's ass, and all conscious thought stopped. Ned stretched his hole, pressing and thrusting until a second finger found its way inside. The world shrank down to his pleasure and their hands.

Jack twitched his hips back toward Ned. Ned's free hand gripped his hip, holding him in place, making him take the decadent torment. Missy's hand slid up and down his cock with the same rhythm as Ned's penetrating fingers. Three fat fingers, fucking his ass. Jack had never let anyone have so much authority over him. Never trusted anyone with such a sensitive area. But *Ned*. Ned owned him. Could do whatever he wanted.

The pace of their strokes increased, Ned still gripping his hip hard enough to mark him. He hoped.

Jack couldn't hold on a second longer. He came all over the towel in huge ropes of cum, calling out their names. He dropped to the side, panting.

Ned stared down at him, a self-satisfied smile playing at his lips. A gleam in his eye promised more. But Jack had plans. Not that he minded where the activity might go, but Ned wasn't excused from truly participating. It was a risk, but if he couldn't get Ned over his inhibitions then they had no future.

After a few moments of recovery and some cleanup, Jack gazed into Ned's eyes.

"Your turn."

~

NED blinked and took a step back. He'd had no intention of having *a turn.*

"If you hate it, we'll stop. Say 'red.'" Jack held his arms open, but low, non-threatening. "You have nothing to fear."

Fear. Damn, Jack saw everything. Always.

The breath Ned had been holding released slowly. He rubbed his hand down his face and cleared his throat. But every nerve was on high alert.

Missy sank to her knees. "Please?"

They asked for his trust. If he couldn't give it to them, then—

Ned stepped close to Jack and tugged him in, one arm around his waist, one hand on his neck. He dove into Jack's mouth with all of the passion and possession the man created inside Ned's chest. He controlled every part of Jack's body. Muscular, rough thighs scraped against his. Jack's cock stirred, tempting his own to awaken. Jack's chest pressed so tightly against his, he could feel the vibration of his lover's pounding heart. Softening his hold as he softened his kiss, he allowed Jack a breath. Kissed him lightly once again before releasing his neck. Jack's eyes were dilated, and he leaned into Ned for support.

He skimmed his free hand down Jack's shoulder and arm, soothing him.

Blond hair caught the corner of Ned's eye. Missy was still on her knees. Her eyes locked on them, and her mouth slightly parted. "Come here."

She crawled forward. The submission was a siren call to the side of him that demanded control, that drove him to be the best and protect those he loved with everything he had.

Perfect.

She was perfect. He held out his hand to assist her, but she didn't take it. She pressed her face to the juncture of his leg and hip and licked the crease. It was like she'd licked his sac. But that wasn't what he wanted right then. He wrapped his hand in her golden tresses and guided her where she was supposed to be. Standing, with them. Her silken skin pressed against him. Jack's arm wrapped around her hips as Ned tugged her hair back and dropped his greedy mouth to hers. He kissed her, hard and possessively at first and then gentling. Jack's hand brushed against his lower back, closing their circle.

Ned savored the warmth flowing through his veins. The constant heaviness around his heart lifted. He'd been labeled successful. Amassed money and possessions with his hard work. But he'd never experienced the sensation of abundance. Until that moment.

He eased back. Released them. Then he turned around and braced his arms against the wall. He was theirs as much as they were his.

Missy caressed his legs, and Jack massaged his shoulders. Slowly, the last bit of hesitation, resistance, left his body. It was everything he'd been afraid to want. He'd been a fool.

Missy kissed the backs of his knees, his thighs. Her soft lips sent quivers up his body. Her shoulders moved between his legs, and he widened his stance reflexively to accommodate her. More attention on his inner thighs—those tingles went straight to his cock. Her hands moved to the front of his legs, still stroking his skin and kissing him with gentle lips.

Jack continued to rub his back, working even lower now, but still not touching his ass. Ned bit his tongue. He wasn't in charge. Didn't have to be. He released the stiffness in his neck and rested his forehead on the wall.

Missy reached between his legs and stroked his cock, kissing and licking his balls. His dick was hard and straining for her. For them. Her warm touch was sweet and gentle, but he craved rough and hard, too. Didn't want one without the other.

As if he'd heard the demand, Jack gripped Ned's ass cheeks, digging his fingers in and pressing them farther apart. Missy released his cock. Jack held him open, and a moment later, delicate fingers slicked up his tight hole. She continued to roll her fingers around his opening. When her tongue hit him, Ned let out a strangled moan.

Jack's fingers replaced Missy's mouth. He rubbed Ned's pucker until he gained entrance. *Fuck.* Ned had forgotten how intense penetration could be. Missy teased his perineum. He closed his eyes and let them take over. Fell into the pleasure that was just for him. Gifted by the two people he loved.

Missy returned to stroking his cock. When Jack worked a second finger inside him, hitting that magic spot, Ned choked back a howl of pleasure and grabbed Missy's hand, squeezing back his orgasm. "Don't want to come...on the wall."

She turned his hip and crawled around him. His raging red hard-on was in her mouth in seconds. After she caressed his balls, she returned to massaging behind them. The roar he'd held back erupted along with an explosion of cum.

Slowly, he returned to his body. Missy was on the floor in front him, smiling. Jack was no longer inside him but still pressed along his back. Ned reached down and lifted Missy to her feet.

"I think we all need another shower," Jack said, guiding Missy in front of him, away from Ned.

Ned followed them under the spray. He wrapped Missy in a tight hug and kissed her. Then he turned to Jack and did the same.

After the second shower, Ned wasn't anywhere near done with his lovers. All the touching and intimacy of washing their bodies left him aching for more of them. In the bedroom, he handed Missy one of the two condoms he pulled from the box.

"Come here." Ned held out his hand to Jack.

Jack took it, and Ned led him to stand between him and Missy, who was seated on the bed. Ned took Jack's relaxed cock in his hand and whispered in his ear, "Missy hasn't had you in her ass." He stroked his hand down Jack's length, pumping the blood into it to make it hard. "She wants you deep inside her. Fucking her." He released Jack only to grip his balls, not too hard but enough to get his attention. "I'm going to watch you taking her, sliding your thick cock in and out of her until you both come." Jack was erect enough to be covered.

Ned held out Jack's shaft to Missy. "Put that condom on him, and then I want you to bend over with your chest on the bed."

She leaned forward and took Jack in her mouth, sucking him up and down while Ned held on. Her lips bumped into his hand. Slurping off the end, she rolled the latex down Jack's head, smiling devilishly. God, she was fun.

Missy rose slowly from the bed, turned, and bent at the hips. The same position Jack had been in earlier. Then she relaxed her arms and let her chest rest on the mattress. Ned let the image sear itself into his mind. A memory he would cherish. Trust. Perfection.

He snatched the lube from the nightstand and handed it to Jack. Jaw clenched, he let Jack take over.

"You ready for me?" Jack asked as he loaded his fingers with the slippery liquid.

Missy wiggled her hips. "You gonna be naughty with me, Jack?"

Ned bit back a laugh.

Jack smacked her cheek and then opened her up. Ned could see the happy pucker waiting for Jack to claim it. "Yeah, sugar. I'm gonna be real naughty with you. So bad, Ned's gonna have to spank us both." Jack winked at Ned over his shoulder.

Ned gripped his erection, trying to keep control.

Missy and Jack laughed while Jack notched his purple head at her private opening. He pressed forward, and Missy sucked in a breath, pushing back into what he offered. Slowly, her ass swallowed his entire length.

Fuck. Ned's cock ached with the ghost sensation of a hot, tight channel holding him in, tugging him deeper until he couldn't be any closer. His eyes lowered to Jack's pumping ass.

Ned ripped open the second packet and covered his cock. He picked up the open lube from where Jack had discarded it and liberally covered his length and two fingers. He dropped the bottle and grabbed Jack's ass with his clean hand while pressing those coated fingers into his crack. Jack moved faster in and out of Missy while Ned rubbed, requesting entrance. When his fingers popped in, Jack nearly pulled out of their girl.

"Keep going," Ned grunted. He removed his fingers and opened Jack so that his dick could take over.

Jack froze.

"Please," Ned whispered, his lips on Jack's neck. He caressed Jack's thigh, moving his hand around Jack's hip to his taut abdomen, just above where he was joined to Missy.

After what seemed like a very long moment, Jack tilted his pelvis back and nodded.

Relief washed through him. Ned took the opportunity to take over completely. He shoved deep into Jack's tight passage and at the same time pushed Jack to the hilt into Missy. *So tight.* Ned held, afraid to move. Jack groaned and then pushed back to Ned. They moved together, Jack following his rhythm, fucking and being fucked. Power flowed through Ned's veins, surpassed only by love for the man and woman who would allow him that even once in his life.

Ned pressed Missy and Jack into the bed, gripping Jack's hips as if his life depended on it. Sweat trickled down his back, and musky air sawed in and out of his lungs. His body demanded more, faster, deeper, trying to merge with them forever. Tears formed in his eyes.

"How are you doing?" Jack asked Missy.

"So good," Missy wailed.

Jack reached between her legs. Her keening grew louder. She craned her neck, and her amber eyes, inflamed with passion, locked onto Ned's.

"Oh my god," she cried. Her body shook and her head dropped forward.

Jack started babbling and shaking. His ass clenched Ned's cock hard and wrenched the orgasm from his balls, tearing all of his control with it. Perfectly connected and entirely shattered at the same time. He'd never again be the man he'd been before them.

SOMEONE HAD OPENED the blackout curtains, and sunlight streamed into the room. Missy could have slept all day. Instead, she rolled over and stretched like a cat. Muscles she'd never used before and tender places reminded her of everything that had occurred. Her mind struggled to resolve the events from the night before. When the guys had first discussed the sexual bucket list, she had put anal sex as a no. Okay, not a *hard no*, but still.

But they'd made it so good. Lube and condoms and lots of showers had meant she wasn't icked out. The fact Jack had encouraged her to explore their assholes, tonguing, and fingering, had made the whole thing much naughtier and hotter. In the heat of the moment, there had been no hesitation. She'd been sexy and wanton, just as they'd been for her.

In the light of day, she questioned what she'd done. Heat crept up her cheeks. Had she let them go too far? What would Ned and Jack think of her?

"You gonna get up, sugar?" Jack drawled from the chair across the room. His voice dragged her back to the present.

"Maybe." She wasn't sure she was ready to face the day and deal with—everything.

"Breakfast and coffee are made. Ned's working in the study, but I'm gonna talk him into a drive out to the lighthouse and a picnic later. You can take pictures."

She groaned, but she was going to be leaving in a few days. And she did want some pictures of them and the lighthouse. Pictures no one but her would ever see or understand the significance of.

"I don't want to wake up, because then it will be tomorrow."

He laughed. "It's already tomorrow. You're wasting it." He plucked her from the bed and guided her to the bathroom. "Come on. I'll draw you a bath. Lavender Epsom salts. You can soak, and I'll even bring you coffee."

"How can I say no to a bath and coffee?" She was going to miss these men so much it would hurt. It would be safer to start pulling back emotionally, but she didn't want to. She should savor every second with them. The pain would come either way.

Jack helped her into the tub. "Be sure to eat—you'll need your energy. I want to play again tonight."

And there was that heat, only it wasn't just her face. It rushed all over her body. Desire. Embarrassment. But Jack wasn't treating her differently than he had on the first day they'd met. She gave him a small smile and nodded.

"Tonight, I plan on getting out the restraints."

CHAPTER 20

*J*ack paced by the windows in the study. Ned was on a call with what sounded like his office in New York. Finally, he finished doling out advice and hung up. Jack sat down gingerly in the chair in front of Ned's desk. He was sore from last night, but he was doing better than Ned, who still had yet to acknowledge him. "You done freaking out?"

"No."

Jack was glad he wasn't pretending. "Which part has you questioning your sanity? The part where you let Missy and me own your ass, or the part where you stuffed your dick up mine while I was fucking her?"

"Both."

"Why?" He could guess, but Ned had to talk to him.

Ned blew out a breath and crossed his arms. "We didn't agree to that, didn't talk about it first. I thought I was just going to…"

"Watch and masturbate?" Jack provided.

"It felt right at the time, but now it doesn't feel right at all."

"It felt right to me. Still does."

"A threesome would never work anyway."

"Don't see why not." Jack wasn't ready to give up on his dream.

193

He'd fight for Missy, but first he had to get Ned on board. Get him over his belief that he had to conform to some imaginary standard. Love. That's all they required. Everything else could be overcome.

"You're bisexual, Jack." Ned played with the coffee cup on the coaster in front of him. "So am I."

If Jack hadn't been sitting, he'd have fallen over. What the fuck did Ned just admit?

"I'm not completely in denial." Ned finally met his gaze and half-smiled. "Maybe I have been. But—we both need a woman to make this work. And Missy's going to leave. She made that clear from the beginning."

Silence hung like a pall.

"We'll just find another woman to be with us." Jack said it like he agreed. There was no way it could be anyone other than Missy.

"Yeah, another woman." Ned's slight tone of sarcasm and his shaking head told Jack he didn't believe it either. No one else would fit so well or elicit such love from both of them. She was unique perfection.

Jack lifted his chin and stared at the ceiling as if the answers would suddenly appear. How? How could he get Missy to see what he did? What Ned was starting to understand?

Jack leaned toward Ned. "I don't know what we can do to convince her."

"We shouldn't *have* to convince her." Ned matched his low tones. "It only works if she wants this, too."

The smell of defeat, or possibly old law books, filled Jack's nose. It was as if the ending of their relationship had already been recorded.

Fuck that.

Jack had never given in easily to anything, and he wasn't about to start. It could work. There had to be a way. "No convincing. We can support her dreams *and* be together. We'll figure this out."

~

Missy tucked her hair in a ponytail and headed to the kitchen. Jack had promised a picnic, but it was still early. Coffee and breakfast. She could sit on the deck and enjoy the ocean. Burn it into her memory.

She slowed as she neared the door to the office. The project was on a tight deadline, and her men were trying to neutralize the problem CEO, but she craved Ned's and Jack's attention, their reassurance. She bit her lip. Interrupting was the worst plan. She pressed her ear against the door. Maybe if they were at a stopping point, they could join her for one cup.

Jack's confident drawl carried through the wood panel. "We'll just find another woman to be with us."

His words stabbed her in the gut.

"Yeah, another woman." Ned's voice dragged the virtual blade into her heart.

Wrong. She'd been completely wrong. Missy swallowed back tears. Forced herself to move before she vomited in the doorway. The scenes from last night flashed through her mind like a bad porno. Spanking. Anal. All of it. The entire vacation. Tinged sickly yellow-green.

Her phone in one hand, she pulled out her suitcase. A quick call to the airline and her flight was moved up. Three hours and she would be on her way. Away from there. From them. She dialed her landlord in New York as she threw her toiletries on top of her clothes. When he agreed that she could occupy the space a week early for the prorated rent, she knew it was the right decision.

At the bottom of her purse, she found the card she was looking for. Not Ned's. The taxi driver. The one who'd been trying to help her all along. He answered immediately and assured her he would be there in minutes.

Hefting the bag so the wheels whirring on the wood floors wouldn't give her away, she tiptoed out of the beach house. The sheets were still rumpled from their daring night and already they discussed replacing her. That wasn't something to hang around for. Better to leave, on her own terms.

"Need a hand?" a deep voice boomed from behind her.

Missy bit back a squeak. Nick. "No, the cab will be here shortly."

"Wasn't aware you were leaving today. I should drive you." Nick's forehead wrinkled, and his gaze drilled into her.

"I...um...got a call to start early. Unfortunate, but I have to go. First job and all that." The lie slid down her throat in a toxic glob. She didn't owe the man an explanation, and Ned and Jack had just forfeited their rights.

Nick nodded gravely.

The taxi pulled up, and the driver jumped out. "I can take your bag."

"Thanks for everything, Nick." Missy shook the bodyguard's hand.

"Trunk's full," the driver said as he opened the back door and shoved her bag onto the seat. Then he opened the front passenger door. "You can ride up here."

"Aren't the guys coming out to say goodbye?" Nick's confusion was obvious.

"Already did. They have a conference call." More lies. She had to get out of there. She settled into the front seat and shut the door. Seat-belt clipped, she gave a little wave to the man who knew something was up but didn't have the authority to stop her. She dropped her head back on the headrest and closed her eyes.

The car accelerated down the driveway, away from everything she wanted but couldn't have. The locks engaged with a click.

"Hey." At the cabbie's sharp tone, Missy lifted her head.

The cab was stifling, and the stench of stale sweat made her empty stomach roil. The brown eyes she'd thought of as sympathetic during her first ride were cold and piercing.

She straightened.

"Which one is your boyfriend?" There was menace in his tone.

Both. Neither. "None of your business."

"You," he spat. His grip on the steering wheel was so tight, his knuckles were white. "You live with men who are not your boyfriends. You show them your body in public. Kiss them like a lover. Do you kiss everyone like that?"

"Excuse me?"

"Do you *fuck* everyone, too?"

Missy sucked in a breath, unable to believe what she'd heard. "Stop this car. Let me out."

"No. You're mine." He turned the wheel hard, and she slammed into the door. "But first, you're going to confess your sins. You're going to tell God what a whore you are."

Whore. The word rattled inside her head. "You threw the rock."

"It was supposed to be a warning. But you didn't listen. Now you have to be cleansed before I can have you."

"Let me out," she screamed. Missy threw herself at the door, wrenching on the handle, but the lock held. They were on a side road, heading away from the airport. No one would know where she was. She scanned the street through the windows. If only some other driver would notice her. She could mouth *help.* But, there wasn't a car in sight.

He pulled behind a church and parked. Instantly, she grasped the door handle.

"Don't move." He pointed a gun at her.

Missy's hands went numb. She gasped. Tried to find enough oxygen to think. Her life couldn't end that way.

He opened his door and with his free hand grabbed her by the ponytail and yanked.

Her scalp was on fire. She had no choice but to scramble as fast as she could out the driver's door before he pulled all the hair from her head. She was too scared to speak.

He half-dragged her toward the building. She struggled to keep up at the awkward angle she was forced into. He jerked her through the back door and into the dim, cool interior. Decaying incense and burnt wax permeated the sanctuary.

"Father," the driver called out when they reached a side entrance to the nave.

"Dwane? What are you doing?" A large man dressed in black came into view. His deep voice resonated a sense of calm control.

"This woman is a sinner, and she must confess." Dwane waved the handgun where the priest could see it. "She must confess before I take her. She has to be saved, Father."

Save. Take. The words didn't sound scary until the cabbie, Dwane, used them. She shivered all the way to her soul.

The priest moved toward them with his hands open at his sides, showing he was no threat. "Dwane, you cannot have a gun in God's house. Why don't you put down the weapon and let her go?"

"No!" He aimed the deadly metal at the priest.

The holy man continued toward them, still using a gentle tone. "Dwane, don't do this. You're disrespecting God. Yourself. And this woman. I know you. I knew your mother. What could this woman have done to cause a good man to act so wickedly?"

"She must tell you, Father. She must confess."

"She can't when you're holding her hair. Let her sit beside me on the pew." The priest's voice was so reasonable. He shot a brief glance at Missy. His calm didn't reach his eyes. "You can watch us, and if she wishes to talk to me, I'll listen."

"She has to." Dwane shook her fiercely, ripping more strands from her head. "I want her clean again, for me. Like she was when I met her."

"Release her, son."

Missy felt the grip on her hair relax. Someone had to have heard him yelling. Called the cops. It was only a matter of time before help would arrive. She tried to imagine it was going to be all right.

The priest patted the space beside him. Missy dared to hope that he could save her. Dwane shoved her down the aisle, forcing her to catch herself on the other benches.

"I'm watching you. Don't try anything or I'll shoot." He focused the gun on her. His eyes were crazy, like a rabid dog's. She didn't doubt for a second he would shoot her or, worse, the priest.

She sat next to the priest, shaking uncontrollably.

∾

"You're done." Dwane raced toward Missy.

She'd run out of words although she'd tried to keep talking for as long as possible.

"Dwane. Please. We need a little longer."

Missy cringed. She hadn't told him everything about Ned and Jack. Only enough to explain what was going on. Her faith didn't require confession to a priest. And some things couldn't be explained to a stranger.

"No. We need to leave now."

"But son, I would like to pray with her for a few—"

"It's unforgivable." The crazy man shook his gun at her.

"God loves all of us. It is not for us to judge each other." His hands held in a prayer position at his chest.

"I'm taking her."

Missy clutched the preacher's strong forearm. *Don't let him.*

"Leave Missy here, son."

"No! She's mine." He grabbed Missy by the arm, sighting his gun on the holy man.

Missy released her grip. She didn't want to be the reason another person died.

"Dwane, she *isn't* yours. Please, let her go. You can stay here, too. We can talk. Your mother wouldn't want you to do this."

"My mother's dead. Don't try to stop me or you'll join her." Dwane pulled Missy back to the hallway where they'd entered. She stumbled but kept going. If someone got killed because of her, she would never forgive herself. Better they got out of the church. Maybe the authorities would already be there.

The taxicab was exactly where Dwane had left it. No police. The flicker of hope she'd been nursing extinguished.

Dwane shoved her into the front seat, forcing her to crawl over to the passenger side with the gun directed at her the entire time.

"Where are you taking me?"

"Home." He put the key in the ignition with the hand not holding the weapon.

"There are people who will be looking for me."

Dwane leaned over and hit her with the end of the gun.

Pain shattered her vision, and waves of nausea rolled through her. She brought her hands to her head and pressed herself against the door.

"Shut up." He didn't scream, and that made him terrifying. Her temple throbbed.

He drove like he'd driven her to the diner, calmly, following the traffic laws. No one paid any attention to them. She considered yanking the steering wheel, but life wasn't like the movies. If he lost control, they could both be killed or live with permanent injuries.

But the farther he drove, the more certain she became. She was going to die.

Alone.

As soon as they parked in front of a small neglected home, Dwane tugged her out of the car. He dragged her across the asphalt before she could get her feet under her.

Two vehicles pulled up behind them. Men screamed at him to drop the weapon and get down on the ground.

A sparkle of relief flittered and died.

Instead of freeing her, Dwane wrapped his arm around her throat and held the handgun to her head. She couldn't breathe. Everything moved in slow motion. One of Nick's men opened his driver's-side door and stepped out.

Nick stood behind the protection of the passenger door, weapon drawn. Dwane started to pull her backward, toward the house. Nick didn't move. Didn't say anything. Why wasn't he saving her?

"Let her go." Ned stepped into the open on her right.

At his deep, calm command Dwane removed the barrel from her head.

Movement on her left triggered Missy to act. She stomped her foot down on the gunman's and slammed her head back into his face. Jack hit Dwane's body. He went flying.

But not before the gun fired.

Ned dropped to the ground.

"No!" Missy's keening wail merged with the sounds of approaching sirens. She fell to her knees, her legs unable to hold her.

CHAPTER 21

*J*ack sat hunched over in a green vinyl chair, elbows on his knees. He rubbed his thumb over the knuckles of his scraped fist and exhaled a long breath. The smell of hospitals made him twitchy. Growing up on the ranch, someone frequently ended up in the ER. But he wasn't sitting there because of an accident.

He'd spent hours with the police, answering intrusive questions about how long he and Ned had known each other. And how they'd met Missy. The nature of their relationship. That had been a fun one. Then a review of the rock incident and an explanation of why Ned had a security team but hadn't notified the police. All the while, he'd been waiting for an update on Ned. But he wasn't going to get one, because he wasn't family. He'd hated every second of waiting for Ned to be alert enough to ask for him. Jack crossed his arms. They'd be fixing that issue legally, soon.

Ned lay in the bed, finally quiet after fussing about being held overnight. The bullet had only grazed his arm, but it had knocked him off his feet and he had a lump on the back of his head. A mild concussion most likely, but the docs weren't taking any chances.

"I can rest at home," Ned insisted for the umpteenth time in the last hour.

"You're a lawyer, partner." Jack tried for levity. "They're afraid you'll sue."

Ned grumbled under his breath.

A uniformed officer opened the door and entered the private room. The same cop Jack had spoken with while Ned was being scrubbed, scanned, and checked into Not-Club-Med.

Jack stood.

"Just a couple more questions, Mr. Strauss. If you'll excuse us, sir?"

"Need anything, partner?" Jack asked as he reached the door.

"A getaway car," Ned quipped but extended a hand to the officer. "Please have a seat."

Jack stepped into the hall. Missy sat on the floor across the corridor, leaning against the wall. She lifted her gaze to him. His instinct to retreat back to the room made him freeze mid-stride. Tear tracks lined her cheeks. Her blond hair was a tangled mess, and a purple bruise had formed above her cheekbone. He held back the part of him that would have scooped her up and soothed her pain. The situation was all on her.

"Is he okay?" Her whisper-soft voice shook.

"He will be." Jack retreated to the far side of the door. He couldn't walk away, but he didn't have to be any closer.

"I'm so sorry."

"For what?" Jack shrugged. She should be sorry. Running away again. But like hell was he going to get into it in a hospital hallway while the love of his life sat in a hospital bed with a gunshot wound. A wound she'd been instrumental in causing.

"For leaving. For getting you two involved in..." Missy swiped at more tears. "For everything."

"Why *did* you run? And why are you here now?" He hadn't intended to ask, but the questions burned in him. First, she'd disappeared for a few hours, then, only hours later, she'd packed her bags and planned to leave for good.

"I...I heard you guys talking. About finding another woman. And I just wanted to make sure Ned was going to be okay." She rose from the floor.

"We didn't—"

But they had.

The conversation came back to him.

Shame gored him like a pissed-off bull. "You misunderstood. Why didn't you say something? You could have opened the study door, right then."

"I was angry." She crossed her arms. "And embarrassed. You guys left me, went right back to work, like nothing'd happened...planned to replace me. Like I was a toy." Her skin, which had been blotchy, turned bright pink.

Jack closed the space to stand next to her, but not touching. "We have *never* treated you like a toy." He dragged a hand through his hair. He'd been concerned about the fallout with Ned and hadn't recognized she'd been feeling vulnerable when he'd left her alone. "We deserved a conversation. And you knew there was a threat, that someone was after you."

"You're right." Missy nodded. "This is all my fault."

"That's where you're wrong, sugar. And Ned and I were discussing the fact that neither one of us wants to let you go. We should've had you in the room for the conversation. All of us handled this badly." Jack held out his hand, palm up. Missy lifted her chin and her watery amber eyes locked on his. Slowly she placed her hand in his. He squeezed it briefly. "The only person to blame is that damn cabbie. And he's going to be locked away for a long time."

They waited, only their hands touching. Jack closed his eyes. He had to find forgiveness. Missy'd left, but she wasn't Katherine. Wasn't married to him. And she'd apologized. He shouldered some of the blame as well. Instead of spending the morning cuddling, he'd left her after a quick chat—no wonder things had gone sideways. The overheard conversation had only twisted things more.

"Can I see Ned?"

"As soon as the cop's done. They already talked to you?"

"Yeah. I told them about the window. And the driver stalking me."

"Stalking?" Jack turned to face her.

"I didn't realize it at the time, but he's been everywhere I have. I think he was...watching us."

Jack's chance to dig into that information was sidelined when the officer emerged from Ned's room. He and Missy dropped their hands.

"He's all yours," the officer said as she strode down the hall.

With any luck, that was still true.

Jack opened the auto-closing door. Ned sat propped up by a couple of pillows and peered past him. "Missy."

She moved from where she'd halted in the middle of the hall and rushed to Ned's side.

"You're still here." He held open his arms, and she wrapped herself carefully around his torso and sobbed.

RELIEVED TO BE BACK at the beach house even if it was temporary, Missy lazed on the couch. Ned lounged at the other end. The hospital staff had finally released him in the dawn hours, probably glad to see him go. The man was a terrible patient. He shouldn't have been in the hospital at all. She could never make it up to him.

"You're frowning." Ned's forehead wrinkled.

"Just thinking about starting my new job." It wasn't a lie. She didn't have a plane ticket, and her starting date was less than a week away.

Jack handed her a cup of hot tea. "This will help."

"Thank you." She wrapped her hands around the warm ceramic. "But I'm fine."

"You're not fine." Ned waved off the cup Jack tried to give him. "You were kidnapped by a gun-toting lunatic."

"And *you* were shot," Missy said. "He tried to kill you."

"A scrape."

"He didn't want to kill me. He wanted to..." Her throat tightened, and she couldn't finish the sentence. He'd kidnapped her and planned to rape her. She wasn't okay, but she couldn't break down. It was time to end the fantasy, get to New York and resume her life. "I have to go."

"The jet will take us back tomorrow."

"So soon?" Jack asked from where he sat on the chair.

"There are some things I need to do in the city. And we can check out Missy's apartment. Nick is doing a full security inspection. We'll implement anything he recommends before we leave."

"Nick?" Jack's voice was heavy with derision. "He froze."

"We talked. I trust him." Ned's tone made it clear that it wasn't up for discussion.

"You don't have to do all that. I'm sure I can talk to the airline and explain." A clean break was the only way she could leave them. The urge to cling and let them handle everything was so strong. But she had to end it.

"Tomorrow, we're taking the jet. Tonight, you're sleeping in our bed. And you *will* have the best security I can buy at your new apartment."

"I'm sleeping where?"

"Missy, we don't want to let you go."

Missy turned to Jack. He tilted his head slightly before nodding in agreement.

"I can't stay," she said.

"We know that, sugar."

"Just because you're going to be living alone doesn't mean we won't still care about you. We're still friends, right?"

Ned's words warmed the final chill from her bones. They could part as friends. Keep in touch occasionally. She could pretend it wouldn't hurt when they moved on with their lives. It would take time, but she could find a way to be okay with…friends.

MISSY'D PLANNED to take the subway from the airport to a stop near her apartment, not arrive in a limousine. But there was no arguing with Ned. He was in full protector mode.

Nick scanned up and down the street and then inspected the entry.

Ned took one of her bags from the driver. "We'll call you when we need to be picked up."

The trio entered the elevator, and she pushed the button for the twelfth floor. She hadn't seen the apartment in person yet, only online. They exited and walked down the hall to 1223, her new address.

She used the key the landlord had left with the superintendent and pushed open the door. Her stuff had been delivered as planned, and there were boxes and upturned furniture everywhere. A slightly musty odor combined with the stale scent of cardboard wafted out. She missed the ocean breezes already.

"It has good light," Jack said in a conciliatory tone.

The entire apartment could be seen from the front door. Would her queen-size bed fit in the tiny bedroom? Maybe, if she didn't put the dresser in there.

"You did well for a starter apartment in the city. It's much nicer than I anticipated." Ned's approval had her breathing a sigh of relief. He was more familiar with New York properties than Jack.

"Well, we better get started." Jack stepped around a tower of boxes.

"You don't have to move my stuff. It won't be a big deal. You didn't come here to do manual labor." They were supposed to inspect the apartment, set up some security if needed and let her go.

"We came here to take care of you and make sure you're going to be okay. So, we're going to help you settle in as much as we can while we still have time together." They began moving the metal bed frame.

"You've spoiled me." And it was only going to make separating harder.

"We'd spoil you for longer if you'd let us, sugar." Jack lifted one end of the box spring onto the frame.

Ned looked skeptically at the bed. "I think you should stay the night with us at the hotel."

"I need to get settled here." She wanted them like an alcoholic wanted another drink.

"And I need one more night with you. If we try to stay here, I'm afraid Jack will end up on the floor."

"Why would *I* end up on the floor?" Jack demanded with mock-seriousness.

Ned just looked at Jack.

"You should stay with us at the hotel. We'll have dinner brought up, and you can take a long soak. It might be a while before you have a chance again." Jack spoke from the door of the bathroom that boasted a coffin-sized shower.

A hot bath. A delicious meal. Together with her men. One last time. "Fine, but I need to unpack as much as possible first."

"Perfect. That will give Nick time to install the additional security before you stay here by yourself," Ned said.

It had been so long since anyone had taken care of her. No wonder she wasn't ready to give it up. Carter had done things for her, but only if they were in his interest, too. She was going to miss them so much.

Instead of crying, she picked up a box marked "kitchen" and went to the alcove with the tiny fridge and the two-burner stove. How would she ever make homemade biscuits there? It would be an adjustment, but she'd figure it out. Besides, it wasn't like she had anyone to make them for.

NED RUBBED at his chest and stared at the bathroom door, the covers of the hotel bed at his hips. Jack lay next to him facedown, sprawled in the space Missy had occupied until a short time ago. She refused to have breakfast with them or even wait for room service. Didn't matter they'd made love last night. Didn't matter that he had a house she could live in. Didn't matter how much he needed her to stay.

The logical part of him understood she had a life plan that didn't involve him and Jack. His heart hurt. He closed his eyes and tilted his head back against the upholstered board, only to snap back when the door to the bathroom opened a moment later.

Missy played with the zipper on her bag, not meeting his eyes. "Um, well, I guess…"

Ned tossed the sheets back, not caring he was naked. If he could, he'd show her his soul, show her how much their parting hurt. He stopped in front of her and lifted her chin with the tips of his fingers. Her skin was rosy pink, but her amber eyes were nearly gray.

"You don't have to go." He resisted actually begging, but barely.

"I do." She placed a cool palm on his chest. "I have to finish getting settled. Make a good impression on my first day."

He put his hand over hers, letting his body heat warm her fingers. "I'm a phone call away."

"I know." She leaned into him.

He wrapped his free arm around her, memorizing exactly how she smelled, like water and flowers. How the weight of her body rested against his, where she fit perfectly. He pressed his lips to her damp braid. As he was about to release her, she squeezed in tighter, heavier. Ned lifted his eyelids. Jack. He'd joined them and made them complete. Ned swallowed back the lump in his throat. Once again, he was on the verge of losing everything, and there was nothing he could do.

"I love you, Missy." The words escaped his lips. He couldn't hold them back.

"We both do, sugar."

Missy stiffened. "I have to go."

Jack stepped back, and Ned dropped his arms. "The car is waiting for you downstairs."

Missy opened her mouth and then closed it. She picked up her purse and pulled the strap high on her shoulder.

He should walk her down, but he didn't have the strength to watch her drive away. A last hug and a kiss. Some sweet, dismissive words before the door snicked closed behind her.

Jack's arms wrapped around him. "We'll see her again, partner."

"Hope so." Ned gave Jack a one-armed squeeze. "Breakfast?"

"Yeah, order something." Jack let him go and turned away. "I need to shower if I'm going to make my flight."

Ned froze in the middle of the well-used hotel room. It was nice. Luxurious even. But it was empty. As empty as his house would be later. When he would give in to the overwhelming urge to curl into a ball and weep.

He swiped his hand across his eyes, picked up the phone, and ordered enough food for three people.

CHAPTER 22

*M*issy got a text from Jack two days after she'd started
working for the law firm.

Jack: *How's the job?*

Missy: *Good so far. I've been assigned to a senior. She's nice to me.*

Jack: *Everything you hoped for?*

Missy: *The work is interesting. How's your project?*

Jack: *Got the problem CEO out of the way. It was ugly.*

Missy: *It's going to work?*

Jack: *Thanks to your help with the contracts.*

Missy: *They're talking about having me review some here.*

Jack: *Acquisitions?*

Missy: *Yep. Seems we may be merging. All hush-hush for now.*

Jack: *You're perfect for that.*

Missy: *Thanks!*

Jack: *Miss you.*

Missy: *Miss you too. Have you seen Ned?*

Jack: *Not since our last night. He said he'd be in the city for the Fourth.*

Missy: *Can you come too?*

Jack: *I always come with you. ;)*

Missy: *You should visit.*

Jack: *I will.*

Missy wanted to cry. At least Jack had contacted her. Ned had been silent. She missed Ned and Jack so badly she ached. It was different when people died. Her family was gone and it hurt, but nothing could change the situation. The very definition of "it is what it is". This was different. Ned and Jack were gone due to circumstances. Well, not any circumstances—she'd run away and got Ned shot. Then she wouldn't even stay for breakfast.

Scrolling through her contacts she paused at Ned's number. What would she say if she did call him? She dropped her phone into her purse and clicked the mouse on her computer. She couldn't keep falling back into them. It was past time to move on.

THE FOURTH of July was Missy's favorite holiday because there were no expectations for the event. Just show up dressed casually and enjoy yourself. In the past, she'd always gone to the town parade with her grandparents. But that Fourth, she was alone.

Jack had his business in Texas. He'd said Ned was going to be in the city, but she hadn't heard anything. The thought of Ned all by himself made her sad. She'd fallen in love with them both. But they were gone, and she was there, chasing her dream and keeping her promise to her family.

At least she had the company party to look forward to that night. The executive floor would be opened so everyone could enjoy the fireworks from fifty stories up. There was a perfect view of the harbor. She was sure there would be champagne and fancy hors d'oeuvres instead of the hot dogs and potato salad she preferred.

It was still early; she threw on some shorts and a tank top and put her hair in a ponytail. She could grab coffee and a bagel and go mingle with the crowds on the streets. She could enjoy the freedom of her nation and the freedom of her new life. Soon she would make more friends, and she wouldn't be so alone.

Finding herself at Battery Park, she caught the ferry to the Statue of Liberty. It was on her bucket list. Her new list. She'd filled it with tamer things like attending a Broadway musical and going to the top of the Empire State Building. The main problem with her new bucket list was that she'd be doing everything by herself. With her hands wrapped around the railing, she fixed her eyes on the statue of a lone woman in the harbor.

Hours later, wearing her new little black dress, a smile plastered on her face, Missy tried to make small talk with her co-workers. She turned at the sound of her boss calling her name and gripped her slipping champagne glass. She blinked, unable to believe the tableau in front of her.

Ned. Standing next to her boss. He had a slight smile on his face. Katherine stood next to him with a smirk. As surprised as she was to see Ned, it was the two other people with him who made her gasp and shake.

Carter. And his father was there, too.

Of the five people in the group, three had seen her naked.

Icy cold threads of dread wound their way down her limbs. A disaster had been inevitable. It was the way her life went. Only she hadn't been prepared for it to all fall apart so soon. Knees shaking, Missy responded to her boss's call to join the group. A vision of a lit match falling into a puddle of kerosene flashed through her mind. She glared at Carter, but he wouldn't meet her gaze.

"Melissa, I want to introduce you to some people. This is Edward Strauss. He's a partner here, but we don't see too much of him because he's semi-retired." Her boss smiled as if he were aware of a secret joke. Did Ned tell him about her and their summer? She fought to take a breath when Ned thrust out his hand and said, "Nice to meet you, Melissa."

"Nice to meet you, too," Missy responded with a slight tremor in her voice. It was all she could do to contain her body's reaction to touching him for the first time in too long.

"Ned insisted on meeting our best and brightest new hire, so I had to introduce him."

"Thank you, Mr. Wallace." Could the man really have no idea that her life was exploding like a fiery wreck before her eyes?

"I'm sure you know my daughter, Katherine."

"We've...met," the woman said frostily. She leaned into Missy for an air-kiss and hissed into her ear, "You're really going to pretend you don't *know* Ned?"

Before Missy could come up with an appropriate response, Mr. Wallace continued, "And these two gentlemen are with a little firm in St. Louis with which we're preparing to merge. I think you've been assigned to the contracts?"

Her boss gestured to the two hateful demons on his left. *That* was the contract she was supposed to review starting Monday? If the merger went through, she would be working at the same firm as Carter and his father? The Shit still wouldn't look at her.

From nowhere, a bubble of rage rose, killing any sense of self-preservation. "Oh, I know these gentlemen, one of them quite well. Carter, how are you?"

"You've met this woman?" His father turned to his son, smiling broadly.

Before Carter could answer with what would be a lie, Missy interjected, "Well, I did come to your house a few times over the five years we dated. I'm surprised you don't remember. It must run in the family. Carter, you still owe me money from the rent on the bungalow that was *returned*. You forgot to tell me our reservation was canceled because the place was uninhabitable. I'm sure you wouldn't take a questionable ethical stance and keep it."

In the back of her mind, a small voice insisted it was neither the time nor the place for that conversation, but she was done being the quiet mouse.

"Please, excuse us." Missy stepped in close and gripped Carter's arm, pulling him from the group. Noises of protest and shock peppered her ears, but she didn't stop or look back.

The office door closed behind them. She was alone with him for the first time since he'd walked out on her. Her mind, usually filled with plans and analyses, was blank. But, in actuality, Carter should be doing the talking. She tapped her foot and tilted her head at him. If he valued his balls, he'd better say something soon.

"It wasn't my fault," he blurted out, then tucked his chin to his chest.

"Really, Carter? *That's* what you have to say. *It wasn't your fault?*" She crossed her arms. "Then whose was it, 'cause it sure wasn't mine."

"I'm sorry." He wrung his hands in front of his crotch as if he knew on some instinctual level how much she wanted to knee him. "Look, I should have told you what was going on then. I shouldn't have shut the door on us like that, but I didn't have a choice."

"Bullshit," Missy hissed between clenched teeth. "Everything is a choice. Just because some choices are more difficult than others doesn't mean you didn't have one. You just didn't like the other options."

"You're right." He put his hands out plaintively. "But I never thought you'd get on the plane by yourself."

"I didn't have a lot of options. The lease was up on the apartment. Where was I supposed to go?"

"I don't know. I didn't think it out. I was under a lot of pressure." He ran his hands through his hair and peeked up at her.

"If you had a problem, why didn't you talk to me about it then, when it would have mattered? Because I'll tell you right now, I'm truly having trouble giving a fuck *what* your problems are."

"My dad—the firm was, *is*, in a lot of financial trouble. He needed me to try to save the company." He finally looked at her, like a little boy hoping to get away without being punished.

It made her gag.

"The ink was still drying on your degree. How were you going to save a law firm? Superpowers I don't know about?"

"No, an engagement. My dad promised I would marry his crony's daughter if he would invest in the firm."

Missy shook her head. She couldn't have heard him correctly. "What year is this, Carter? Your dad tells you to dump your girlfriend and marry someone else? Like for her dowry? Are you seriously trying to tell me you dropped me after five years without a word of explanation because your daddy *told* you to?"

Carter winced. "I didn't think I had a choice. And...and he didn't *know* you were my girlfriend, just that I dated you. And, be honest, you weren't completely happy with our relationship."

"Wow. Who *don't* you lie to?" Missy closed her eyes briefly and took a slow breath. "You're right. I wasn't happy. But I was willing to try. I was willing to go on an island vacation with you and try to change the situation so I could be happy." She uncrossed her arms and pointed her finger at him, almost poking his chest but unwilling to touch him again. "And you know what? I went to that island. And I did find my happiness, and for that, I have to thank you, Carter. Because if you hadn't been the limpest daddy's-boy prick on the planet, I might still be with you. I can't imagine that now."

"I told my father I wasn't going to marry Susan. With the merger—"

Missy gasped. "You *knew*? You knew when I accepted the job here that your dad's firm was merging." She shook her head, unable to believe the layers of deceit.

"No. I..." Carter held his hands up in defense. "I swear I didn't. Not until I started working there. And by then...well, I figured it was a big firm and we wouldn't see each other."

"Yet here we are. You destroying my life, again."

"I...I want you back."

"I would rather be alone than waste one more second with such a weak-willed, spineless excuse for a man."

A welcome knock sounded. Any pretext to get away from that slime. "Goodbye, Carter."

She strode to the door and stepped out, practically into Ned's arms. If she fell into them, he'd catch her. But she was done. Done relying on others to save her.

"Mis—Melissa." Ned's voice rattled her resolve.

"No." She held up a hand. "I have to go."

"Don't act rashly. Say goodbye to Wallace. You don't want to burn a bridge you may need." Ned held out his arm to her.

He was right. She could hold her head up and be a professional despite the fact her entire personal life had been dumped in the middle of her office for all of her co-workers and the partners to see. Missy straightened her spine, lifted her chin, and took his offering.

"Mr. Wallace?" Missy addressed her boss where he stood among a small group of the more senior lawyers. He acknowledged her but said nothing. "Thank you for a wonderful party, but I don't think I'm going to stay for the fireworks."

"I understand. I wasn't aware there was history between you and the Simmons family."

"You had no reason to be, sir."

"We'll talk on Monday."

"Yes, sir." Her job was probably over. No one survived a train wreck of that proportion.

"Relax and enjoy the rest of the weekend."

"Thank you," Missy said, confused as to what would happen next week. The fact that people couldn't read Mr. Wallace very well made him a good lawyer. Could she ever cultivate such a persona?

"I'll escort Ms. Winter out." Ned took Missy's elbow. "I'm calling it a night as well."

As soon as they were in the lobby, Missy pulled away. "How long have you known?"

"About the merger? It was the meeting I went to, but I swear I didn't know it was your ex."

She crossed her arms. "No? How long have you known I worked for your firm?"

"I didn't. The background check didn't show—"

"*Background check?*" Missy gaped, her whole body rigid. She couldn't have heard him correctly.

"Uh, Jack. The first night on the island. We didn't know who you were, but I swear, there was nothing about the firm."

Missy turned on her heel. "I'm going to grab a cab."

"I have the driver ready to take us. I was hoping you'd stay with me."

She walked through the large glass doors. "I can't. I...need to be alone."

"You aren't alone. Jack and I—"

"No," Missy snapped. "I'm done with everyone hiding things from me. I've probably lost my job. And sex isn't going to fix this. Sex is the root cause of this disaster. It was a fling, Ned. A bucket list. The fantasy is over." She lifted her arm, and a yellow cab pulled up.

Ned opened the back door and assisted her in. "Please, Missy. Promise you'll call."

She turned her head to hide her tears. The door shut, and the taxi pulled away.

CHAPTER 23

*T*he long weekend and several pints of ice cream gone, Missy set her coffee on her beige laminate cubicle desk and tried to focus on work. Already she'd wasted several minutes in the break room. But everywhere she went, the conversations stopped and her co-workers scattered. She logged into her computer and opened her email to plan her day. There were some links to contracts she'd been assigned early last week and plenty to keep her busy until she could hide in her apartment again.

Her phone rang, disrupting her thoughts. It was an internal line calling, but she answered professionally. "This is Melissa."

"Melissa, this is Patricia Chen. Can you please come to my office?"

Human Resources. Despite the fact she'd feared it, the shock of the actual call hit hard. Her bowels turned to ice, and she thought she might throw up. HR didn't call unless it was in response to a question you'd raised or they were going to terminate you. Her gut said she was being fired. "I'll be right there."

The woman didn't even say thank you, just hung up. For a few frozen seconds, Missy stared at the handset of her phone until the dial tone startled her. Dully, she assessed her little cubicle. Not much to pack. A plant and a personal calendar with an island theme. And there was a small bag of emergency toiletries in the drawer. Not even enough for a box.

She replaced the receiver. Standing, she straightened her skirt and slowed her breathing before facing the gallows. The elevator ride was blessedly short. HR was on the executive floor, one floor below the partners. Missy paused to admire that particular view of the city for the last time. Resolved to maintain her professionalism to the end, she turned and addressed the admin at the desk. "I'm Melissa Winter, here to see Ms. Chen."

The woman's head popped up, and she stared at her with rounded eyes. "Oh. Yes, of course. One moment." She must have been new to HR because she couldn't mask her thoughts at all. Her reaction only confirmed what Missy suspected. The admin whispered into the phone and then instructed her to take a seat.

She didn't have to wait long. The oversized door swung silently, and Missy stepped into the cheerful, tidy office. A polished middle-aged woman sat at the desk, facing a computer that was angled away from visitors.

"Melissa, please close the door and have a seat." She gestured to one of the two chairs without bothering to make eye contact.

Missy turned to do as instructed, and the handle slipped from her grip. Katherine, a cold glint in her eyes, stood in the corner of the office next to a large indoor plant. The door had blocked her from view until then. Why would Katherine be there? The woman wasn't her boss, didn't work in HR, and from what Jack had said, did marketing for the firm. Whatever calm Missy'd found burned away in a cloud of adrenaline.

The door clicked as it closed, locking her in with her prosecutor and executioner. It was too late to run, so Missy swallowed and took the chair farthest from Katherine.

"Thank you for coming, Melissa. Unfortunately, I have to inform you the firm can no longer continue to employ you."

"Why is she here?" It wasn't like Missy was going to be un-fired. She might as well ask the question burning in her throat.

"Mr. Wallace asked her to be a witness to the conversation so there would be no misunderstanding." Ms. Chen's voice was calm and reasonable.

"Why exactly am I being fired? I've received nothing but positive feedback on my work."

Katherine huffed out a breath. "Your work isn't relevant if you can't represent the firm in a dignified manner."

"You're referring to the holiday event?" Missy didn't know why she was arguing. She'd seen it coming.

"The holiday event is only one example." Katherine stalked over to where Missy sat and loomed over her. "As I discussed with my father, there were several instances of impropriety. Using company assets for personal benefit."

"Company assets?"

Katherine reached down and lifted a stack of paper-clipped documents off Patricia's desk. Slowly, she turned back to the first page. A line was highlighted on the second, but Missy couldn't read it. Katherine cleared her throat dramatically. "You were logged as the only passenger in a car owned by the firm, driven by our company-paid driver, leaving the Plaza Hotel to go to a residential address. One that matches your personnel records."

The last day she'd spent with Ned and Jack. Her ride back to the apartment. Missy's blood ran cold.

"I hadn't started yet."

"You had completed your new-hire packet and submitted it. You'd read the employee manual. I have a signed document that says you did."

Missy swallowed the lump that formed in her throat. She'd completed all the paperwork before she'd left St. Louis. And yes, she'd read every word of every document. Her worst fear was coming true. Hard work, doing a good job, should be enough. It wasn't. If she didn't get out of there, she was going to cry in front of Katherine. It wasn't sadness, it was anger at herself.

"Then there's the matter of you seducing a board member."

Liar. Missy sucked back a scream. If she slapped Katherine, it would be assault. Missy tucked her hands under her thighs. "Personal relationships have no bearing on my performance. Besides, I didn't know he was a board member."

"Sure you didn't." Sarcasm dripped from every word.

"Are you sure this isn't about your ex-husband?" Missy couldn't generate enough air to speak above a whisper. She *had* been having a sexual relationship with a board member, even if she wasn't aware.

"The list of people you're fucking or have fucked related to this firm seems to grow longer every day. Edward Strauss. Carter Simmons. Anyone else we should know about?"

Missy gasped. The insinuation was like a slap. Katherine might as well have called her a slut.

"That's enough." The HR executive stood and gestured for the paperwork. Katherine smacked it into the woman's hand and stepped back. Her face was twisted in an evil scowl, half-rabid, half-victorious.

"Melissa, this firm is not a good fit for you." Ms. Chen's voice soothed with its low steady tones. "You're bright and talented. I'm sure you will land on your feet. Mr. Wallace has *generously* specified a month's severance in lieu of *any* wages owed."

Missy hadn't been there long enough to get her first paycheck. The only way it could be worse was if her family were alive to see her failure. Her face heated. "Thank you," she stammered, and stood on shaky legs. Check in hand, she bolted for the door, only to be greeted by a security guard. Could they do anything more to humiliate her?

"I need to get my purse and my personal things."

"Yes, ma'am." He followed her to the elevator.

"You're going to watch me until I leave, aren't you?"

"Yes, ma'am."

The man stood by silently as she tucked the calendar and toiletries into her handbag. Heads popped up from the surrounding desks and dropped the instant she made eye contact over the fabric half-walls. A ridiculous urge to wave and yell goodbye surged through her. But she gritted her teeth, picked up her plant, and entered the elevator for the last time with as much dignity as she could muster. Unbelievably, she'd been fired by Jack's ex-wife. She could feel a huge cry coming, but she wouldn't give Katherine any more joy.

Sure enough, as Missy walked into the lobby, there was Katherine with a smug look on her face. "All set?"

"Yes, I'm going home. Then I'm going to call Jack and have phenomenal phone sex with him. Should I tell him you said hi?" Missy replied with as much snark as Katherine had spewed at her. She wasn't a fucking doormat for anyone anymore.

"You do that, you little country bumpkin." Katherine's icy glare raked her body slowly from top to bottom. "You have your phone sex and your nasty threesomes. But know this," she said in a low rasp as she leaned closer, "they will tire of you. You'll be alone. And no one in this city will hire you. I'll personally make sure of it."

"Are you threatening me with slander?" Missy asked her as she took a step forward.

Katherine stepped back, her stiletto stuttering on the floor. "It's not slander if I tell the truth."

"You wouldn't know the truth if it was drawn in a coloring book and you were handed a pack of crayons. Good day, Katherine." Missy spun around and walked out of the building with her head high.

She made it home without losing it, but just barely. The door to her apartment closed, and the sob she'd been containing erupted. She dropped her bag and set the plant on the nearest surface before flinging herself onto the bed.

Why was she always the one to lose? Even when receiving an unbelievable gift, two men who loved her and wanted her, she ended up with nothing.

All she'd ever wanted was to be a lawyer like her father. Practicing in New York was the definition of success. She'd done everything right. She'd worked hard all the way through college and done her time interning in a local firm. She'd been the loyal girlfriend to a man who was born to that life.

Gone. All of it. Her entire future was snatched away.

She'd known it was going to happen as soon as Ned, Katherine, and Carter had all been in one room. There was no other way for it to end. It was her life that everything good would be taken from her, and at the worst possible moment.

Giving up wasn't an option. With only herself to depend on, there was a single course of action to take. Several months of studying and then she was going to nail that bar exam. At least she'd have plenty of time to bury herself in the material. And since she was going to be homeless, she could spend all her time at the city library.

Missy sobbed until she fell asleep.

CHAPTER 24

*F*our days. Ned had been trying to reach Missy for four long days. Ever since she'd driven away after the party. Not knowing if she was okay, was torture. Unable to rest, he sent another text. Maybe that would be the one she answered. He dropped the phone on his desk and went to the window of his home office. The view of the canal, surrounded by trees, was spectacular. It did nothing for him. He was tired of New York. Tired of inhabiting a large, empty space. Tired of being surrounded by his past. He'd bought the house thinking he and his wife would fill it with children. That dream was dead. His wife was dead. His relationship with Missy and Jack appeared to be slowly dying. Despite the July heat, cold, gray nothingness pumped through his veins.

With a deep breath, he turned from the view he no longer cared about, picked up his phone, and dialed.

"Hey, partner." Jack's Texas twang gave Ned a small measure of relief.

"Has Missy contacted you?"

"I'm great, thanks for asking."

Ned heard the playful teasing or he would have apologized. "Did she call you after the party?"

"What party?"

Shit. She hadn't reached out to Jack. Ned paced the length of the room as he filled Jack in on the debacle.

"Aw hell." Jack sighed. Ned imagined Jack running his hand down his face. The image of him was never far from his mind. An ache formed in his chest. It should be his hands touching Jack.

"She's not returning my texts or phone calls."

"I thought it was just me," Jack said. "I sent a text on Saturday."

"I'm going to her apartment." Ned could no longer stand by and do nothing.

"Wait. Can't you just go to the office? Check if she's okay but not invade. Why didn't you go in today?"

Jack's suggestion was probably sound, but, in all honesty, Ned preferred to see her in private. Exactly what Missy didn't need.

"I had a client meeting in the Hamptons. I'll go in tomorrow. How soon can you be here?"

Silence filled the line between them. Finally, Jack said, "I can get a flight…"

"What aren't you saying?"

"The business. Moving it. It's not coming together." Jack sighed. "I've been on the phone with real estate agents and every county office within fifty miles of you."

"Let me help. Make some calls."

"Partner, if there was anything you could do, I'd have asked. I mean, I can move, but the costs are prohibitive. I can't make New York work. You know how it is with a startup, every dollar counts. There is no way I can move the manufacturing there."

Ned dropped into his chair. All the strength left his body. Jack wasn't moving. There was no end to the loneliness. No way to recapture the magic they'd found.

"I'll book a flight." Jack's soft tone soothed his ragged nerves slightly. "Be there as soon as I can."

"Good. I'll let you know what Missy says when I see her."

"Give her a kiss for me, too."

The call ended. Where was she? Why wasn't she responding? What if something had happened? Sickness swirled in Ned's gut. He dragged himself up the stairs. Only three in the afternoon. He'd call it a nap even if he didn't get up again until the morning.

~

MISSY WAS DREAMING. She had to be dreaming, because she did not operate a jackhammer doing road construction. She woke enough to realize it was not a jackhammer but someone pounding on her door. And calling her name.

Ned. Bad news traveled fast. The thumping hurt her head. She untangled herself from the covers. She probably looked like death warmed over, but she couldn't work up a single care.

"Stop." She flung open the door. Ned's fist froze mid-knock. He must not have heard her turning the locks over all the hollering and pounding. She would get scowls from her neighbors, but she wouldn't be staying long enough for it to matter.

Ned rushed into the apartment and shut the door. Missy dropped onto the couch, exhausted despite the sleep she'd had.

Ned's arms were crossed, face red. He loomed over her. "They told me you no longer work for the firm."

"Heard that, huh?"

"Why didn't you call me?" His growly voice teased her insides, but she wasn't going to soften.

"It didn't occur to me to call the man who caused my termination."

"I didn't get you fired." Ned dropped his arms and took a step back. "I would never do that."

"Our unique situation did. Or at least was part of it. I didn't think running back for more of the same thing that ruined my life was the best plan." She scowled up at him, embracing her anger.

"If it makes you feel better to take it out on me, go ahead. When you're done being mad, we can figure out what we're going to do next. That's we, little girl. Because *we* are a *we*. People in relationships work on problems together. I already called Jack, and he's on the way."

"Seriously, Ned? I don't know where to start with that. First, I'm not a little girl. I'm a full-grown woman who made a decision that has led to the demise of her future. Second, we *aren't* in a relationship. That ended at the end of last month. And third, why would you call Jack? There's no reason for him to come here because I got fired for being a slut."

"Wrong. You got fired for revenge. Your brains and beauty threatened a shallow woman who has too much influence over her father." Ned sat on the couch and pulled Missy to him. She struggled on principle, but he held her tight. His firm thighs and solid chest anchored her. "I called Jack because you call the people who love you when you're in trouble. You don't have to do everything alone."

"I don't know how to do things any other way." Missy laid her head on Ned's chest. There was a hint of leather and spice on his skin. Tears formed in her eyes, but she refused to cry again. He had a point. It was comforting to know someone cared for her.

"We've taught you—and you've taught us—some other wonderful things." His voice was seductive. "I'm sure we can teach you how to rely on us, too."

Heat climbed up her face when she recalled all they'd taught her. His words kept stealing her anger and replacing it with desire. It was dangerous. She couldn't fall into the trap again. "Every time I rely on someone, they go away."

"Maybe that's why you have *two* men who love you and want to be with you. Maybe you need a backup." There was a grin in his voice, and he held her a little a tighter. "Jack and I want to be with you. I'm not going to lie and say nothing is ever going to happen—you know better than anyone that's a promise no one can keep. But I can tell you, as long as we breathe, we're going to love you. You mean the world to me...to us."

"I love you both, too, but—"

Ned leaned back and peered into her eyes. "Don't think for a moment I don't respect you, your talent, and your intellect. I know you're brilliant." He tucked a stray lock of hair behind her ear. "But you don't need to be the strong one with us. You've had to be too strong for too long. Let us care for you. Please."

She nestled in closer to him and nodded. They sat like that for a long time. Just being together and breathing in and out.

Missy was the first to stir. Her nose wrinkled. "I need to take a shower."

"I'll order food." He helped her off the couch. "I need to look at my email and see what time Jack's getting in. Can I use your laptop?"

"Of course." She waved her hand in the direction of the little table where it was charging. "I still can't believe he dropped everything to fly out because I got fired."

"He dropped everything and flew out because you didn't call us and you disappeared for an entire week."

Missy froze and turned back to Ned. "I got fired yesterday."

"Missy, it's Wednesday. You got fired Monday. You haven't returned any calls or texts since the party."

She'd lost days. No wonder he'd been worried.

"I was about to call the police if you hadn't answered the door." Ned moved closer and wrapped her in his arms again.

"I'm sorry."

He loosened his grip on her and placed a sweet kiss on her lips. "Go take your shower."

She squeezed him tight and let him go. Three days, no wonder she stank.

After washing up and brushing her teeth, Missy felt better. She was pulling on jeans when she heard Ned open the door. She assumed it was Chinese food being delivered until she heard Jack bellow, "Where is she?"

He quickly stomped through the apartment and flung open her bedroom door without knocking. He threw himself at her and grabbed her by the shoulders.

She'd never seen him like that—wild with tousled hair, a wrinkled shirt, and an air of stale coffee. "Jack?"

"You scared the shit out of me." He pulled her in tight to his body and just held her. The soft cotton of his shirt was warm and familiar.

After a few moments, he eased his grip on her. In the depths of his crystal-blue eyes, she recognized unending adoration. Even though she'd hurt him. She dropped her gaze to the ground. "I'm sorry. I didn't mean to scare you or make you fly all the way out here. But I'm glad you did."

Jack lifted her chin with calloused fingers and kissed her deeply, owning her mouth. She was breathless when he stepped back. "Don't ever disappear like that again, sugar."

She dove back into his arms and held him as close as he'd held her.

Jack whispered in her ear, "It's going to be all right. We'll fix this."

"You can't fix it."

"Then we'll make it better than fixed."

CHAPTER 25

*N*ed tidied up the last of the chicken chow mein and egg drop soup, surprised at the emptiness of Missy's fridge. He held back comment and joined Jack and Missy on her tiny couch. He lifted her into his lap. It was heaven. "You should move in with me."

"That's crazy," she answered. Her voice was relaxed, though. The response almost automatic. Ned should have expected an argument.

"Why is it crazy?" Jack asked.

"I have an apartment and enough to pay next month's rent. I'll find another job. It might not be at a law firm—those take a while to get—but I'll find something to make do."

"I have a huge empty house. You should be there, with me. Take your time finding the right position and spend your time studying for the bar." Ned didn't want to tell her it might be challenging for her to find a new job in a law firm after being fired. It was a big city, but lawyers loved to hear themselves talk and they gossiped worse than old ladies at bingo.

"Very tempting, but it's ridiculous to move in with a man I've only known for weeks."

"You're arguing from a place of logic. You need to think from a

230

place of love," Jack countered. "We love you. I hate that you're here alone. What are you willing to do? For the love we all share?"

Ned resisted the urge to pile on. Jack should take his own advice, to act from a place of love and move his business to New York, no matter how illogical.

"You're playing dirty," Missy said.

"Not yet." Jack's voice was provocative and teasing.

Ned bit back an inappropriate grin.

"Besides, I'm not above playing dirty to get you somewhere safe. I've hated this apartment from day one." Jack picked up Missy's feet and started massaging them.

"We don't have to make the decision tonight." Ned would be patient if he had to. "Let's pack up some of your things and go to my house for a few days. Spend some time together."

"Fine," she said, as if agreeing was a hardship.

"Jack, you're staying through the weekend, I assume?"

He nodded.

Ned held back a chuckle as Missy launched herself off the couch and hurried around, pulling things from piles and shoving them in a bag. It was obvious she wanted to go with them. A warm wave of contentment washed over him, but he didn't cling to it. Missy was only half the battle. He still had to get Jack to stay.

MISSY SCOOPED the bath bubbles to her chest. She'd missed the hell out of Ned and Jack. Being in Ned's New York home was a dream. It was a place she'd never expected to see, and nothing like his beach house. Although secluded with all the trees around, it was in a neighborhood. The modern architectural style belied the dated interior. Missy eyed the large abstract wallpaper with the maroon background. It must have been decorated years ago with an expensive budget, but it didn't feel like Ned. At least not her image of him.

Ned came into the bathroom with a fluffy pink towel draped over his arms.

"There's room in here if you want to join me."

"Next time." He held the oversized towel open for her.

She slowly rose and let what remained of the soapy foam slide down her body.

"Jack's waiting in the bed." Ned's voice was husky and low. Her little bit of teasing had worked.

She let him wrap her up and rub his hands along the thick cotton, tracing her hidden curves. After a few minutes, he led her back into the cavernous space with the huge bed. Jack, hair damp from a recent shower, reclined against the tufted leather headboard, naked and slowly stroking his erect shaft. Her mouth watered, as well as other parts.

"See something you like, sugar?" he drawled, his heavy-lidded eyes tracing over her covered body.

Two could play that game. She untucked the corner that held the bath sheet in place and let the fabric slide down to her feet. "Sure do."

"Come here."

Slowly, placing each foot carefully in front of the other—and letting her hips swing not just for Jack but for Ned ,whose gaze she could feel on her back—she went to Jack's side. Missy wrapped her hand around his and helped him stroke his big, beautiful cock. When their hands reached the base, she leaned forward and took him in her mouth, swirling her tongue around his head and over his slit. He groaned. She teased his thighs apart and cupped his balls.

Ned's naked thighs grazed against hers—his hair tickled. He ran a smooth, warm hand down her spine as he dug into the box of condoms on the nightstand. "Keep going, but I need to be inside you."

Moments later, his hands spanned her hips. Jack pulled the elastic from her hair, letting it fall free. He ran his fingers through it. Ned pressed his covered cock to her opening. She arched her back, encouraging him. Needing him. Remembering every sweet moment on the island and desperate to return. Not to the place, but to them. That was home. It might not be right for anyone else, but it was perfect for them. He slid deep inside her and jerked her hips into his thrust. She mewled around Jack's cock.

"Fuck. Do that again," Jack said. She sucked him into her throat and hummed. Ned thrust into her again, and she swallowed on Jack's cock. They found their rhythm. Pulsing need cascaded and echoed between them. The thumping beats of their hearts kept time. Jack fell first, shooting his hot cum into Missy's waiting mouth. Ned bellowed as she clamped around him in quivering contractions that squeezed him until his thrusts were reduced to uncontrolled twitches.

All night, they slept wrapped together. Woke. Made love again and again.

BEFORE DAWN, Ned slipped from the bed, carefully moving Missy's arm from his chest to his pillow. He didn't want to wake her. Didn't want to explain his plan for the morning. He showered in the guest bath and left coffee and a note in the kitchen.

The hectic commute reminded Ned why he used a driver in the city. Finally at the firm's office, he strode down the plushily carpeted, wood-paneled hallway to the corner office. It was too early for the staff to be there, exactly as he'd planned. He opened the tall wooden door and was greeted by a bank of floor-to-ceiling windows. The view of Central Park no longer interested him, and the man behind the enormous cherry desk no longer commanded his respect. He relaxed into one of the leather chairs set at a perfect forty-five-degree angle. "Wallace."

"Strauss." Richard acknowledged him and then laced his fingers together, resting his hands on his desk blotter. "If you're here about the HR issue we had earlier this week, we have nothing to talk about."

"I've decided to fully retire, effective immediately. I'm cashing out my shares."

"You can't come in here and demand to be bought out," Wallace sputtered. "We have to do a valuation. There are procedures. You have to give thirty days."

"Here's my written notice." Ned dropped a sealed envelope on the edge of the desk. "The original has been mailed with a return-receipt request to the business office. Do whatever you need to do, but I'm done. I've already sent an email to my clients and the rest of the board."

Wallace's face was nearly purple. "You have no right to communicate with the company clients about internal issues."

"It's not internal. I'm retiring." Ned leaned forward, placed his forearm on top of the letter, and locked his gaze to the doughy man's glare. "Your affair with your secretary, that's an internal issue. The fact Rubin is shtupping a nineteen-year-old from the mailroom while his wife is at home with brand-new twins—that's an internal issue. The fact you pay your daughter a quarter of a million dollars a year to run errands, that's an internal issue." He kept his expression blank despite the thrill of satisfaction. He'd caught the bastard completely unaware. "I haven't shared any of that."

"That's slander," Wallace blustered.

"Not if it's true."

Wallace fiddled with files on his desk, clearly delaying as he searched for a new tactic. Ned bit back a laugh and relaxed back into the chair. It was a standoff, and the next person who spoke lost.

"We don't have the funds right now. They're allocated to the merger." The whine of Wallace's voice scraped up Ned's spine.

"*Un*-allocate them."

"I can't do that." Sweat had popped out on the man's forehead. Time to finish it.

"You will. Or in addition to suing the firm personally, I'll hire the best employee-rights lawyer I know to represent your former employee. The one *your daughter* fired. The irony of terminating Ms. Winter for unbecoming conduct will be illuminated with the examples I gave and more. I'll especially enjoy your explanation of how you knew Melissa was engaging in unbecoming conduct. I'm sure the judge will appreciate a story about a jealous ex-wife seeing a younger woman with her ex-husband and talking *Daddy* into firing her for no cause."

"You'll have no credibility with a judge after it comes out what you three have been doing. Katherine gave me all the sordid details."

"First of all, I'm not a party to the potential lawsuit. I'm retiring." Ned leaned forward and rested his laced fingers on the desk, locking his gaze to Wallace's. "Second, my relationship with Missy and Jack isn't legally or morally wrong—none of *us* are married." Ned lowered his voice. "And third, you're worried about the judge? I'm sure the board will be fascinated to learn Katherine has such influence over—personnel decisions."

"You'll never win." Wallace pounded his fist on the desk.

Ned rose from his seat. "We don't have to win to ruin the firm's reputation. Clients trust this firm with their most sacred personal and professional issues. They won't when I'm done."

"You can't threaten me."

"Thirty days." Ned tapped the letter, turned his back, and left. A desperate voice called after him, but he didn't stop. He left the building for what he hoped was the last time.

CHAPTER 26

$\mathcal{M}$issy was deep into preparing for the bar. She still hadn't agreed to move in with Ned, but she found more and more of her things were at his home. He'd provided her a private study with beautiful light and a view of the forested land that edged a canal. She shouldn't get used to it, but it was damn hard to turn it down.

She refocused on the words in front of her, trying to commit the details to memory that would help her pass the test. Her phone rang. Probably Jack. He'd been calling every day since he'd left. She loved hearing his voice and answered without looking. "Hello."

"You fucking bitch!" Carter's venomous voice boomed in her ear.

"Excuse me?" Missy checked the number but didn't recognize it. "What the hell is your problem, Carter?"

"You stabbed me in the back. I can't believe I loved you once. Even wanted us to get back together. I took care of you and your every whining, sniveling need for *five years*. And this is what you do?"

The razor-blade quality of his voice dulled any potential remorse on her part. "*You* broke up with *me*—"

"I don't know what you did or what you said to get this merger off the table, but I will never forgive you."

"This conversation is over." She hovered her finger over the button.

"Don't you dare hang up—"

"Or what?"

"Or I'll be there in person. If you see me, turn around. Don't come to St. Louis. Don't ever be near me again."

"Trust me, I don't ever want to see you either." The crazy ass didn't know where she was, yet he threatened to find her? "Besides, I have no idea *what* you're talking about."

"The Wallace merger. It's dead. Now I have to marry that horse-faced cow and be her daddy's little bitch."

"Carter, I don't work at the law firm anymore. And whatever went wrong, it's nothing more than you deserve. You're a self-centered prick, and karma is coming around to kick your ass." Missy hung up on him and blocked the number in case he wasn't done with his insane ranting.

"Dammit." She'd lost her studying zen with an overload of adrenaline. She'd been firm on the phone, but he'd rattled her.

"What's going on? I heard you yelling." Ned entered the study, frowning.

"It was Carter, hating on me because the firm canceled the merger. Like I had anything to do with that."

"I can get you a new phone."

Missy narrowed her eyes at him. "Why aren't you surprised? You didn't mention they'd changed plans."

"They're having some cash-flow problems." Ned's handsome face was expressionless.

She suspected there was more to the story, but she could tell by his tone he wasn't going to be forthcoming. "I don't need a new phone. I blocked his number. It's fine."

"Tell me if he contacts you again."

She agreed and went for a run to get the ick the Shit had spewed out of her head. When she returned, she'd find her focus and get back to studying.

237

~

NED HATED BEING IN LIMBO. Three long weeks had passed since he'd seen Jack. Missy was living in his house like a guest, not leaving but not moving in. She studied like the earth was going to end and humanity would cease to exist if she didn't pass the damn bar on the first go. Hell, it'd taken him two tries to get it. He admired her dedication, but his heart and other parts missed his lovers. Full retirement wore on him, too. He could only call and pester Jack about the companies so often. Something had to change.

He marched into his study and sent Jack a meeting request for seven that night. They were going to have a come-to-Jesus session and get on the same page and any other cheesy corporate expression he needed to employ to convey the urgency for all of them to be together sooner than later. He followed up by interrupting the studying machine formerly known as Missy. "Hey, I need you to be on a call tonight."

"Uh-huh," she replied without looking up.

"Melissa," he barked.

Missy jerked and looked up at Ned with huge, round eyes. "What?"

He'd startled her. Good. Everyone had to wake up. "We have a call with Jack tonight. The three of us need to talk."

"Is everything okay?"

"No. Everything is not okay. You have your plan, and Jack has his plan, and I don't have a plan, but none of them are about how we're going to be together." Ned scrubbed a hand through his hair. "I barely see you. It's been two weeks since we had sex. I miss you. Both of you. This can't continue. You haven't even moved out of your apartment."

"I don't—"

"Not now," Ned interrupted her. "Tonight. We'll all agree on what needs to happen so we can be together like we're supposed to."

"Are we?" Her voice was small, and she stared at the desk.

"Are we what?"

Amber eyes filled with doubt lifted to his. "Supposed to be together?"

"Don't you want to be?" His whole body tensed.

"I do. But I don't know how it will work or if it *should* work. And no one asked me. We've just kind of been together through circumstances."

A wash of relief relaxed his muscles. "I think those circumstances existed to bring us together, and it's up to us to figure out how to make it work, forever."

"Forever?" She said it like an unknown foreign word.

"Yes, forever. What do you think I've been saying all of these weeks?"

"Not that. I heard you and Jack both say you loved me. I love you guys, too, but no one said this was permanent."

He moved closer and went down on his knees. "I want a life with you. You and Jack are mine. This isn't a proposal, it's a promise." Ned gripped her hands in his. They were shaking and ice-cold. "We'll find a way to be together, for the rest of our lives. That's what I want."

Missy sucked in a breath. A single tear traced down her cheek.

"Me too." Her voice was husky with emotion.

Ned stood. He pulled her from the chair and held her close. "Tonight. We'll figure it all out."

She tilted her head up. He kissed her, softly at first and then deeply. He guided her from the study to his bedroom. He needed her, desperately.

~

JACK LOGGED in at five o'clock Texas time. Ned and Missy were already there sharing one chair, Ned's arm wrapped around Missy's middle.

"Hello, beautiful," Jack said to draw their attention back to the laptop screen.

"Hello, yourself," Ned replied.

"Hi to you, too, Missy," Jack teased, following Ned's lead. "So, what has you all fired up, demanding a meeting and being a pain in my ass?"

239

"Keep that up and I'll be sure to be a *real* pain in your ass." At Ned's words, Jack ached to be in New York.

"Well, it can't be that serious. You're in a chipper mood, and Missy's glowing." Jack faked a pout. "I'm jealous."

"He was a bear this afternoon," Missy said. "At least he was before we had amazing sex."

"Now that's just cruel. Couldn't you have waited and at least let me be a video voyeur?"

"Mmm. Maybe next time." Missy wiggled, and Jack chuckled but wished she was on his lap moving like that.

"Focus, you two," Ned said, interrupting Jack's sexual musings. "We need to come up with a solution. And I can't do that with an erection, thinking about performing for Jack over the internet."

"A solution for what?" Jack settled in. Ned had a bee in his bonnet. He didn't get like that often, but when he did...

"Forever," Ned answered.

"So, no big deal, right?" Missy smiled, her warm eyes sparkling.

"I want Missy and you. I can't keep doing this where she's living out of a suitcase and you're flying in randomly." Ned's gaze blasted into him through the screen. "We need to be in the same place. Together, all of us."

Ned wanted him. To live in the same place. A relationship. A balloon of emotion expanded in Jack's chest. He crossed his arms to keep from bursting. But there was one more question.

"Is that what *you* want, Missy?" Jack's voice was a rough whisper—he was so afraid to hope.

She leaned forward. "Yes, with *both* of you."

"I think you two should move out here." It was a stretch, but Jack had to ask.

"I need to stay in New York." Missy sat back sharply. "I can give up my apartment, but I still need to take the bar exam. Besides, Ned's working for the firm part-time."

Ned cleared his throat. "Actually, I retired. Completely."

"You did? When did this happen?" Jack and Missy spoke over each other.

"A couple of weeks ago. It seemed like the time to do it."

That must have been what triggered the termination of the merger with the Simmons Law Firm. Missy had told Jack about the nasty phone call from her ex. He didn't say anything. If Ned didn't want to spell it out, he wasn't going to go there. Besides, retirement freed Ned to live anywhere. He just had to get Missy on board. "You should both move here."

"But I'm supposed to be a New York lawyer. I promised my grandparents." Missy's eyebrows had drawn together and her lips were firm.

Her answer stung a bit, but Jack smiled. He would win their long-standing argument. "What did you promise them, *exactly*?"

"That I would use my parents' inheritance to become the most successful lawyer I could be. That means passing the bar here."

"How long do you need to prepare before you take it?" Jack asked.

"It's only offered twice a year. I'm scheduled for February."

"That's six months away—Ned will go crazy before then. Can you take it somewhere else, like Texas?" Jack winked at Ned.

"What about New Mexico?"

This was the question Ned had called the meeting to ask, his low, nonchalant tone gave him away. But only because Jack had long ago cataloged all the man's tricks. Crafty as always.

"New Mexico?" Missy echoed like it was Pluto.

"I have a house in Santa Fe. It's a much shorter flight to Texas if we need to deal with the business."

"That has real possibilities." Jack was surprised Ned had property in the Southwest but imagined moving to be with his soul mates. "I could probably relocate the R and D. That state has some attractive tax incentives, as well as a pool of engineers and scientist-types from the research labs. This might be doable."

"What about *this* house?" Missy looked around the stuffy and dated man-cave like it was irreplaceable. Jack wasn't sure how to break it to his buddy that the place was a decade overdue for a remodel. The wallpaper was the stuff of nightmares.

"I'll sell it," Ned replied. "It has some great memories, but it also has a lot of tragedy for me. I would love to have a fresh start with you and Jack. Jack's willing to move his business to be with us. What about you?" Ned tucked a blond lock of her hair behind her ear. "Is New York the only place you can be a success? Is practicing here more important than having a family?"

"Family." Missy took a shuddering breath. It was hard to tell over the video, but Jack bet the sheen in her eyes was unshed tears. She leaned over and put her head on Ned's shoulder as she stared at Jack in the monitor. "I've never been to the Southwest. What if I don't like it?"

"We'll handle it. Together," Ned said.

CHAPTER 27

*J*ack stretched in his chair. The new furniture in their Santa Fe home office was even better than at the beach house. They'd been hard at work all morning. He studied the current profit and loss statement for his merged company, and Ned finalized the New Mexico state paperwork for the private law firm he was creating with Missy. An unfamiliar chirp sounded on Ned's cell phone. Jack stood up from the desk and picked up Ned's empty coffee cup.

"Edward Strauss."

Jack filled their cups, emptying the carafe. He'd have to make more if they were going to work much longer. He set one cup in front of Ned and moved to the fireplace. The high-desert blue skies looked warm, but it was cold.

"Katherine? Slow down." Ned's voice was low and soothing. The same tone he'd used on Missy when she'd panicked before the bar exam last month.

Ned flashed him a concerned look, but Jack waived him off.

His ex-wife was calling his lover. Jack waited for an internal reaction. Just a few months ago, rage would have sparked through him. Instead, he was mildly curious. He gazed out the window, cradling the warm mug in his hands. Ned had a knack for picking properties that seemed secluded. There were houses nearby, but you wouldn't know it from the gorgeous view of snow-dappled chamisa and piñons.

"I can't commit to that. I'd have to discuss it with Jack and Missy." Ned ended the call after promising to get back to her.

"What's going on, partner?"

"Seems your ex-wife had a falling out with her father. She's been living in Colorado, and Richard is trying to tie up or steal her funds. But I won't help her if it's going to be a problem."

Jack considered for a moment. No anger, but no trust. "She could be double-dealing."

"I'm aware, but I don't think so. She was extremely apologetic. Sounded sincere."

"See what Missy thinks. I don't care either way." And it was true. Jack was over Katherine. His dream was a reality, and his past no longer stung. "Let's finish up. I promised a sexy blond woman she'd be tied up and ravished as soon as we're done."

JACK COULDN'T BREATHE. Missy lay on the bed, naked and spread out as he'd requested and Ned demanded. She'd been as eager as they were to resume the fantasy from last summer. He hadn't even begun to restrain her and already she was a vision. Against the white sheets, her lightly tanned skin appeared gilded. It didn't matter how often he saw her naked—she enthralled him.

"How do you want to do this, partner?" Jack popped the button on his jeans and stripped off his t-shirt, dropping it on the tooled-leather chair in the corner.

Ned slowly rolled up his shirt sleeves. "Let's tie her first and then the blindfold."

"Arms together overhead?" Jack asked to confirm so she would hear and the tingles of anticipation would tantalize her as they did him.

"Absolutely. I've got her ankles." Ned picked up one of the silk restraints from the pile Jack had gathered earlier.

"Ready, sugar?" Jack asked her as he stared into her eyes. The sparks of her beautiful soul shone back.

She nodded.

The trust she gave them had him choking up. He purposely slowed his breathing until he found his control. "What are your words?"

"*Lemon* to slow down and *mandarin* to stop," she replied in a breathy voice.

Jack slid the sleek black length through his hand, eyes locked on hers. "You know you're in control, Missy."

She nodded and offered her hands. He carefully wrapped soft silk around her wrists, then anchored it to a slat in the headboard. The bed they'd custom-ordered would be better for those types of games, but it wasn't done yet.

Ned tied her leg to the bed frame.

"Answer me." Jack purposely lowered his voice, emphasizing the command.

"Yes, sir." Her voice quivered, but there was no fear in her eyes. Anticipation. Desire. Perfect.

"Good girl." Ned trailed his fingertips up the inside of her restrained leg as he moved to the other.

Missy shivered, and a soft moan whispered across her lips.

Ned finished tying her and tested each restraint. "How are you doing, Missy?"

The care that Ned showed her, making sure her ties were loose enough not to harm, raised Ned a little more in Jack's estimation. The man was so careful with both of them. It was an unexpected blessing to have found the perfect lovers.

Jack drew the tip of his finger through her glistening pussy and then slid it into his mouth, eyes locked to hers.

"Missy?" Ned's voice was sharp.

She panted and nodded, her focus on Jack.

"I need the words, Missy," Ned prompted.

She turned to Ned. "Good."

245

"Good, what?" he corrected.

A naughty smile played across her lips. "Good, sir."

Every time she said "sir," Ned stood taller, and Jack's dick got harder. God, he loved playing with them like that. It had been too long since they'd done anything wild. But it was time. Missy was laid out like an upside-down Y, utterly open to them. A pink-hued light filtered in through the gauze-covered window from the setting sun, kissing her golden skin. She was so gorgeous, his heart ached. Her body begged him to dive face-first into her—instead, he licked his lips and swallowed her taste that lingered on his tongue.

"We're going to blindfold you. Are you ready?" Ned used his commanding voice, and it went straight to Jack's balls. "When I ask you a question, answer out loud."

Jack's throat tightened as he held back the compulsion to respond.

Missy's thighs tensed against the restraints. She bit her bottom lip and dropped her lids before purring, "Yes, sir."

"She loves your dominance," Jack whispered in Ned's ear and then flicked his tongue up the edge. "So do I—sir."

～

NED GRIPPED Jack's straining dick through his jeans, physically taking control. Control he'd nearly lost a moment ago. Ned released him. "Jack, blindfold."

Jack grinned at him. Cheeky devil. But he picked up the remaining piece of fabric and covered Missy's eyes.

When Jack stood back, Ned asked, "Missy, can you see?"

"No...sir."

"Nice save." He rubbed her arms gently before moving toward her breasts. He stroked over her soft skin and tight nipple, sitting on the bed next to her. When he pinched her bud, she gasped and arched up as much as she could within the restraints. It was heady and humbling to see her so vulnerable under his authority. The trust she gave him made his chest swell.

Jack sat on the other side of her and matched Ned's movements.

246

She wiggled and moaned as they stroked and licked and kissed down her abdomen, taking turns tonguing her navel. Jack's eyes met his, and Ned leaned forward over Missy. Jack met him and they kissed, tongues tangling, the taste of the three of them merging. Ned could savor the taste all night but pulled back. He had plans. He rose from the bed, and Jack followed, removing all contact.

Missy turned her head back and forth, searching without sight. "More."

Silently, Ned stripped off his clothes, and Jack dropped his jeans, the only item he'd been wearing. Jack reached toward Missy, but Ned stopped him with a hand gesture. He opened his top dresser drawer and extracted the feather ticklers he'd ordered weeks ago and handed one to Jack. Missy whimpered. Ned stalled, waiting for the perfect moment. Finally, she stopped writhing and quieted, cocking her head.

Ned touched the feather to her toes and dragged it up her leg from the bottom of her foot to her inner thigh, but short of her sopping center. Jack mirrored the movements. She sucked in her breath and writhed in her ties, so beautiful Ned wouldn't have been able to speak if he'd wanted to.

Ned moved the feather toward her neck. Jack traced up the opposite side in perfect synchronization. Starting at the top of her neck, he drew the wand under her jaw and moved up and around her ears, back down to her collarbones and then over her armpits. She squirmed and giggled, and Ned noted her ticklish spots but remained silent. They glided down the edges of her chest, grazing the sides of her breasts, down to her hips and across her belly. She was incoherent with arousal. They dusted their feathers up the center of her abdomen and then around and around her breasts, getting closer to the areolae but avoiding her tight little buds.

"Please," she cried out.

Ned gave Jack a look, and they both dropped the feathers and dove down on a breast each, nipping, suckling, and tonguing her. She cried out as her first orgasm hit her, and she shook from the intensity, pulling at her restraints.

"More," she demanded.

Ned nodded toward her pussy, instructing Jack wordlessly. They moved their hands over her mound and fucked her with one finger each—in and out, in tandem, in opposition. Jack rubbed her bud with his thumb, and Ned used her cream to tease her anus with his.

"Oh yes. Please, please…I need…yes," Missy babbled. Ned enjoyed her torment.

Jack pulled away. He handed Ned a condom and then covered himself. Her clit was swollen, his body ached to give in to her demands. They each untied a foot and moved her legs to a bent position, opening her completely.

"Fuck me. Please," she screamed.

Ned spoke for the first time as he smacked her pussy. "Address us correctly."

"Please, sir. Fuck me. Please," she begged.

"I think you need something in your sassy mouth." Ned dropped the unopened packet on the nightstand.

"Yes, please, both," she whimpered.

Ned slapped her pussy again. Then pointed for Jack to take his place.

"Sir," Missy said in a teasing tone.

Ned didn't miss the mischievous smile that flashed across her face either. He knelt on the bed to the side of her and lined up his cock, then waited until Jack was in position between her legs. "Open your mouth, Missy."

Jack slid inside her pussy as Ned pressed between her lips. Her warm, wet heat gripped him. She swallowed, taking him deeper. She moaned and sucked noisily. Ned set the rhythm and Jack kept pace, pounding into her. The tension of her sweet mouth, sucking him, her tongue dancing on his shaft, made him wish he could remain like that always. Jack's length thrusting in and out of her pussy, glossy with her juices, shot desire down Ned's spine to his balls. He wasn't going to last.

He caught Jack's eye and held his hand out to him. Jack placed one hand in his, and Ned sucked two of Jack's fingers into his mouth, using his tongue to slick them perfectly. His cock in Missy mouth and

Jack's fingers in his threatened his control. He released Jack and bit his lip. Jack used his wet digits to tease Missy's clit. The man was shaking, about to blow. Good. Missy screamed around Ned's cock, and he leaned back, took his erection in hand and spilled on Missy's breasts. Jack gripped Missy's hips, threw back his head, and pumped out his ecstasy with a roar.

Several moments of recovery later, Ned untied Missy's hands. He laughed when she hummed as she rubbed his cum into her tits. Jack pulled the blindfold from her eyes. Missy blinked up at them and smiled like a Cheshire cat. Jack settled in behind her, and Ned lay down and snuggled close. He leaned over her naked body and kissed Jack before bending his head to kiss her.

"That was awesome." Missy sighed and stretched.

Jack dropped a chaste kiss on her lips, where Ned's had just been. "You like that, sugar?"

"Better than I expected. But we have a problem."

"What's that?" Tension gripped Ned's shoulders.

"Our list is empty." She stuck her lip out in a fake pout.

He breathed a sigh of relief. She was so damn adorable. But his hand itched to spank her ass for scaring him, even for a moment. Instead, he sucked that pouty lip into his mouth and gave it a nip before he released her.

She laughed and briefly tucked her head into his chest. Love and warmth pumped through every vein in his body.

Jack traced circles on her stomach. "What do you want to put on our list, Missy?"

"I don't know. It can be anything, right? Not just sex?"

"Anything you want, my love," Ned answered.

EPILOGUE

Missy padded barefoot over the Saltillo tiles, warm from the radiant heat. She carried a glass of water back to the bedroom, where her men were waiting for her. Both of them had insisted they would go to the kitchen, but she had to collect her thoughts to find a way to say what she'd been holding back. The last few months had been a whirlwind, and it was about to get a whole lot crazier.

"There she is." Jack smiled at her. He was sitting in their new California king bed that had been handcrafted and stained with a dark finish. It was a perfect fit for their Santa Fe home.

"Put down the water and get back in here. We're not done with you." Ned pulled the white duvet off his body, inviting her to return to her warm spot in the middle.

"We might as well spend all day in bed. The roads are going to be treacherous with the storm." Jack patted the mattress.

Spring in New Mexico had brought a variety of crazy weather. She set the water on the chest at the end of the bed and then crawled as seductively as she could between the two sexy, naked men. She wouldn't be able to do that for long. "I see you both are recovered from your blow jobs." She eyed their erections. Her mouth watered, and her pussy twitched.

"Get in here and be our Missy sandwich." Jack grabbed her and pulled her up the bed.

Ned rolled her over so she faced him. "We both need you, now." He pressed his hard dick into her belly. Jack was pressed in behind her just as hard. The conversation could wait a little longer.

"Mmm," she moaned and moved against Jack. "How do you want me?"

"Together," Jack answered. Exactly the way she liked.

Ned rolled her some more so she was on top of him. She felt Jack spread her ass cheeks, and lube hit her pucker. The icy cold gel made her squeal. "A little warning would be nice."

"We should get a warmer," Jack said to Ned over her shoulder.

"I'll find something online and have it shipped."

"We need heating accessories for lube?" She held back a laugh. Did such a thing even exist?

"If you like this as much as I think you will, absolutely," Jack replied as he worked his fingers inside her ass.

"So far, I like it a lot." She tilted her hips for him.

Ned pushed his cock between her thighs, toward her gushing pussy, and against her clit. His head was slipping in between her lips, teasing her with the threat of penetration. Jack withdrew his fingers and pressed his mushroom head at her back entrance. Slowly, they both moved inside her as if they had been practicing the move. She was full and stretched and closer to her lovers than ever before. They continued to press until they were both balls-deep inside her. Missy exhaled into the blissful sensation of the three of them so completely united.

"Yes. Just. Like. That," she purred.

Ned pulled out by lifting her, and Jack tugged her closer to him. Then they reversed the move. She pressed down on Ned and slid almost off Jack. The men were controlling her every movement, and it was glorious. Missy gripped Ned's chest. She moaned and begged, her body so sensitized already. She'd come twice that morning from the oral sex each one had insisted on having with her. Not to mention the orgasms last night. She may be with older men, but they were in great shape and knew how to play her body. They stretched her, gliding against each other inside her. Heat and tension built between her legs and radiated outward. She shook her head, jaw clenched. It was going to be too much.

"Yes, let us have it. Let us see you come, sugar." Jack spoke the soft words into her ear while he gripped her hips even tighter, the warmth of his chest pressed to her back. They moved her faster and harder against their cocks. The stretch and friction heated her core. A fire that burned so good.

"Missy," Ned growled in that way he did when he was close to coming. It was the perfect blend of sweet softness and hard command to get her to erupt. She couldn't imagine living without either one of them. She cried out as her entire body tightened around them. Her body clung to them, never to let go. Electric tendrils of pleasure shot out to every nerve ending. Their eruptions added to the intensity of hers. She shivered with the final contraction and collapsed bonelessly on Ned's chest, with Jack wrapped around them both.

After a few moments of recovery, Jack retreated into their custom three-sink bathroom to clean up. Missy lay in Ned's arms. His solid warmth connected them as she floated in post-sex bliss. Jack returned and gently pressed a warm, wet cloth between her legs, caressing her skin with his free hand.

Jack got rid of the towel and flopped into the bed next to her. The three of them lay there in a peaceful stupor that could only be achieved after multiple rounds of lovemaking.

Missy contemplated the pines and bare aspens frosted with snow through the window. She loved living in Santa Fe with Ned and Jack. She couldn't believe it was her life. And it was about to get even better. Her earlier anxiety was gone—time to tell them.

"What are you thinking about so loudly?" Ned asked.

"I have something to tell you, and I'm not sure how. It's going to be as life-changing as when I passed the bar and as mind-blowing as the hot-air balloon ride."

"That was a great bucket list experience." Jack trailed his calloused fingers up her arm. They'd chartered a private balloon last weekend to celebrate her success on the test.

"What?" Ned rolled up onto his elbow to face her.

"Well, we've all been a little busy and distracted since the time on the island." She grabbed Jack's hand. "You were reforming two companies into one and relocating the company here." She placed her other hand on Ned's chest. "You were selling your house in New York and paring down all of your things from an entire lifetime. I was homeless. Falling in love. Studying and getting fired. Moving, twice. Starting our own firm, and well—" she glanced quickly at each of them "—I didn't have insurance, and I meant to find a doctor, but I didn't, and I forgot to get my shot, and... I'm pregnant."

Missy bit her lip and waited for them to say...something.

"Repeat that last part." Ned said.

"Did you say *pregnant?*" Jack sat up, spine stiff.

"Uh-huh." Missy looked back and forth between the men, hopeful and nervous. When she'd been planning to work in New York, there would have been no time for children. But Ned's insistence that they start their own business after they moved meant she could control her hours and embrace their unexpected blessing. At least she hoped that's how they saw it.

"You're sure?" Ned shifted into a seated position and stared down at her. His face was creased like he was going to cry.

"As sure as I can be from a drugstore test."

"Oh my god." Jack leapt out of bed.

Ned pulled her into his embrace. "I always, always wanted children. But I'd given up."

"Jack?" She turned back to gaze at him over her shoulder. Jack's mouth hung open, his lower jaw flapping up and down like he wanted to form words but couldn't.

Ned relaxed his hold. "Jack, buddy? Are you okay?"

"I'm going to be a father," he finally said.

"You are. You both are." Missy put as much enthusiasm as she could in her voice, uncertain where Jack was falling on the issue.

"It's amazing. It's more than I ever dared dream. I can't believe—"

Jack froze, a panicked grimace taking over his face. "We have to get you to a doctor."

"I have an appointment," Missy said, but he wasn't listening.

He moved frantically around the room, grabbing clothes, most of which weren't his.

"In two weeks," she clarified, trying to get him to calm down.

"Two weeks? That's ridiculous. You need to see someone now. What if something goes wrong? What if we do something wrong? Oh shit, we just did double penetration. We can't do that anymore." Jack was shaking his head like a wet dog. "This is the most important thing ever."

"Jack, you need to calm down or you'll stress our little momma," Ned said in his low, commanding tone.

"It's going to be fine." Missy reached out her hand to him. "We have plenty of time."

"Oh my god, you're having a baby. Our baby." Jack knelt by the bed and held Missy's hands. "Thank you. I love you so much. You don't know how much I wanted to be a father and never thought I would."

Jack rested his head on her still-flat belly. Ned ran a hand through Jack's hair.

"I love you, too, little one," Jack said into her belly.

Missy laughed. Ned and Jack were the best thing that had ever happened to her, and they were hers. Her family. Forever.

***

ACKNOWLEDGMENTS

First I have to thank my husband who gives me all the time and space to write and never gets upset when I use him for research. I love you!

Thank you to the Land of Enchantment Romance Authors (LERA) who provided a place of support and education, especially BP. I would never have met my critique partners without LERA.

To my Reines, without whom, this book would not be what it is. Thank you for making me go deeper.

ABOUT THE AUTHOR

Award-winning author, Jordyn Kross, is an unapologetically naughty novelist who spent years honing her writing skills with tech manuals and marginal poetry before finding her passion for writing sexy, boundary-stretching happily-ever-afters.

When she's not writing, she's attempting to garden in the desert Southwest, hiking with her insane pound posse, and admiring that handsome man wandering around her house who continues to stay.

Jordyn enjoys saucy double entendres, pretending to be an extrovert, and is well-known for having no filter. And when she's not in social media jail, she can be found on Facebook, Instagram, and Goodreads, or hiding in a dark cave peering out at Twitter. Or subscribe to her monthly newsletter at her website: jordynkross.com

Made in the USA
Monee, IL
19 April 2022

94995023R00156